The Masque
of
Saint Eadmundsburg

The Masque of Saint Eadmundsburg

Humphrey R. Morrison

Blond & Briggs

First published in Great Britain by
Blond & Briggs Limited, Dataday House,
Alexandra Road, London SW19 7JZ

Copyright © 1982 by Humphrey R. Morrison

British Library Cataloguing in Publication Data

Morrison, Humphrey R.
  The Masque of St Eadmundsburg
  I. Title
  823'.914[F]

  ISBN 0-85634-127-4

Photoset in Palatino by
Rowland Phototypesetting Ltd,
Bury St Edmunds, Suffolk.
Printed in Great Britain by
Billing & Sons Ltd, Worcester.

To all those of my friends and family without whose advice and encouragement this book would not have been finished, and in particular to Joanna Korner and Michael Rhodes.

Acknowledgements

I would like to express my gratitude to Professor Walter Ullman of Cambridge University, who inspired in me a fascination for past perceptions of society.

Foreword

Marsilius of Padua was born in 1270 in the city from which his name was taken. He died in about 1342, his major and controversial work, on Government and Law and entitled *The Defender of the Peace*, having been first published in 1324.

Prologue

'Of all institutions the university is closest to a perfect model of a society which is not blindly drawn behind the inconsistent and peculiar talents of individuals. Its purposes are clear and time-honoured, though the achievements of its great men are diverse and sometimes strange.'

These were the famous words of Lugwig Aicha, written around the year 1460, when he was a member of the University of Saint Eadmundsburg.

Doctor Dolke, in spite of his acceptance of this long-revered assertion of his university, asked himself what that institution would be without great men. His question was the more pointed in that his own university was that of Saint Eadmundsburg. Had Aicha's clarion words referred to the University of Saint Eadmundsburg? Its Senate had erected a statue to Ludwig Aicha in their Great Hall of Convocation with the words of his precept inscribed on its pedestal.

Dolke had paused abruptly, quite on the lip of one of the coursing gutters of the street. He now continued on his way to the Aula Senatus, the Great Hall of Convocation, where today's meeting would be the most important of the academic year.

Indeed, he told himself, had it no great men, the university would nevertheless today be celebrating its founder, the holy Saint Libori. He walked on, frowning. The saint had a name day; today, July the 23rd. The university celebrated it with utmost ceremony. Doctor Eberhard Dolke privately suspected that Saint Libori had not been a great man.

However, it was not to be forgotten that he, Eberhard Dolke, was of some standing in the university. If to him that institution seemed of little account or purpose without men of genius among its members, this was not to say that the achievements of men of talent were insignificant. Such men – he would include himself among them – were also needed. His own researches had not

1

been negligible, he suggested to himself. The note of diffidence was perhaps spurious.

His respect for individuals and their work led him to see them as the essence of the university. His own capacity for work, and a sometimes upsetting desire that its products should receive respect, drew him to the same position. His reverence for creative work – or for that elusive realm of creative work which he might achieve – led him, as he contemplated the imminent ceremonial of Saint Libori's Day, to ask himself again the question: What would the university be without great men?

Merit was not always recognised, he reflected (with a sudden feeling of weakness inside himself, as if he had laid open to discovery some guilty secret of his own). He at once dismissed from his mind a temptation he had felt increasingly: to examine his own long career. It was true, and he should not forget, that within the university he was of some standing. His college had resolved that he receive – when the time came – a gilded tomb.

He rehearsed its details with a curious care. It was to have a carved Saint James the Great and, below his own effigy recumbent in robes of a master of the university, a cadaver behind delicate openwork. This monument he had recently designed himself. He had delineated it on parchment and had chosen for it words of another great jurist but longer dead than Aicha, Marsilius of Padua. They were to appear in gold on the open pages of what all would understand to represent that eminent man's *Defender of the Peace*. It was to lie as if fallen by the Doctor's side, his right index finger still touching the place.

He remembered, with the sense of pride that may be felt for something achieved, though vicariously, a certain late afternoon with Doctor Michel. Ambrose Michel – his friend, dead now sadly – had told him of one of his forebears who had conversed at length with Marsilius. It had been passed down as a tradition, almost as an inheritance, among a family of controversial academics: how he had heard Marsilius expound his doctrine of law which was not fixed, imposed once and forever, but might evolve with and spring from the very society to which it gave cohesion. That incorrigible heretic, that man who dared reassert the rôle of individual and social creativity in the making of law, had come to find refuge from the rigid, hierarchical laws of the Avignon Pope.

2

Work on the graving of the monument and the plans for its erection were in hand. Every day for the last thirty days Dolke had visited the cramped workshops in the precinct of the Benedictines to confer with the craftsmen. Already he recognised that when the time came for its erection not a day would pass on which he did not spend at least one hour watching the work, tempted throughout to direct the labourers.

It was the invincible desire to create, and moreover to construct a thing complete in itself, set in permanent balance, which would compel his presence. It was a strange compulsion. Was he not conscious that his desire for law which welled from a sympathy between the ideas of many individuals – which welled and ebbed and again sprang out – as Marsilius described, somehow contradicted the aim of a complex and artificial monument, the pristine masterwork of a solitary?

Permanence and constant creation; he longed for both. Once he had read as a lawyer the *Defender of the Peace*; but that work had provided him with something more. Within him were chaotic, mutually repellent forces; it had made some reconciliation. Between an awareness of imperfection which justified effort and an ideal of perfection requiring no substitution he had achieved a balance. Between his individuality (above all in him the overbearing awareness of his own limitations, his ultimate insignificance) and the great university there could appear an eye (as Marsilius had put it of law), made from many such eyes as himself.

And his monument? It was to stand in the fine new chapel of his college, Ulpian. Indeed he too, he supposed, was one of those who might be said to have ornamented and embellished the university with his works, to be one of its great men. He no longer attempted to compute the volumes, tracts, monographs and published lectures that there were signed 'Dolcchius', Doctor of Laws and master in the College Domitius Ulpianus. All this had been for the greater glory of God and according to His purposes through His foundation, the most famous of the university's houses for knowledge and exposition of the laws.

Among these works, however, the burden of many and the unspoken premise of them all had been the desirability, even the inevitability, of a fluctuating, evolving law of men.

Whatever his status, he thought, the day was so cheering; and he enjoyed a whimsicality – ordinances of irrational chance he

3

called them – that he found in the way his reflections had come to mind. When, as so often now, he looked back into the history of the university, all was vivid. Even their names seemed to possess a music, a flame: Guillaume of Juvigny, Heraclius of Acre, the friar Wolfried, Athellus of Outremer (called Athellus the Englishman) and more recently the sombre and subtle Ludwig Aicha, whose words on the nature of a university, as a perfect model of a perfect realm, God-given and immutable, had been in his mind a little earlier and had lightly disturbed him.

Ahead, Doctor Dolke could already make out the white stone of the Forum Academicum – so much, he thought (with a slight awareness of doing justice), so much in the spirit of the Saint. Then there to his left, suddenly, was the view! At that point, just at the last bend, there was the space in the sinuous and majestic progression of colleges! Tenth Day Street (so named from that day of each month on which the Doctors had always thronged it on their way to their regular council) seemed to fall away to one side. He always paused here to look out, at this space among the colleges, across the river to the royal palace. He stopped to glance; to do so made him so happy that he wanted to laugh aloud. He felt the force of the impulse. The irrationality again filled him with joy. He could have laughed aloud with defiance. The sun shone. The forum lay four-square at the centre of the city, at the heart then of the university; the goal of the last, long bend of the winding processional way. He threw out his chest; his full beard jutted. Raising his arms forwards slightly, so that they were stiff, he strode along.

It was a familiar sight to the university people, the Doctor's peculiar gait when pleased and debonaire. His straightened arms displayed to himself and all others the claret-coloured silk of his master's summer robes; and at the same time they raised from the dusty way the pendulous sleeves that fell away at the elbow – like a thirsty tongue or the dewlap of an ox, he thought. It was only when his body contracted and his face lowered that he was full of pride, whose nature in him, not often seen, could be so intractable and scathing.

The university was the city; today was the most important day of the year for them both. The Aula Senatus would entertain the undivided spiritual, legal and academic personality of the university, embodied in the doctors, the masters and, supremely, in

4

the Seneschal. These three estates, Dolke silently recited, formed the whole. In the numerous houses and schools of the university existed a multitude of ranks and degrees, but these three were the only distinctions known in the government of the whole. All this was brought together to the greater glory of their founder, holy Saint Libori, on his festal day. Rejoice! Bells were singing; his name and purposes and his foundation are surely protected.

Nonetheless it was surely obvious that without great men a university was nothing. There was such vehemence in this silent thought that Doctor Dolke felt a sensation close to pain between his eyes and in the crown of his head. Around him that day, however, the university seemed quite capable of continuing interminably, whether he or indeed any of his fellow masters were there or not. Their differing status and achievements seemed to him for the moment of no more effect within that sphere than to diversify, by the various colours of the academical robes to which they had become entitled, the patterns of their processions and convocations.

Chapter 1

The peal of Saints Ulrich and Afra, the principal church of the university, swung out. Its music seemed to infect the colleges and other churches with jubilation. Their peals swayed and swelled, while the great bell of the grey tower of the College of the Three Archbishops (called 'Electors' College') sounded beneath the tumbling and pitching as soft and insistent as the indeterminate sound of the deeper sea, beneath and between the breakers that draw and hiss, heard from the shore.

In the Great Hall of Convocation Doctor Feucht took the place next to Doctor Dolke with something like an excuse. He was a man diffident and ceremonious in the same instant. Dolke accepted his presence as tolerantly as he felt able, with a movement of his open right hand which might be taken to say, 'Do sit here, Doctor Feucht'. After fifteen years as colleagues they were still on those terms, 'Doctor Dolke' and 'Doctor Feucht'. Doctor Feucht rarely hoped for more.

To Dolke's astonishment he thought he heard Feucht murmur in reply, 'An honour, Doctor Dolke': or some such words. He decided that, if he had caught the remark correctly, it deserved to be ignored. Some academics acted like courtiers.

Doctor Dolke had been in the hall for about ten minutes. Around the two of them other doctors of the Law Faculty were beginning to fill the benches. They clustered into knots of figures which painstakingly kept distinct, but which, somehow inevitably, stretched out, touched, and coalesced.

It was the university's, not the colleges', day; the doctors congregated according to their disciplines. Traditional, honourable places in the rows remained free for professors.

There was a little time to wait. Most of those entitled to sit in the Senate were at High Mass in the university church, or now perhaps in the process of crossing the forum – Saints Ulrich and Afra lay just to the east. When they entered, with the drifting sound of bells, those who, like Dolke and Feucht, were masters, entitled to participate in college as well as university government, would precede those who were merely doctors teaching at the university. And all would give precedence to the Regents, the heads of colleges. Thus individuals did not possess merely academic and governmental functions. They were also as bricks built into a tower, and the bricks themselves embossed or coloured. The tower was of a shape visible and intelligible at least to the bricks themselves. Or rather, at any one moment they sensed its solidity, which must (inferentially) have shape. Dolke believed that he still shared this sense of cohesion, of presence. At one time he had been confident, on close scrutiny, of the subtle outline of the tower, its orders and proportions.

He had attended early Mass in college but had evaded what others perhaps regarded as the further obligation. For some reason he rarely felt of late that awe of the processing and kneeling, of the high and sublime choirs. He stared up to the coffered ceiling of the hall. Its cream and grey and its friezes of acanthus were temperate and harmonious. Yet he was not satisfied. Was it that its mood did not change? It could not suit all moods. It failed to lead them. Least of all was it alive with associations, with the conflict between forms and associations. An harmonious dignity always prevailed. It remained in obedience to the rules according to which it had been designed. Never was there an effect, a response to an intruder, but that intended by its architect. Whatever was the quality it lacked, Dolke told himself, this chamber could never exercise over him any such fascination as that which held him on even a glimpse of the royal palace.

'Undergraduate affairs have been oppressive': Doctor Feucht had felt no time for preliminaries (and he knew of no formula for the occasion). Doctor Dolke had not spoken a word to him. Feucht's tone was understandably forced.

'How then would you describe this affair?'

Dolke was only too easily irritated by the irrelevant or superfluous; which included what was irrelevant or superfluous to his undisclosed train of thought. Moreover it was clear that Feucht's words were a mere gambit. An elaboration was to be expected.

'As a result I was not at High Mass – of course you can see that.'

Dolke briefly nodded an ironical concurrence.

'You had intended to be?'

As he spoke he turned abruptly and stared fixedly at a group of colleagues newly entered. Doctor Feucht would not be so rude as to interrupt almost anxious attention elsewhere. Yet Dolke had not wished to sound quite so dismissive. As he considered those whom politeness referred to as his 'brother academics' his concentration was genuinely absorbed by the return of earlier reflections. For a moment half aware of this mental shift, he was pleased at the sense of being preoccupied, and so not obliged to talk.

In truth it was difficult, Dolke told himself as his eyes passed over the faces of those brother academics, to say who at present were the great ones of the university. His own features, he well knew, did not enjoy the conventional aspect of greatness; for his monument his image had been taken in silverpoint, and by Master Pius, the most skilled draughtsman at the Benedictines. Both men had been concerned that it seem to live and so contrast (assertively perhaps, rather than submissively) with the *memento mori*, the pale skeleton which was to lie carved beneath.

Dolke's skin was very white and thin. That did not matter. His hair had been red. Marks of gold still lay in his beard where the summer light glanced upon it and in the final volutes of its longest, straggling hairs; the rest had resolved into an earth brown. All so unimportant. But his robust body, he thought – that signified.

He regretted dimly the lack of a courtly education.

What was essential was the mobility and energy, his expression when he fixed his eyes on a problem. They had discussed the almost insuperable difficulty of suggesting that; Master Pius had drawn his attention to the problem. And it was in this alone that his mind's activity – both his observation and imagination – were apparent.

More often his eyes opened – inexpressive, wide and bland. They were very blue, and some remarked that they were typical of an active and inward fantasy of imagination. Others, observing how they lit on woman and boy with equal indifference, saw in them only his complete innocence.

It was Feucht's way, however, that Dolke's last remark should require him to justify his prospective attendance at High Mass, even as his actual absence had required excuse. Dolke, at first absorbed, had begun to scan the ranks of faces distantly. Lower-

9

ing his voice confidentially, as if others might not have understood, Feucht explained:

'It was to be of unusual magnificence . . .'

'For Saint Libori.'

It was not possible to tell whether these words contained some colour of derision. Dolke's tone might have indicated approval. They might merely be anticipatory of the likely end of Feucht's own sentence.

'A chorale of the Sieur de Gallus; the Cross of the Blachernae. The Seneschal was to enter alone to a voluntary . . .'

Dolke was not averse to pomp. Perhaps his present lack of interest was lethargy, age perhaps; or Feucht. At one time Dolke had acquired an exhaustive knowledge of the etiquette of the law. He was an authority on that of the university, and this standing he had won early in the more than forty years spent there since his arrival as a student. As a master in Ulpian College he still taught above all the Law of the Constitution: of the Empire then, and of the King. Once he had felt its harmonies, its almost architectural certainties.

The intended excuses were all but forgotten. Dolke's empty expression struck Feucht as sympathetic. He went on:

'Music! Surely we are fortunate to have such music here.'

'As compared with that of the Benedictines?'

'Indeed no! There is no need for the invidious. . . . Their music is very fine, is it not? But here . . . musicians and connoisseurs have agreed that there is a harmony here, not merely musical.'

'Celestial perhaps?' Dolke interrupted, disliking an appeal to connoisseurs, but at last smiling.

'A harmony . . . surely . . . of taste. Of sympathy,' Feucht corrected himself.

A smile aggravated his confusion. One part of him could not resist the desire to see what he so needed, some hint that disagreement was academic – thus really a sort of intimacy.

'The Benedictines, by comparison, are rampant individualists.' Dolke was almost laughing.

'I dare say,' Feucht replied in a low voice, and he used that phrase when he felt keenly the solace offered by smiles dissolve and a bitterness infect his speech, 'that other bodies possess sympathies in common. But at least do we not also feel . . . share?'

10

He had succeeded in what he least intended; Dolke pouted his lips and frowned energetically, as if to say that, as he did not understand what Feucht was saying, he must agree and would say no more.

Feucht was not ashamed to be openly moved by these occasions; this point formed part of Dolke's revery. It was not entirely Feucht's fault that excitement reduced his speech – his thought – to chaos, and even to platitudes. At such times it was to be observed that something happened to Feucht's face; a space of quite unnaturally white skin on his forehead stretched, tighter and tighter, as if it would snap. That was the symptom of the disease. And only too often Feucht was in that state. Dolke smiled to himself.

On the other hand, apology only temporarily corrupted a collected mind. An intelligent mind was there, sometimes hidden. When pressed, Feucht could be obstinate, even resolute. And he had his enthusiasms; even if they did not broaden him. Would it ever be within rational bounds to conceive of Feucht composing even a short fugue, Dolke wondered? He was obliged to keep himself to a narrow and certain track. Its measurement was the sole aim of his work, and that of his life was to belong; as if the university were like a city in the distance, glimmering and wonderful, and yet he belonging to it while he stepped, with regulated step, forward along the path. When he took his ground there, he could stand on his punctilious rectitude; then you could see how he took the pain as the blows went home. All this (which in less exact creatures produced a saint – perhaps a martyr) Dolke associated with a high, rounded cap of soft grey felt which Feucht customarily wore, and which he wore even today. It seemed to make an assertion, not quite clear to Dolke, through its insistent presence in place of the gold-embroidered, black satin coif of a doctor.

Half-observed ceremony flickered before Doctor Dolke's eyes. There were dashes of gold, and dimly he caught the intonation of archaic forms and titles. Sumptuous brocades and silks, as stiff as caparisons, alternated with figures in black robes. All faded, taking their places.

Two gaunt creatures appeared, each with a cumbrous staff on which he leant at every stride as if the staff were a third limb, yet portentously, as if it contained some hidden motive force. These

11

men, the Doctor knew, preceded the Seneschal. All rose.

The subdued brush of shoes over marble and of hems of robes against the wooden benches drew a sound like a sigh or a dour murmur. A spare, angular man entered. He stepped with long strides to the centre of the fore-ground of the dais. There he took his place, a round-backed wood chair with carved, curving arms. He doffed his cap once with an easy and urbane gesture. For a short moment he busied himself almost inconsequentially in settling and rather fluffing out his voluminous and awkward robes, while his narrow form remained apparent beneath. His gown of white silk brocade supported a cloak of state, for he, the Seneschal, was elected of his peers of the Senate and confirmed by the King to have charge of the university for a term of five years.

There followed the usual and expected form of celebration. Dolke was struck only once or twice by a graceful or rolling cadence during the long Latin oration. In essence it was a recital of the prerogatives and acts of the Seneschal during the preceding year.

A man not younger than forty-five, but with an extraordinarily boyish face, made responses on behalf of the doctors. He was almost ungainly in his height and his auburn hair curled careless-ly and artfully from below the brim of his flat velvet bonnet. This was the legatus, Arcute, advocate to the university. There were historical allusions, and a spiced little gloss, thrown off casually to all appearances, on words of Aicha, expressive of the certainty of glory for the successors of the Glorious. In short the speech was of the almost unvarying type of protestation, of thanks from the senators to the Seneschal and to history, which nevertheless confesses the truth of sundry self-flattering, self-depreciatory admissions. This was the wit of oration and response. Andreas Arcute was, though, someone impossible to ignore. His English features were so young. His declamation and the fluent anima-tion of those features in sympathy with the succession of moods communicated to his audience something which seemed to approach a youthful exhilaration, self-conscious and yet fun-damentally innocent.

Figures shifted and bowed. A young man drew back from before the dais and, in the very moment of this step, slightly stooped head and knee and touched his breast. His right hand he

12

withheld, as he might holding a doffed hat. Dolke approved in the young man the courtliness of gesture. He was Friedrich von Fluorn, a pupil under Dolke's tutelage and a member of an old and honoured family. Dolke had played some small part in persuading him to accept the coveted duty of presenting the response of his fellow students. Von Fluorn's speech had been controlled, with, nonetheless, a careful expressiveness; the effect was complemented by a relaxed and posed stance. Dolke felt slightly guilty for having failed to take in quite what he had said.

After the mass at Saints Ulrich and Afra; after the giving and receiving of thanks, came the distribution of honours, the worship of God, the praise of Saint Libori and the salutation of the various degrees of the university hierarchy, succeeded by an even more important stage of the celebrations. That extraordinary organism, the university, relied for its vitality, as did its colleges, on a series of adjustments. Often they were referred to as the fine tuning of a musical instrument or, on half-confessed occasions of crisis, as a focusing (certainly by adjustments almost imperceptible to the world at large) of energy, talent and power. They constituted a gradual but continual process of regeneration and redirection.

Dolke, however, was completely unaware of what was about to happen. Senators had, one after another, been called from all parts of the hall to make an obeisance before the Seneschal and receive from him some words signifying a work completed or to be undertaken. Suddenly he heard his own name announced. (It had been called quite unmistakably by the more venerable of the two staff-bearing attendants of the Seneschal.) He heard his name acclaimed! He rose with the instinct of custom, but stood still.

The generous applause was sustained. Had he then achieved something of weight or subtlety in these last, enervating years?

He felt a hand lightly tug one of his pendulous sleeves.

'My dear Dolke.'

It was Feucht. For the first time, in his excitement, he had allowed himself to forget their unvarying formality. Dolke recognised this; somehow it released him to make his way forward until he was close to the Seneschal and his accompanying officials, in front of the dais. Having made his bow, he strove to concentrate on their lack of consideration, their lack of sense of what was fitting, to prevent his being overwhelmed. These men had caused his exposure to scrutiny without preparation. Failure to give the customary intimation must so obviously induce a pointless apprehension. In the short time during which he stood silent and looked once to right and left, he clung to these thoughts, little more than momentary mental sensations as they were, so that he would not have to struggle against incoherence. Applause had meant far more to him still, he found, than he had expected. He had almost to struggle against tears.

'You are the last, Doctor Dolke,' said the Seneschal, as if the words held some obscure but particular compliment.

'Sirs – sirs – you have the advantage of bestowing honour on one who, given time to investigate his own limitations in that regard, might have evaded it.'

That, he felt, implied sufficient rebuke, and he was almost overcome with emotion. He was disadvantaged unfairly by the absence of anything on which to support himself, or so his awareness of his dignity and his embarrassment made him feel.

The Seneschal had expected Dolke's reaction; indeed he was slightly relieved to have received no more cutting reprimand from the ironical and formidable old lawyer. The two had never known each other very well; the Seneschal was a Doctor of the Liberal Arts. He correctly understood that such contact as there was between them was complicated by Dolke's sense of greater age and less exalted rank. To one or two other colleagues (not, strangely, to all of whom it might have been expected, though the Seneschal could draw no conclusion from this) Dolke was known to be, for similar reasons, by turns paternal and deflatingly dispassionate.

Whatever the risk (and he was phlegmatic in the face of rudeness), the Seneschal had determined to ignore the conventions for the very reason admitted in Dolke's reply. The coming year would be the last of his office as Seneschal. While he had observed Dolke with accuracy, he was perhaps less aware of his own sense of rank – not exactly a personal pride, but a consciousness of fulfilling at every moment his exalted office. It was almost as if he were two persons to whom he himself owed different degrees of respect.

When he had been confirmed in that status, as Seneschal, a previously inchoate aspiration (which he, when detached, might almost have dismissed as childish) had received its fullest possible satisfaction. At the time he began his regency this consummation was less intense only than that which was evoked by the very enactment of his various formal rôles. The donning or removal of his cloak of state, the taking of his place in the firm, unadorned seat on the dais and, above all perhaps, the ceremony of homage with his hands between those of the King aroused in him almost an ecstasy; the reception of a monograph of his had never awoken such feelings. Since then a new desire, perhaps the creature of a kindred or even of the same aspect of his nature, had begun to occupy his mind; that his regency should be memorable – and not merely memorable (though much that was of practical value had certainly been achieved during it) – but scintillating, dazzling. It was to this end that he turned automatically towards pageantry.

Exactly one year from today there would be a celebration worthy of five years of prosperity. He had fixed in his imagination an event crowned with glory – with the academic and perhaps more material glories (for he was not a man to undervalue them) of a triumphal masque of the university.

He had not settled on this idea lightly. Caution, and even more a self-possession, were important influences on all his decisions. Throughout the last year he had, according to his own reckoning, wasted time turning the matter over and over in his mind. That year was now clearly to be seen, however, as another stage of a reign of almost unbroken triumph and happiness. The Seneschal was sufficiently modest to own to himself that good fortune and peace were due more credit for this result than was his own effort. His own contribution had been thoroughness and dedication to his duties: holding the balance between the various colleges and faculties, and maintaining the rights of the whole body in its dealings through him with the city and with the King. Influence, in the absence of power, could be exerted. Through tact, it had been exerted successfully. Tact in particular had been required in dealing with the colleges, for each jealously preserved the letter, and often the advantage, of every right and privilege it possessed.

The Seneschal's passion for ordered forms of alternate supplication and exaltation was restrained by common sense, and indeed by a degree of thrift. With these went a reverence for taste in the arts and for erudition, neither of which, in his present

15

company, he felt that he possessed. The vulgar panoply of municipal and even ducal triumphs, with their spurious trains of wild-eyed Moors, Bulgars and Orientals, he had himself seen and freely despised. On the other hand he understood the emotions, the awe, that even these had succeeded in awakening in people's minds. The masque must be a procession and a celebration, but it should also be an evocation and an explanation. In so far as it was a progress, it would display to the city, the university, and to the King perhaps (he dared to think), the rights, form and hierarchy of an ancient and glorious foundation. In so far as it was a dramatic representation it might display its history, its achievements and its ideals. His heart beat with a curious tension at the mental sensation of the stylised drama and ceremonial poetry of this extraordinary art, whose tight and mannered restraint excited his eager belief in sentiments and ideals higher than the common, and than his own. It was almost as if – for he had witnessed once a royal masque of France – these finer feelings were indeed personified in those who, in radiant costume and with ideal gesture, impersonated them. In all its parts his masque would bring together not merely costliness and splendours, but also craft and music; feeling and elegance and beauty.

In his imaginings the Seneschal was without caution. His masque would be the climax of that art. It would not merely represent, it would be the university. Such inspiration in the Seneschal remained airy, however; vague in spite of the time he had spent, and perhaps wasted, musing (as even now at these celebrations of Saint Libori his mind wandered to his favourite scheme). He remained incapable of inventing or borrowing more than a few precise images. Dolke's exactness, his undoubted authority concerning the university and his long association with it made his participation of importance. The Seneschal had even resigned himself to the possibility of surrendering a substantial part of the glory, or at least of the public acclaim, should that be entailed in the choice of Dolke and his effective execution of the design. He had considered with his usual perspicacity the note to strike and had even composed, as a natural progression from a consideration of probable eventualities, a number of suitable phrases for his own reply.

'My dear Doctor,' he began, speaking to the hall. 'It is no obligation that I would impose upon you; it is recognition. Your

16

great works, "On the Traditions and Forms" and "On the Statutes and Precedence" of this university, are not forgotten. They have not been sufficiently celebrated.

We call on you to lend your name to a committee to be constituted for the purpose – which my inner household of the Senate has this day approved – of the creation and execution of a masque of the University of Saint Eadmundsburg.'

He paused. The applause so anticipated matched his expectation. The occasion had been made an emotional one in every aspect. The Seneschal allowed himself to smile affably and to resume, with something of an air which was yet without warmth or laughter.

'Doctor Dolke, your knowledge would supply the want of confidence on my part either to cite those ancient authorities which founded the peculiar right of the Seneschal to imbue with splendour his final Saint Libori's Day or to example the witty innovation of previous Seneschals on that festival for the benefit of the university:

'There would be, I confess, one obligation; it is the only one. If, Doctor, if you will it, select those who by learning or long familiarity with the university are most worthy to represent us on your committee, and, if you will, guide them by your example.'

The applause was irresistible. Doctor Dolke, having accepted, returned to his seat. He wondered how many of those around him had known before he did. Doctor Feucht had known, he was sure; that was why Feucht had been so obsequious. But that was a harsh judgment, he told himself, and he could forgive Feucht.

A trifle effusive, but the effect of the little speech clearly gave no cause for concern; even his own faculty were no judges of rhetoric: the Seneschal was not inclined to self-criticism when he had got what he wanted, while his manner had suffered from his own discovery, during years of university politics, of his possession of tact. Dolke had accepted graciously, he mused, watching with an almost solicitous interest as the Doctor returned to the benches. Having given his name to a committee, Dolke would never permit the exclusion from it of his knowledge and understanding. If there was anything to remark (and it was not the sort of thing the Seneschal would have failed to remark) it was the degree of regard apparent among the senators for Dolke, who

17

had never been given a Chair let alone held the office of Seneschal.

'The Seneschal will surely speak with you in the gallery,' Feucht whispered, his eyes alight and his lips shaping like an actor's close to Dolke's face the soft sounds of his private supposition; he would have felt it an honour. Dolke was too distracted to think the remark insensitive or even tactless. It could be put down to the fact that Feucht was ten years junior to Dolke, just as the Seneschal (and Feucht knew it) was ten years Dolke's junior in the Senate.

Feucht failed to notice even Dolke's silence. He leaned forward again as they rose with the whole Senate for the Seneschal to lead them out:

'But your robe! I fear your seat was excessively dusty.'

Dolke seemed to draw back with a start. He intended only to dismiss the inappropriateness which threatened to break the spell of the moment:

'The Seneschal will not feel obliged to dust it for me, Doctor Feucht.'

And with that they returned to their old terms.

Behind the Classical façade of the Senate and the Great Hall of Convocation lay, untouched and unreformed, a labyrinth. Galleries and passages intersected or slipped one to another by landings and newel stairs. Minute flagged courts, across one of which a man might just lie, gave ingress to the light.

The doctors, having risen in the hall, filed towards one or other of twin pairs of lofty doors. These exits matched each other at the farthest extremes of that part of the wall, below the dais, which faced the windows and the Forum. Through them the doctors could reach the hinter world; in front of them the pews were angled like a mason's square to match the geometry of the hall, and impeded the way.

The doctors hesitated, thwarted by these obstacles. Each party was confined and spread from its route as if into a pool. From this a trickle of figures made its way forward. All were silent and thus seemed to follow as if impelled by some unspoken sympathy. If so, Dolke was not of their mind. He watched to left and right, moved with them nonetheless, and reflected that the procession imparted a sensation that was almost religious. Today perhaps there was something besides. He was not aware of eyes turned on him with a certain naive discretion; but it was not mere vanity, he told himself, which discovered amid all that venerability an air almost of excitement.

As they passed through the doors the doctors were confronted with what momentarily seemed, after the light and the receptive materials of the Aula Senatus, an almost impenetrable gloom. Each sought to adjust his eyes and entered the maze of circuitous approaches, the sudden stairway and the extravagant but misleadingly inviting door-cases. Some of the doctors almost felt their way; some had to repress the pricks of a temptation to find between their fingers the reassuring silken robe of whoever was closest by them; until again they won the light.

It was all at once apparent beyond an open and expectant doorway.

The chamber to which they had come was the Library Gallery. It was not so bright as the Aula Senatus, but struck them as brilliant after the half-light of their tortuous route. When first erected, as part of the focal square of the then still modest, if already ancient, university, and an accretion itself to the fortress-like solidity of those low and vaulted closets through which the doctors had just come, this gallery had indeed been considered splendid, at least by comparison, and that with anything but naked sunlight itself. It had served as the library of the university, or more exactly as the room to whose array of desks books were conveyed from the safety of concealment for study by scholars. This history had given the room its name.

Dolke paused at the entrance and found the Seneschal by him. He slipped his arm through Dolke's and they moved through a press of their colleagues. At the same time they observed the entry at the farther end of the gallery of the members of the second group of senators, whose exit had led them by another way. The width and length of the gallery were such that it rarely seemed crowded, even on such an occasion as this, when almost all the doctors were gathered. Its perspective was accentuated by gracefully moulded and cambered beams which spanned the ceiling at regular intervals and, in supporting the rafters, lent to them their own subtle curve and pitch.

This room seemed to relax the silence of the doctors. The note of conversation of those at the opposite end could be caught between the clear exclamations of those at hand. The warm sun fell obliquely towards the party of the Seneschal. Its light rarely lay perpendicular to the gallery, which extended along a range of the Forum, at right angles to the Aula Senatus and facing to the east. Rectangular windows contrasted with the woodwork of its beams and of a Gothic frieze of marvellous beasts and fabulous deeds. Outside, these windows were brought into harmony with the uncompromising façade of the Aula Senatus only by the uniform whiteness of the stone and the ornamentation of their intervals through two storeys with pilasters, which stretched downwards, superimposed on the pillars of an arcade, to reach the ground.

Within the gallery the sunlight could now be seen to fall, strict and parallel, marshalled by velvet hangings which themselves hung like fluted columns. A suspension, fine and flickering, seemed to illuminate the rays rather than to be illumined by them. Wherever was not directly covered by this flow of light, especially at the end farther from the Seneschal, where hangings were drawn against the sun, the shadowed spaces lay undisturbed, the rich woodwork and the tapestries remained in darkness.

Most important of all the contents of the room were its paintings, on board or canvas, in tempera or oil. Each remained almost invisible until its nearest window's hangings were fully parted. The gallery now contained the university's collected treasures of this art. The senators might go there to inspect them at their ease or jealously compare them with their college collections. Particles of colour, on one picture beyond another into the distance, were picked out by the streams of light, which succeeded and, where the farthest perspective narrowed the distance between them, overlaid one another as if into a haze or screen made up of multiplied layers of gauze.

The almost motionless scene perturbed the Seneschal. Nor did he approve, on such an occasion of rejoicing and informality, the separation of the senators, as it seemed to him, into distinct groups. He released Dolke's arm and took a long step forward. Dolke was obliged to follow, and the Seneschal advanced with a dignity and an inevitability in the manner he drew on those about him that suggested to Dolke a royal progress in the stately Polish

Dance, or the solemn revels of the doctors whose dances had long celebrated Midsummer. The groups mingled and a new and almost busy atmosphere attended the throng, as if radiated by the Seneschal. He, however, turned and singled out Dolke again.

'You will have twelve demanding months, Doctor Dolke.'

'Not oppressively,' Dolke answered, with courtesy. His pride was already less defensive; it was increasingly confident of his just status.

'It would seem strange for me to congratulate you on what must appear my own enthusiasm?'

Dolke at least thought the remark curious. He doubted whether the Seneschal was so extravagantly vain as to be compelled, by an irresistible desire to make some reference to his own scheme, to make a sort of compliment of it. The next words of the Seneschal seemed obscurely to suggest another motive.

'Only in its vaguest outline is the scheme my own. Others also have a part in it.'

That was scarcely likely, thought Dolke. The little he had heard of it bore the hallmark of the Seneschal.

'Others, that is –' continued the Seneschal, though remarking Dolke's silence, 'who have an interest in it.'

The company was polite, the conversation animated. Doctors passed them two-and-two. A tall man permitted himself to acknowledge them with a grave smile.

'Professor Kutten.' Both the Seneschal and Doctor Dolke returned a greeting as they passed.

This was the man Dolke would have desired most to assist him with the masque, had an unfettered choice seemed to be his. That work was, however, the consolation for the approaching retreat into old age, a specific for becoming of no consequence. His present clammy companion, almost like Death in his indefatigable but cold perseverance, made him aware of it, though without inducing in him any rancour; the man who had passed them reminded Dolke that he might hope to do something. The achievement would be exposed to an almost public scrutiny, but it would be an achievement. Indeed the thought of the coming year was pleasant.

But the task would be unworthy of the abilities of a man like

Kutten; he, without doubt, was one of the great men of the university. His talent, Dolke remembered, had required drawing out, not unlike that at present of the young von Fluorn. Like the professor fifteen or more years ago, his present pupil was reluctant to expose himself to the curious, and had once been so reticent as almost intentionally to disguise the extent of his understanding. For Vaslav Kutten had also been Dolke's pupil, perhaps the ablest he had ever instructed.

Memories of the present and the former youth charmed Dolke. As a professor, however, Vaslav Kutten was also a true familiar of the Seneschal; only this, remembered, hurt Dolke in a pang of envy.

'That man . . .' he began abruptly, unconscious, as was his way, that his rambling thoughts had not been apparent; and, correcting himself, 'Professor Kutten would raise my efforts for your masque above the merely accurate.'

'He would not importune you for the honour.'

'You foresee that he might devote himself to it were I to importune him?' Dolke's tone was dry, almost acid.

If the Seneschal willed it, a cutting and ungrateful remark would fail to have any effect on him. He was even able, in the same instant, to congratulate himself on his self-control. He was concerned only that their conversation had not progressed sufficiently in the direction he had intended. He could not afford much more time on it. In deciding that Dolke was 'the man'; in canvassing the agreement (rather than the opinions) of heads of colleges and of men who held college purse strings; in his presentation of Dolke to the Senate, his confident opinion of Dolke was of a pedantic, painstaking man who knew the hierarchy and its formulations and badges – the whole edifice of the university; and moreover knew it minutely. If perhaps without finesse, Dolke was known to have a spark of that inspiration which both felt the greater power of some of those formulations and was not unresponsive to the splendour of the whole foundation. The Seneschal knew (and without making conscious reference to the uneasy vagueness of his own image of the university) that Dolke was the only possible man.

A few, however, had doubted the choice.

'I meant only his reticence. He might not press himself. But Professor Kutten's talent and enthusiasm are boundless,' the

Seneschal found himself answering, modestly. 'And there seemed something in his expression as we passed just now.'

It was Kutten who doubted, a voice in the Seneschal repeated. That grave man's first silence, when the matter was broached, had been eloquent. The force of that memory – that courteous but unmistakable doubt – reminded the Seneschal now of the only knowledge of Dolke he possessed to have made him waiver.

Moreover the goal of his path of diplomatic inquiry was for the moment obscure. Dolke was irrevocably chosen (although it was in the Seneschal only to hear some such words as 'more or less irrevocably'). What more might he do? What more, rather, was he obliged to do? For the Seneschal did submit to his own belief that in the fulfilment of his desires lay the benefit of the university. He was but its human mechanism, moved by the impulse of the elixir of rank.

As for the knowledge that had given birth to doubt, to uncharacteristic fear, it lay in the design of Dolke's tomb: and most particularly in that sinister motto which was not at one with the idea of the Seneschal or with his looming sense of the ancient foundation in which he sat enthroned. And those words were to be inscribed on the tomb in letters of gold! He, the Seneschal, must now reach the point.

'But without doubt I need not praise Vaslav Kutten to you. I should rather be congratulating you on the monument – the work of art – you have designed.'

'You have seen it?' Dolke did not conceal his surprise and pleasure. The Seneschal had changed subject with that habitual elaboration which always fell somewhere short of elegance: also however with an apt and perhaps unconscious forgetfulness of Professor Kutten's rank that touched Dolke. Might the Seneschal have visited the masons slowly persevering in the chapel of Ulpian? Must he not see that the college held him worthy of a memorial, though the university had never condescended to grant him a Chair?

'I saw your drawings,' replied the Seneschal, almost apologetically. 'It was at the Regent's lodgings; he took the liberty of showing them to me – at my request. You must know they have been a topic of conversation.'

He was sensitive to an advantage over Dolke, from a view of drawings left with the Regent of Ulpian for private scrutiny.

'I took advantage of a visit . . .'

A tit-bit of gossip, a hint of wider concerns, might compensate: 'We were to discuss this affair of the university's land at Heching-en. The monks of Zwiefalten and the lords of Mindelheim have been pressing.'

It was now time for Dolke to respond to his interest in the tomb. He had allowed Dolke the initiative.

Having approached with an eye to Dolke's innocence, the Seneschal was quick to suspect him of evasion. During the further steps of silence, he felt an unaccountable but prickling temptation to place the palms of his hands flat against one another and press the very tips of the fingers hard into one another: almost (but quite unthinkable) a loss of will. The sur-rounding hubbub was being muffled by their silence.

The Seneschal was obliged to compliment Dolke on his 'most natural perspective'.

'You might have been a master-painter,' he added.

'Master Pius, of the workshops in the Benedictines kindly showed me – admitted me into some of his art.'

He stopped before a large panel, an Adoration of the Virgin.

'And I have studied some of our Flemings. In this very room.'

Dolke added this, and then the painting held him.

Its colours were more translucent but less artificial than enamel. The Virgin sat beneath a cloistral arch as if enthroned. One pillar spiralled to the left, one to the right. In the farthest distance was an ideal Gothic city.

Only such a city, Dolke thought, may be perfect and give perfect satisfaction. The imagination which had so created an ideal, unexhausted by the effort, remained free to be safely exercised – in the invention of numberless ideal cities. It need not be tempted to find its first creation suddenly unsatisfactory in order to justify its further use – in alteration and, incidentally, in destruction. Its value, and the value and beauty of its creations, were never impaired by the elusive but haunting memory of things replaced.

Its creations – these images – were only a pale tracing of what might have been achieved in some tangible, some realised architecture, but these achievements did not expect their own certain change. Its ideal city had an appearance of total perfection which no worldly city had enjoyed, even for a moment. It neither

24

displayed nor contained a seed of decay; nor did it evoke that disturbing sense, met with in the finest real city, that one would never see the whole in a condition of ultimate and equal perfection.

The Seneschal claimed his attention.

'Your columns are as delicate as these. These are by Master van der Weyden?'

He leaned over and was looking at the picture. Dolke, asked about the efforts he must have made, described how he had made three full sets of designs for Master Michael.

'Master Michael chose those which best suit his skill . . .'

As Dolke explained, his strong hands pushed forward together with smooth but insistent force, as if he felt the fluent sinuosities natural to the carver's hands.

The stone, he went on, ought to be hard-wearing; the best limestone. Master Michael's apprentices were to carve the indented panelling of the revetment, the columns, the quatrefoils and the pinnacles. His voice contained now a note of awe, disturbing to the mind of the Seneschal. He ended:

'But the Master will carve the canopy, the effigy, the cadaver and the Saint James.'

Was this reassurance? the Seneschal wondered. He had hoped not for knowledge but for reassurance. Dry Dolke was, but his eyes and touch were clearly prone to intoxication; his heightened tones betrayed him. Yet the subtle play and shimmer of forms might make any man's head reel a little; as had his own in the Aula Senatus. Some men in such intoxication were prone however to find a new significance in the objects which made them sottish, and thence to believe in the superiority of their own perception, and so at last to insist on an explanation of things around them which gave due weight to the contribution of such as themselves. Such men blinded themselves to the intrinsic character of their setting; the play of their senses filled their sight. Was Dolke such? Or did he remain at one with the old foundation?

'A cadaver indeed! It is sublime, but quite Gothic.' The Seneschal managed this, though his discovery of Dolke's sensuousness was more painful to his own superiority than he could have imagined. Such faint praise relieved a weight in his heart and even whispered that the choice of canopy and effigy, and perhaps also the words of the old Italian lawyer might mean that Dolke's

25

senses rose to the certainties of the old forms and new glory of the university.

'And the inscription – from old Marsilius. It leaves the soul to fend for itself.'

'With other souls.'

'But nothing to stand between him and God. Not perhaps Gothic.' The Seneschal saw himself the embodiment of tradition, yet in tune with the most recent advances of the university. He believed himself, though faithful, yet modern in his confidence that, though God had placed men, ranks and institutions on earth, He had placed them there to reflect His magnificence.

Dolke was uncertain how to respond. The remarks broke into his enthusiasm. He scarcely discerned their edge however. He was not sensitive to elaborate irony and there was a conventional uniformity of tone in these as in so many of the Seneschal's statements. It awoke Dolke however to the Seneschal's persistence on the subject of the monument, scarcely likely to interest him more than politeness required and delicacy allowed. He temporized:

'Ah, theology.'

'Perhaps I do not have the courage to face my soul laid as bare as a skeleton. Some say it lessens the man, but there is comfort in having rules to obey, in knowing oneself to belong.'

'It is less comforting if one has no rôle.'

'Are we then tempted to persuade ourselves that the rules, the place, do not exist?'

'Well, I dare say one looks for a rôle – if one does have none.'

'A rank only.'

Dolke half-turned towards another picture.

'That inscription must have entailed careful thought; not words of the Scriptures,' the Seneschal persisted. His tone now seemed significantly elusive.

'Not a maxim of the Church,' Dolke said, as if correcting him, 'but an observation of nature. As you said – by Marsilius of Padua.'

His tone was ingenuous, but he was now quite certain what the Seneschal wanted. He hoped to shift the course of argument.

The Seneschal remained confident of his own tact, and of the identity of the Church and theology. His voice remained level:

'I am no lawyer; the university statutes seem so dry. Do they offer scope for finding a rôle?'

'Why, some are very recent. You might be surprised how many have been made in the last hundred years.'

'Yet your "observation of nature" – How does it go? "The law is an eye made of many eyes".'

It had given life and breadth to his long consideration of the law. Yet at this moment he saw the importance of the sentiment only to this one aspect of his life. What was its relevance to the university, or even to the decrees which founded it? Such irrelevance was painful. He paused before he could reply. Even spoken in such a tone as the Seneschal's, those words possessed for him a drama.

'Certainly. *Lex est oculus ex multis oculis.*'

Without those eyes, an inward voice now muttered, is there anything?

'And you sense . . .' The memory of his earlier thoughts made the Seneschal's voice stumble guiltily, and he inspected his fingers. 'You hear – their resonance.'

'I have lectured on them.'

'You value them?'

'I feel the Latin has a peculiar tautness. Do you agree?' Dolke meant conciliation, trying to convey the conversation of other doctors, but catching their half-tone of contempt.

There was another, an acid, pause.

'Old Marsilius. Yes, a taut phrase,' the Seneschal confirmed, 'but would he have wished to see one of his aphorisms enshrined?'

He stopped. He dared put into his words no more than a musing lilt. Anger was a state of mind he could hardly imagine. It was something to be suppressed with both hands. Dolke had casually exuded consciousness of superior perception. As he spoke, the Seneschal forced from his sentence sarcasm and near-bitterness. 'Enshrined in a church' he might have ended of that Godless man; and of his human, Godless 'law'; of his transient, incoherent world.

Then that intoxication of Dolke again. Ceremony could not be forgotten; but he, the Seneschal, indulged that rationally, cautiously. Dolke was one of those capable of believing his reactions to be truths. The truth of resonance. Perception which

27

could not believe in the permanence of an institution because that might make the perceiver insignificant. Such men saw what was great as small and ephemeral as they feared themselves to be. For himself, he called these 'truths' a reaction of the senses to a turn of phrase – or to a piece of stone. He did not share them. Something in Dolke's answer of which he was innocent – pride of intellect – hurt him.

The first weapon of the Seneschal's self-control was fear. The Seneschal was afraid. Neither his precarious self-satisfaction nor his choice of Dolke might be put in issue. To what end? They argued that Dolke would not be convinced without debate; that Dolke's appointment was not to be dependent on compliance.

Then came a sudden jink. In him was almost laughter. A deeper self-control (a mechanism of his endangered vanity) came to his rescue. It was strong enough to flood his mind and bear rancour away. In the same spate it rounded on and dismissed with finality the silently accumulating, nagging suggestions of his inferiority. His final weapon – his inescapable weakness of imagination – now braced him as he stood back from the brink. Could an aphorism hold a man's mind? Could a motto mean that Dolke had come to a conclusion, or mark a change, a rupture, in his character?

The Seneschal could not long believe that conduct might be affected by theories, or made less than polite by the turmoil of inner academic uncertainty. A natural love of stone statues was more significant in Dolke, he saw, than a brocard on which he had lectured with advantage. It was others who had doubted. It was Kutten. Despite that first silence – courtesy to his old mentor – it was Kutten who always came back to Dolke's theories.

'Then it is up to you, Professor Kutten!' He had put that to Kutten without equivocation. 'You know his mind.'

Another shadow of silent laughter passed over the Seneschal's imagination. His fears were obscured; which was tantamount to reassurance. He was reminded that he had been too skilful a politician to commit himself at that moment.

They were talking again. He said, with cold jocularity: 'We deserve a debate. You must have poured over our institution. And I am no lawyer. I may have to take up your theory!'

'His writing has all the arguments. My oratory would be a paraphrase. My lectures were.'

'But you will have given him a lasting monument.'

'Well, perhaps the stone will last.'

'It pleases me that some have confidence to add another monument.'

These were parting words. The Seneschal did not invite a reply. No, he was thinking, Dolke has not changed; he believed in what could last. With those words and a gesture the Seneschal excused himself. There was no need to change Dolke's theories, a more easy-going, more self-satisfied voice repeated; there was no possibility of changing them. Dolke believed . . . but men did not apply to all cases all the implications that might be derived from their own beliefs. The benefit of the doubt should be given. Other attitudes led to persecutions. But yes, there must remain a question about Dolke.

Were anyone to change Dolke's ideas it would be Professor Kutten. After silence, and then his unconscious harping on Dolke's ideas, his fascination by the idea of the masque had been frank – and in any case transparent. He was the proper alkali to Dolke's rather corrosive temperament. He knew Dolke's mind from youth. Better still, he loved his old mentor.

The Seneschal was glad to see the professor circling nearby.

Dolke had a moment to himself. While he might he slipped back to the picture of the Virgin and the distant town. Doctor Feucht was uncomfortably close; Dolke hoped fervently that Feucht's eye would not catch his.

To have approached Dolke at that time was perhaps the last thing Feucht would have done. He was quite certain as he watched Dolke stand before the painting that the Seneschal and he had been discussing the prospective membership of the committee for the creation of the masque. The truth was that Feucht, while seeing Dolke as a man who compelled not merely deference but respect and regard, believed that Dolke must have interpreted his attentions as having some contemptible motive; for Feucht was acutely shy. He would have given much to work with Dolke in representing the university. For both, his attachment was almost filial, the most extreme cases of an exaggerated affection which in his loneliness he secretly gave even to slight acquaintances.

29

Dolke looked up from the painting to find Vaslav Kutten behind him.

'Professor Kutten!'

'Doctor Dolke!'

They laughed aloud; their formalities had been an unfailing source of good humour between them since the young Vaslav Kutten, Dolke's favourite pupil, had achieved his doctorate. Their repetition remained successful despite the poignancy of a certain lapse of time, and though Dolke's delighted exclamation had formerly been a less magnificent 'Doctor Kutten!'

'Vaslav . . .' Dolke said nothing more, nor for him would any further words have better expressed his feeling that a companion had at last come with whom he could share the proper contemplation of his task.

Kutten gave his congratulations. Dolke stopped and said suddenly:

'I tell you what, Vaslav – help me with the masque.'

His index finger was close to Kutten's face, a favourite gesture of certainty. Then he added bluntly:

'The achievement need not be beneath you.'

The roughness needed no explanation. The effort to be himself was betrayed only by a hesitation of the breath.

Kutten said simply, 'I had only wondered how I might persuade you to offer me a position.'

Then they paced the room. They pointed at pictures, discussed the day and repeated whenever possible phrases which had between them the quality of reweaving the strands of their former intimacy.

They displayed at random any fancy or image for the masque that occurred to them.

'There must be chariots,' Dolke urged, 'and a stupendous gilt one, for the Seneschal.'

'With two tritons, Rhetoric and Logic.'

'Entwining their muscular limbs in combat. In God's name,' affirmed Dolke, remembering another expression from days when he had taught Kutten.

'Once I designed stage scenes which moved by their own machinery,' Kutten began afresh.

'There will be plays and verses.'

'One play: "The Masque of the University". Of what value are all those rhymes without the university?'

His own remark struck Kutten as an intrusion. It was proof by admission of his already obsessive wish to bring Dolke to a true portrayal of the university. In the play of Dolke's banter was suddenly audible painful echoes of Dolke's past teachings. In Dolke's mind the law was no more than the shifting product of men's minds. For that reason it was to be feared that of the university *he* could see nothing but settings in which men thought.

But the spoken remark passed. In his revived state Dolke scarcely noticed it, except strangely he sensed a familiar chord struck, which he could not place. He was more alert to Kutten's start, and wanted no interruption of their harmony. He merely replied:

'Yes, there is room here for talent – even perhaps for greatness.'

Kutten was to be away from his college the next day; Dolke, he proposed, might visit him for lunch in his bachelor lodgings in the Barschgasse. It would be easier to enjoy a discussion there. Dolke accepted without hesitation, mentioning only that recently he had himself neglected paying visits. Light-heartedly exchanging formal little bows, they parted. Each was full of a curious exhilaration.

Dolke delayed his departure from the gallery, however. It was rare to have so ample an opportunity to enjoy its architecture and its contents. He dealt briskly with congratulations. The room was airy and placid, qualities complemented here by a mood, Dolke reflected (but he could not exactly fix its source in any object), of restraint and discipline. These were all suited to habits of academic reflection. They were to him so pervasive that they, with other attributes, dominated his whole view of the university. He was aware that these impressions were elusive. Indeed a variety of moods, some among them contradictory, seemed to permeate the old heart of the university; his response to the expected effects of its architectural forms was increasingly secondary to the influence of those others. They were becoming as apparent – as dominant – as in that view of the royal palace, whenever he paused to glance from Tenth Day Street. As when there sometimes, he again sought to decide whether these moods and associations were nothing more than the creations of his peculiar and congenital response to what in fact were lifeless, characterless objects. They had the immediacy and reality of the painted images before him – far removed from mere memories of personal experiences. Was he, he asked himself, becoming aware of some character inherent to these places? It was not that he invested them with any mystical, yet alone magical, existence. He knew himself to be more prescient of antiquity, of achievement, of personal memories perhaps, of sharing the libraries and galleries with his day-to-day colleagues, and of a closeness with the dead.

Even whether these qualities existed in – or were observed by – any other mind but his own, he was too uncertain to say. It seems, he thought, to be in the forms, the ornament, the wood, the light, all shifting in their play on one another; and even in decay (his eye fell on a panel stretched to splitting with dry age).

And he wanted to know, for the influence of the established forms of the university itself seemed to be slipping from him. With this the Seneschal's evasions returned to him. For the first time Dolke began to see that his legal 'motto' might indeed represent a shift of his whole self. He half expected from it – his mind caught at – an explanation which he could prefer, but his thoughts floated on. The sudden clarity, the gap between clouds, was inevitably obscured.

His newly-discovered elements of the university, past and present, might be counterfeit, being no more than the heroes he chose and the ideas he favoured. They were also increasingly more vivid to him than the traditions which merely mimed the past and the forms which merely recited it. He inquired hopefully of himself whether his was not the fortune to be responsive to the truth and fact of its history and nature. If what he felt was true, he asked, was it not in that light that the masque, not merely might, but should portray the university?

The resolution of this uncertainty would perhaps be painful. Such views meant isolation; which Vaslav Kutten would tempt him to forsake.

There was a further danger. However he and others might see the university, Dolke (unlike the Seneschal) did not recognise his incapacity to doubt the existence, the truth, of whatever – even if insubstantial – he perceived to be the essence of an object of his scrutiny. As the Seneschal had guessed, though it was the form of the object that Dolke would always need to be confident of its existence, it was his personal view of it which for him would characterise it. In each case however the form, the solidity of the place or the institution must already be less definite, less compelling when the new and necessary explanation came to him.

For the while Dolke allowed his mind to drift lightly among allegorical figures, mythic deities and echoes of slow music.

Chapter 2

Friedrich von Fluorn, besides being a pupil of talent and having played successfully his small part in the previous day's celebrations, was the centre of a circle of students. Most of the members of this little set were, as he was, from good families from the south-west. It was their fashion to wear French cloaks, yet they insisted in their more tumultuous or imperious public gatherings on speaking the liltingly incomprehensible Schwabian dialect. When, as now, the university year was effectively over, each carried a rapier; some who were not within the group said that they aped the military. In short they affected a gallant, often swaggering, manner; except, that is, von Fluorn himself. He did not need the uniform, though he sometimes assumed it. Somehow he exercised over his friends a sort of moral ascendancy. Whatever its basis, this discipline, and von Fluorn's own readiness for an open-handed redress after excesses, prevented their becoming too unpopular. Von Fluorn had sometimes laughingly attributed this power over his friends, even to their faces, to their lack of sufficient imagination to know what to do without him.

They were advancing down Tallow Gate. Doctor Dolke, pausing a little way up its slope, saw before him a dozen of the companions ranked arm-in-arm. Von Fluorn was conspicuous in the front row and the only one wearing, though so late in June, his demure, clerkish suit of black fustian. The others displayed their most extravagant hats and mantles. For those students who cared to be in the town at this time of year the cut of their clothes was their own affair.

In a few strides they met Dolke. To show his *esprit*, von Fluorn pulled off his soft, almost shapeless student's cap, so that his hair fell about his face, and bowed politely. There was no inkling of his scholastic diffidence. The others followed his example but to uncertain effect; they wished to catch the same note but could not be quite sure what it was.

'Still here, Fluorn?'

'My companions will not let me go.'

He turned to the others and said shortly, 'Go on down into the town, will you? I must speak with Doctor Dolke.'

Dolke could never feel more than a benign amusement at von Fluorn's impudence, even when it embraced him as well as von Fluorn's friends. They waved and moved off cheerfully, calling von Fluorn 'Federigo'. It was a suitable nick-name in Dolke's opinion. Friedrich, he thought – von Fluorn (in his case the Christian name seemed too easily to come to mind) – took the name without exception. It suited his complexion, which was olive, and his hair, which was almost black and slightly long for a clerk or a student, though it would not have been excessive for a fashionable young man of the region. The predominant family in his make-up, Dolke thought, must have been Black Forest people; von Fluorn was not only darker but shorter and slighter, and more deft perhaps, than most of his set. His father was a man of reputation, greater than his standing: a *Freiherr* of five hundred acres of farms and seven hundred and fifty of chase held free of his Duke on the great plain of the south.

'I must press on,' Dolke explained. 'I must be prompt to eat at midday at Professor Kutten's.'

'Would you mind very much, Doctor Dolke, if I were to walk a little of the way with you? I am quite glad to see their backs for now.'

He meant his friends. Hesitancy and dismissiveness were odd bed-fellows: Dolke thought him strange but, at the same time feeling somehow sorry for him, began to walk on in such a manner that his action could only be taken as consent. For the Barschgasse was still some distance away, leaving space at some corner, if he remained alone, for a sudden ambuscade springing from obscure mental recesses, demanding that he learn all Vaslav Kutten's mind on the masque, lest Vaslav seek to know his. At the same time he felt that something – von Fluorn's detachment or his conversation perhaps – required an excuse for him to accept von Fluorn's presence.

Therefore he said as he walked, without accenting the words as a question:

'You have something important to ask me.'

'I just wished to congratulate you on your appointment, Doctor Dolke.'

The remark was neither touching nor obsequious. It was so matter-of-fact that no particular reply, or no reply at all, seemed to be expected. The young man's expression was vacant, as one assumes in close company, when wishing to observe but not participate. The compliment was as frank as his comments to his friends; it did not even draw thanks from Dolke, who, while hearing the words, did not as it were recognise that they were something to which he should respond.

Instead Dolke asked, 'You stayed to hear the "Honours" yesterday, then?'

'Yes. But anyway it is all formally published in the Forum this morning.'

They had already reached the top of the little rise. A gate had stood there until recent years and they now entered what was still called the Upper Town. First there was a narrow way, almost a passage. Its overhanging balconies and its shadow exaggerated its twisting length and every jink and angle. As some of the houses strained back into smooth curves and some leaned out uneasily, they aggravated a sense of precariousness. The first building seemed to win its remaining strength and support from one whitewashed pole which pressed from the earth up to a corner of a ledge. It had on one wall an old coloured carving of the Virgin in a crown, and on the house opposite was another, but of a monstrous creature with a beak. A round stone, resembling by accident or shaping a human face, had been set into the fabric of the same wall.

Beyond this alley spread a large, uneven open space. This was now the fish market and was called after its use. On its fringes was an intricate tracing of straitened, narrow ways. Above, on the highest point of the plateau, stood a broken castle. Four towers of the curtain wall against the city were of sufficient height to conceal all that might lie behind – domestic buildings, a keep or a second line of defence. Despite the fracture of their pinnacles and the collapse of shingled turrets, of crenellations and even of the deceptive and once lethal smoothness of their masonry, these towers retained in their high position and tapered elegance something of the sense of their old dominion and impregnability. They retained something too of their obscure significance in the imaginations of the townspeople, which had anciently been expressed in their familiar names: 'Caesar' (to the doctors,

'Theodosius'); on its right 'Heathens' Tower', then 'The Crucible' and lastly that which adopted the sinister popular euphemism which referred to 'The Question'.

Dolke paused in the deserted square. They must cross it and arrive under the towers to find the Barschgasse and Professor Kutten's lodgings. When obliged to come to the Upper Town on a market day he felt so self-conscious among the fish-wives that he would strut past; and so nervous that he could not adjust his pace even to miss some patch of soft fish slime. And there was something about the wet white hands of the women who cleaned the fish on moist pine boards; it made him stare. Today there was only the smell of brine; it suggested the corrosive but ineffectual remedies applied to open wounds.

'It is an extraordinary place,' von Fluorn exclaimed in a suppressed voice. He was excited, but he also wanted to draw Dolke out, to know his reaction.

'Is it true what they say of Mantua: so well architected that there is no room for ghosts?'

'There was a certain . . .' How was he to reply? Von Fluorn knew he could not say 'emptiness'; yet even here in the pungent fish market, by walls incised with uncertain, provoking shapes, he had to seize on everything, keep himself alert to them, to maintain excitement. And 'academicism'? A wrong impression, a quick, detached voice assured him. His face twitched as if he might have been about to cry:

'A certain pomposity.'

'That is incompatible with ghosts,' Dolke laughed.

'And with fish; I've never come up here before.' He stooped: 'Look! Scales, iridescent scales!'

Dolke was scarcely listening, only distractedly to the distant lilt of the young man's voice. Does he have imagination, he asked himself, watching von Fluorn's hand balanced assuredly on the air. He was intelligent and mannered; it was a pleasure to teach him; it was said that all young men of sensibility and invention were mannered.

'But you learnt much in Italy,' Dolke went on, with a note almost of insistence. He had never had the wherewithal to go.

'Why, I almost ceased believing in ghosts!' Then more seriously, 'Everything there is so cool and measured. The most ancient relics could not harbour something monstrous. Our nearest

37

achievement is the Aula Senatus – and the royal palace.'

'That does not lack drama; and the past is near . . .' The image of the palace was before Dolke with an almost physical presence, and that presence was an attribute of the building itself rather than of anything within it. 'One sees it so well from Tenth Day Street.' Though in fact one did not so much see it there, as be aware of it along its ridge behind the trees.

As they had walked together up the hill, he had allowed von Fluorn to trap him gently. Von Fluorn had persisted in lightly bantering pleas for improving criticisms of his address to the Seneschal on Saint Libori's Day – the shortcomings of its sentiments, his observation of correct forms of address – until it was manifest that Dolke had scarcely heard a single sentence of it. His fear of von Fluorn's disappointment had been dispelled by the young man's obvious concern that he might be upset. Von Fluorn had bent forward to look up, with lines of an almost guilty frown about his eyes, straight at Dolke's face.

Now he was describing, with a relaxed upward throw of his arm, the beauty and height of the palace library.

'My father – he can be helpful really – managed a letter to the Gentleman Custodian. But it's a place to suggest every sort of fable and dream.'

Only the emphatic spontaneity of this commentary struck Dolke. The casual impertinence towards his father was meant as, and seemed only, a form of taking into confidence, of treating Dolke as already a party to his personal world. The company of the young, the enthusiastic, was once again, as in the past, exhilarating and almost intoxicating. There was again scope; there was a purpose in himself drawing out and feeding. Dolke had always liked best teaching within a small group of such men. There he was as the hub of radiating, turning exchanges. If he could keep from his voice that awareness, which defiled all joy and virtue by self-conscious reference, that note of pedantry. Few people knew how much pompousness hated itself. Even now his words, with mind of their own, asserted his:

'But I suspect you have neglected this city. You should explore, while you have the opportunity.'

'I am bent on it, sir.'

The Barschgasse ran off to one side, round the foot of the castle wall. At its entrance Dolke turned to von Fluorn.

'I must leave you now,' he said and, surprised by the way this sentence had formed, felt a wrench, a dismay, close to nostalgia.

The Barschgasse was meagre and uneven. On market days people found unbearable the smell which settled along it. Kutten always insisted that it did not trouble him; he could escape to his lodgings there from his college rooms and work without interruption. University colleagues shirked invitations to a squalid, if not actually hostile, neighbourhood. It allowed enemies to elaborate rumours about the nature of his indefatigable and private investigations.

Most of the lodgings' windows faced south; two however on each of his two floors were to the east, for the house stood on a corner where the lane bent round under the last of the four towers. It was taller than the mean wattle houses which faced it from the south side of the Barschgasse, and more dignified. Its beam-lengths and corbels were covered with deeply, almost obsessively carved ornamentation. The Upper Town had been prosperous until the final abandonment of the castle in favour of the palace on the hill, and in this house a wealthy draper had maintained a last vestige of this substance, despite the long and ultimately suppurating infection of the rest of the quarter. His widow, Mrs Wimpfner, was landlady to Professor Kutten. Through the strength of her hands and the discretion by which she maintained Professor Kutten's dependence on her (not least by a frank admission to her tenant of her dependence on him) the air which to local sensitivity suffused her home had decayed only from that of prosperity to one of simple respectability. Dolke could now see the entrance, deep in shadow even at noon while the sunlight lay on the upper storeys.

Von Fluorn was not interested even to see the house where Professor Kutten lived. Dolke demanded his whole attention. Not long ago he had adjudged Dolke a pettifogger. His companions and he had put their fingers on his brusqueness and *gaucherie*, warranting suspicion of a thinly disguised boor. Now this seemed part of an urgency, a constrained fulness which offered much.

In Italy there had been so much emptiness; but despite moments of self-doubt, Friedrich von Fluorn retained his conviction of the existence of a route of painless escape from this dissatisfaction. His mind's eye obscurely saw himself drawing on Dolke until he was nourished (then vividly, with distaste, as a parasite sucking, practising on Dolke). The sometimes almost anguished hope in him was, if self-centred, not entirely selfish. He longed to be filled, his almost physical emptiness fed to the sudden release of superfluity, when, as by a reflex, his own time of bounty and purpose would come. And what he poured forth would somehow be finer than what he had imbibed.

And he would be filled partly by his own effort! Now he was bent on seeing the city. Those were the words which had sprung from him – and with an unaccustomed spontaneity that had taken him aback. 'Bent on' seeing, experiencing, absorbing the city. He had found this purposefulness, he thought, in Dolke's sense of purpose. He started to hum softly as he walked.

Nonetheless it was an incontrovertible fact that he was in a slow and sordid part of the town. A light breeze touched his hot, dry face without relieving the weight of the summer air. His customary affectation in such circumstances was of boredom or a false confession of laziness. Instead he turned his face into the air, breathing in sharply, and wet his lips profusely with his tongue. He had purpose and he was free. The chance of freedom was rare; for he was not free unless he was alone. Yet the sudden appearance of freedom was a confusing element. He was tempted to run, to play the fool. Unused to strenuous walking, he scuttled forward hurriedly, in the way boys sometimes pretend to march and run at once. He never really ran, least of all in front of his friends, for then he was ungainly and, he feared, ludicrous.

Beyond a corner he found himself against a barrier of roughly scarped, natural rock. It formed a plinth, perhaps fifteen feet high, on which rose a tower and the curtain wall of the castle. The alley opened into a neat and pointless circle. Nevertheless he would not go back. Von Fluorn made up his mind and mastered his irritation. I am not free, he said inwardly, perhaps with the dramatic whisper of an actor. I am under my own discipline. His teeth closed as if to grip. There was a genuine determination in him, exerted more frequently than he and most others realised; when he faced an obstacle it seemed to be reinforced by a sense of disbelief that anything might even accidentally be put in his way. Without further hesitation he climbed the bank of rock and balanced himself erect on the narrow ledge under the tower.

His glance fixed on this scraping of ground at his feet. Pebbles, chips of masonry and knobs of weed, any shade of motion over its surface appeared to his concentration considerable features. After a moment gathering the capacity of his body to respond, he twisted round in a single motion to face the wall. The looming curvature of the tower seemed to press him over backwards towards the edge. Quite coolly he told himself that there was no physical danger, but he shook softly with embarrassment for the thought that his effort might have been seen, his privacy touched; also for the clumsiness which his next, more difficult, steps might discover.

To his left there was only one more tower and just ahead of him in the same direction was the back of a cottage built against the rock. This would give to the little path the safety of a gangway. He pressed on along it and scrambled round the buttress of rock on to which the base of the last tower – Caesar's tower – projected.

In the same instant he half cried out in anger and frustration, and perhaps even in fear, for he stifled the sound with a sharp inhalation of breath. Below him was the river. He called silently on the Virgin with extraordinary bitterness. Then he controlled his wilfulness and considered the position.

There is to be no question, he decided explicitly, but how to go further. The silent words pressed with sharply articulated, uncomfortable presence in the curve of his head.

He had never realised the extent of the drop from the castle to the river. It must have amounted to two hundred feet or more. On the other hand, after a sheer drop of perhaps twenty feet from the foot of the rock plinth, the slope, though steep, was not dangerous. The nearest walls of houses and gardens were not far beyond and seemed to rise up to catch, not to shatter, him. Far below, but also far away, was the slow green-banked river.

On that side of the castle moreover was an outwork, a sort of barbican. There, he argued, must also be a gate or a low wall, a gate probably spanning a path from the nearer of the bridges built under the protection of the castle where the river rounded its heights. Von Fluorn was incapable of, and despised, the impetuous daring of his companions, but he possessed detachment and a sense of shame. They precluded failure through any mental exaggeration of the risk. All he must do, he observed, was to

41

climb to the base of the bare rock, then make his way to the barbican, at the risk of a tumble should he lose his footing.

He crouched down tightly to the ground. Don't stiffen, the thought came to him, don't be absurd! Then he let out one foot cautiously but smoothly over the brink, felt a hold, and scrambled and swung his way, moving continuously as the ground best allowed, across the rock-face.

Through the abandoned postern of the barbican, he clambered monkey-like over a heap of rubble, the last obstacle, and rushed under the inner archway with a cry of triumph.

Almost at once, with the assertion of the dirt under his finger-nails and the dry friction between his finger-tips, detachment returned. It struck him first that the castle seemed to have been built more in opposition to the town than to defend it. The courtyard sloped gradually from the four towers past a well to an irregular jumble of buildings. Just above these appeared the pitched roofs of further towers. But it was impossible to realise the whole plan from where he stood. He scanned the curtain wall and judged what looked the best-preserved stretch of the wooden walk-way. It was next to the alchemists' tower, The Crucible.

At the entrance he pressed his foot hard on the first step, though it was of stone. It won him confidence and he began to climb. At first he strode two steps at a time. But his slight uneasiness was almost dissipated. If the stairway ahead had fallen he would control himself. There was no deeper alarm, no shiver of expectation; the stone was chill and damp but dead. Or was he deaf to its breathing? Was he blind to mystery? He kept his hand on it unhesitantly. He paused, breathed long, and ambled up with loose shoulders until he was suddenly in the sunlight. The roof of the defensive gallery and the rampart above shoulder height had collapsed long ago.

Beneath him the city spread out southwards into an irregular triangle. Von Fluorn looked at its beauty. Then he turned to the castle, bending even as he did so to dust his breeches with quick, deft flicks of both hands. The castle acquired a plan; it was a small additional triangle adding an apex to that of the town. The domestic buildings were nevertheless without order; a series of accretions. There was a chapel and a turreted building with a timber gallery. There were low storehouses with massive lintels and solid, if not quite true beams; they reminded him cosily of the homes of his local farmers, the houses of the most prosperous tenants of his family – of his father. The dry, uneven yard might have been that of his own home, but somewhat grown. He turned his mind abruptly to the last building, more recent and more elegant, he thought, with three tiers of rounded windows. The King had built here within the last one hundred years. There was a ramp for the Junkers to clatter their horses right into the building. His own friends would enjoy the chance to do that. He made a grimace of affected tolerance.

He spent time making further observations. It was clear, for example, contrary to his first impression, that the castle had been built for the sake of (though it somehow also possessed) the town; the forbidding curtain of towers was insignificant compared with the height of the plateau over which the castle extended and around the foot of which the river made its course. It still surprised him how he had failed to gauge this. The bend of the stream and the bridges, one at each end, were hidden from his sight; but a dust road, spectrally clean and white in the summer heat, followed its banks eastwards against the current, across the plain to Franconia and Bohemia. A second road ran straight to the north and in the farthest distance wound into a little valley on its way to the wilder and more solitary mountains of Thuringia.

This was the impression von Fluorn obtained. He caught no atmosphere from the place. He was dimly reminded by superficial similarities of a home he chose to remain away from, and at moments a realisation of height and of radiant distances seemed to promise something.

But he did expect himself to be observant. He took in the general line of things easily, and also incidental details: the guest bell on a wooden gallows, the iron ivy leaves which entangled promiscuously about the iron frame of the cupola on the well-head. For he was conscious of the importance of developing his critical faculties. Observation permitted understanding and comparison. These were the twin keys to rational appreciation and the critical exercise of taste. How often had his father reminded him emphatically and assured him – before Italy – that the grasp and turning of these successive keys led to a love of beauty untrammelled by affectation or fashion, to the overflowing of the cup of a man's genius.

The scene before him, von Fluorn observed, with some pleasure in thus mortifying himself, the scene provided an obvious subject for his father's exercises. In theory he could measure against different criteria its value and effect. There was still glass in the narrow lancets of the chapel and patches of peach-coloured wash on the turreted buildings. That luxurious colour was something he could respond to, particularly against its whitish, dusty foil of plaster and stone and all round each bright patch its papery thin and stiff edges. What else? More rooks and buzzards, he noticed, were to be seen here than anywhere else in the area.

Satiated and bitter, he turned his back on the scene. The sight of the city induced, though not elation, at least a bland contentment with its congenial, familiar forms. His sense of freedom returned with the ability to grasp the scale and relation of the tower of Saints Ulrich and Afra and the apparently diminutive Forum; for it was as if in looking at them he placed them and scaled them down so that each fitted just as he intended into a position in his total view. He looked; there was Tenth Day Street winding south from the Forum. Almost directly ahead, it formed an axis for his scene. There to his left was the main market; his friends would be drinking nearby.

Ultimately it was worse. From this view something might really have been expected. Suggestions of something concealed within the forms and surfaces of the city – behind incoherent sounds, vapours and the haze, all emitted or perhaps conjured or lured by certain districts, beneath abrupt flashes of light – penetrated his numbed consciousness. He started and peered down, but the patterns, materials and monuments below him neither dissolved nor revealed more. They reassembled with the remote beauty of a painted city.

In that moment was vouchsafed to him with bewilderingly merciless simplicity his own inescapable emptiness. For several seconds only he was blindly immobile, looking into himself. Thereafter, through a supreme effort of his will, that knowledge was condemned as despair and banished to desolate regions.

To the west were the luxuriant trees and the curve of the palace hill. It stood out bright and flat and almost yellow against the grey-purple of the distant high pine forests, as if lit, as a single tree often is against a thundery sky, by a low late afternoon sun.

Von Fluorn scientifically identified and numbered the monuments of the city – Electors' tower, the spires of the Colleges of Saint Eustace and Maximilian (apparently touching one another), the new dome of Ulpian, the South or University Gate and many others west to east – gates, flêches, towers, gardens, squares, touching them and passing on, until the last. It stood to his left and was the nearest, the Cathedral Church of the Benedictines. As he scrutinised it, its filigree and flambuoyant crossing tower and its west tower anciently and devoutly unadorned, he could, had he wished, have recited the lines and storeys which buttressed and projected the vast and buoyant structure. It was on a different scale from the palace and magnified by its closeness, even from the hill, or so it seemed. He could not assess it for its significance and size and put it in place. Its almost sudden immediacy startled him from his lethargy.

This alertness, the climb, its pain and wretchedness and fear were surely, he prayed, of a sort of beauty, had given birth to an inspiration to reach this height, had made him ache with an intensity, a violence, surely close to the pouring forth, in a flooding draught of mental and physical ecstasy, of the fulness he would one day achieve. There had been no failure. The absence of response (which might have presaged failure and been unforgivable) instead proved only the need to experience and to be filled.

With this he resumed the mild amusement of cataloguing the smaller towers. Nonetheless he stayed, and leaned on the crumbling parapet in a pose. It became unconscious as he watched more intently. He felt hungry; his friends were eating.

He decided that he would go hungry. He responded to the voices, lights and smells which again came up to him from below, as he was unable to do to the orthodox beauties. He caught the mood or tone, or the suggestion to his imagination of their origin, even the chance concurrence and provocative interplay of two or more such elements from quite different parts of the city. His hunger permitted him to introduce himself, as it were, into the incidents of his imaginings, not literally but as if what he saw was of one substance with his dry emptiness. From this awareness of his body, though uncomfortable, he derived a sensation that he was unable to distinguish from pleasure.

A doctor of the university whom von Fluorn admired found delight in almost anything. Taste, he said, was limited in so far as it could not enjoy some object. It was a pleasure admitted by will, but, the doctor urged, both sophisticated and rational, and in the moment of response exquisite. Strangely von Fluorn had drawn secret reassurance from this doctrine. By breaking the bounds of conventional beauty it confused these sources with those of all other urgent responses of mind and body. He glanced back casually at the castle and the hills. The town smells were sudden and vehement.

A sultry haze now shifted and hovered over the lower roofs of the city. Von Fluorn at last set off along the high-walled pathways, southwards and then east towards the centre of the town and his friends. They would still, he was confident, be where they had agreed to eat, waiting until he came and suggested what to do.

He turned and strolled through a grove of apple trees. They were ancient and twisted, and with an abundance of small, hard fruit. The branches were supported with staves; these pushed firmly but at irregular angles and seemed to von Fluorn a human, caricature, abstract grove among the natural trees. The effect even of such a familiar sight was unreal; his hunger distracted his concentration. The rising irritant smell of grass and the heat were oppressive. As he lingered his stomach felt as flat as if there were a pressure over it from outside and the simple awareness of the surface of his body imposed sexual images on all he saw. Putting his left hand to his mouth, he pressed the soft tip of his index finger hard against the upper edge of his teeth, a faint attempt to detach himself from these smothering sensations. All other reasoning was excluded.

His fantasy concerned Mrs Primel's house and his returning now hot to his young squires with an account of the newest girl there from the country. They would still have been sitting. In his dream, Mrs Primel always chose carefully for her young gentlemen (her 'stalwarts' or her 'yeomen', she called them). Yes, thank God she chose carefully; the uncleanliness, the dangers, scared him even through his dreaming, and the momentary apprehension aggravated his hunger.

As he continued on his way he was hurried by resonant and penetrating voices. He plunged into the first street. Mrs Primel's house was behind the main market. He felt compelled to go at least towards the door; his fantasy was still somehow quite distinct from any decision whether he would enter. The corrosive smells of tanning and the sickly air of a brewery enticed him and excited his frustration. He remembered his black clothes, but they seemed suitable for the business. Even the stickiness of his body in the black clothes no longer offended him.

At the end of a small street – of sellers of tawdry, orange and scarlet stuff – he found himself at a quiet, dull space. To one side was the church of the parish, Saint Lorenz (little, von Fluorn smiled, to do with the hospitable college of that name). It rose, square to the dusty cobbles, as if extending naturally from them. Its colour was the same; its edge to the ground was no more than a line, an angle. There were no steps or a tree or lamp, as one found at any prosperous church. A glance at it lowered his spirits.

As he averted his eyes, he noticed a figure slip forward, from what direction he could not catch, into a patch of light in front of an archway on his left.

'Friedrich.'

It was a cautious voice, not much louder now than a whisper. Von Fluorn's mind slipped further from its intention. He turned to look.

'Tassillo Aicha?'

A soberly and exactly dressed young man, in clothes in fact not unlike von Fluorn's, approached with a clumsy imitation of coolness. Von Fluorn stiffened and the sweat ran in vexation and embarrassment: that his earlier thoughts and companion discomfort might be as open to this other's curiosity as he often found those of others to be to him. In spite of it he managed to scold the man lightly:

'Tassillo Aicha! Whatever are you doing in a far from respectable part of the town? And I thought you never climbed out of the university area!'

'What do you mean "climbed"?' Aicha said seriously, 'Who climbs?' Aicha caught at himself; but he could not stop himself sounding gauche or worse. That was his habitual, uncontrollable tone of response to banter. It said inwardly, 'I could return the same coin, if . . .', but spoke only heaviness.

'You got rather ahead,' von Fluorn interrupted, with the tone of a lawyer putting a leading question in cross-examination. He needed relief to Aicha's pompous literalness. He suspected Aicha had been following him.

Aicha, looking at the church as if he found something interesting there, merely asked von Fluorn whether he had eaten:

'We might see if we can find something to eat. And drink, if you like,' he added as an afterthought.

Though he was still sweat-sodden and damp, the drive of von Fluorn's sexual imaginings had, without an effort of will, left him. It was not possible to return to them now by the usual mental keys: names, sounds, crude evocations of favourite dreams, or the bringing to life of some nerve or muscle whose tension, with the right mood or time or temperature, shut out one world and admitted another.

He looked the incongruous figure of Tassillo Aicha up and down. He had no doubt that Aicha appeared far more out of place than himself, despite the superficial similarity of their clothes. Von Fluorn felt safe: Aicha's sidelong look assured him that he was with someone who would always be more on the defensive than he was himself, yet whose furtive motions invited scrutiny. There was certainly something secretive about Aicha. It gave him his only fascination, a sort of thin glamour. The greater interest stemmed from von Fluorn's awareness of that secretiveness; his sense almost that, if he cared to, he could pull aside the veil and know everything. It was this that gave von Fluorn's voice the promptness of reassurance and the glow of authority. Aicha could, he reflected, be difficult, but Aicha respected him. Respect was a sort of nourishment.

Aicha made a gesture that von Fluorn might make the decision, an interested, insinuating movement.

'I should like to come.'

Von Fluorn put his arm through Aicha's and, turning about with an air, drew him along. He talked gaily and allowed the usual edge of his humour to sound like intimacy.

'It's quite a thing to be walking arm-in-arm with an Aicha. Really my family's positively new. You're founder's kin – almost!'

Aicha smiled awkwardly. He knew von Fluorn was curious – about him and about why he was in this tasteless part of the city. How it disgusted him; why he had come there he scarcely knew himself. Sometimes he found himself following – or just watching.

Aicha would not have presumed to inquire, even covertly, why von Fluorn was there. What he confided in solely was von

48

Fluorn's temporary interest. Like von Fluorn he was a student of law and at Ulpian. His capacity to act – to allow himself to act – as a foil in their discussions and exercises with tutors had struck and perplexed von Fluorn. He knew this: also that when he had silence to gather himself he could, if he wished, unnerve von Fluorn.

His sudden appearance had, then, achieved something; by putting his conclusion in this way, Aicha had to admit to himself that he had followed von Fluorn for some distance. But how was he to proceed? And to what end? All he knew was that, without knowing why, and with embarrassment but without guilt, he had followed an almost painful anxiety to convince von Fluorn that they had something in common. That was all he wanted von Fluorn to realise, he told himself. He did not choose to consider the matter beyond this. Therefore he answered, though obscurely disappointed by von Fluorn's thin politeness, which depreciated a noble family:

'No, not "founder's kin" or anything like. And we've never produced another Aicha like the Ludwig or even one who looks like him.'

'Is that good news? Because of his looks I mean,' von Fluorn grinned. 'I know a good place, by the way,' he confided. 'One can just sit and talk the afternoon away.' Then he laughed like a boy and looked back over his shoulder thinking to himself, I hope the others will not wait all day.

Professor Kutten had been expecting Dolke. In his long sitting room, which overlooked the Barschgasse, Mrs Wimpfner watched from a window for the visitor. She had insisted on stationing herself there while Kutten tried to read in the inner library behind his study. It must not be thought that Mrs Wimpfner ever assumed a rôle as his servant; but she knew how to stand as still as a statue, and somehow to allow no emanation from her presence which might as she waited, or moved behind him, alert the nerves of his back and neck. It was her pleasure (a cool, unruffled, deep pleasure) and her pride to grant him indulgences and privileges; he had the run of the cellars and storerooms and might examine at will her dead husband's collection of Nuremberg prints. Kutten had escorted her more than once to informal civic occasions, though never to any of the university's. No more than this was to be known, but little would have been expected, except to say that she stood and watched, and that when she saw Doctor Dolke dawdling up the hill with a pupil she delayed her call to Professor Kutten until Dolke was briskly approaching alone along the Barschgasse. It was the same possessive affection that both made her disobey the professor's request to be called as soon as Dolke was in sight and made her feel almost hurt that he had as few visitors as she.

'Nearly at the door!' Kutten burst out, 'Why ever . . . ? Forgive me!'

He had been nervously irritable beyond reason. When he had retired to the inner room of his library he had sat himself stock still in his ebony chair. He had bent over a volume of the planets but with sightless eyes. Was he soon to be discovered? That question had filled his attention without his quite knowing to what guilt it referred. Before approaching Dolke in the Library Gallery he had stooped to solicit the Seneschal's politic approval. But this only mocked his pride. His irritated guilt was of the purpose both of that stooping and of his very invitation to Dolke: to insinuate his own vision. Yet he would fail. He had no plot and no cunning to convince. This had almost soothed him. That Dolke would lightly see through everything had almost reassured him. Inadequacy excused guilt. He had smiled wryly, almost sardonically, and had breathed more fluently.

Here, then, lay the deeper springs of his agitation: he wanted to be discovered. To end deceit and to be spared retribution would have been sufficient joy for Vaslav Kutten, for he not only loved but feared Eberhard Dolke as a father. To Dolke even his fear, he believed, must be apparent; such (he had been sure since boyhood) was the almost mystical power of a father. Of his own, who had died far away and long ago, he had no memory. Dolke had taken him up as a son and had acquired thereby a father's powers.

The counterpart in Kutten's mind of this dread was trust. Deceit was certain to be discovered but openness and trust would be returned. The force of this trust was as that of a radiant harmony; its realisation was a half-believed Golden Age once pertaining between the two of them.

A curious dishonesty of his memory, a capacity to separate into

50

elements the compound of a relationship and to place them so far apart that they were no longer related, could revive independently both the dizzying presence of that harmony and the pain of the same occasion on later recognising the (ultimately willing) confluence of his mind in the current of Dolke's; the abject, happy echoing of Dolke's rhythm. In Kutten submission was an element of trust.

Sitting, awaiting Dolke, the warmth of trust for a while consumed guilt. He refined its vague and wisping fume and its exultant light (for its character shifted, its guise changed) by bringing into focus its most precious moments: just when he was no longer a student and they had worked together on a monograph; an afternoon, walking with him under the façade of the royal palace (they had doffed to the King as he rode under the arch); Dolke had given his first spontaneous criticism, without aggression or condescension, almost mellifluous, almost beautiful, of Kutten's first long work. In selecting the perfect there was an inevitable precipitation of memory of the less than perfect; further mechanisms deftly filtered this out; but that harmony as of equals had in fact been unique; that afternoon encompassed the whole life of a perfection which at this and other moments appeared to Kutten the character of a long phase of his life.

At his landlady's matter-of-fact announcement of Dolke's approach he was again possessed by a sort of dull panic.

'Would you wish me to show him in here, Professor Kutten?' Mrs Wimpfner continued. Her voice was unflustered, slightly soothing.

Kutten barely answered. His conscious mind only registered the grating nicety of 'wish' (when placatory she tended to affectation). It does not suit her, he thought. He stared at the dark space which occupied the open door-frame; he did not notice Mrs Wimpfner leave by it. With the identification of a fact, that he and Dolke must soon be talking, the fearful face of his love for Dolke was again before his eyes. How immediate were those open talks which were Dolke the tutor's speciality! His rooms, a small group of students, and talk infectiously opened by Dolke with a remark about a city, a caustic reference to an historical personage. Then they were free, and so compelled to declare their feelings and incidentally their true attitude (it always came to this) to Dolke's teachings. Kutten had since learned self-discipline. In his youth

51

self-revelation seemed inescapable, the duty, the need, to believe in Dolke's maxims irresistible. But his love for Dolke was expectant, no longer in the shadow.

'Doctor Dolke,' Mrs Wimpfner announced.

Kutten stepped towards him, almost overwhelmed with joy.

Kutten dismissed Mrs Wimpfner more shortly than he meant.

'There are preparations to be seen to,' she said, as if accounting to Dolke for his tone. She had almost insisted on these 'proper preparations'; but she had quietly determined to keep herself busy afterwards in her own sitting room and to leave charge to a good, prompt girl she hired by the day. She knew when not to be seen.

'And how is my pupil?' asked Dolke, the moment Mrs Wimpfner had closed the door. Dolke was still buoyant after von Fluorn's company, but a part of his mind was measuring, as it were keeping a hand on, the unease in him which could sound discord.

Kutten closed his mind to all the associations of Dolke's opening.

'One day follows the next; a number of pages appear at the end.' He tapped an irrelevant sheaf of paper which lay nearby and tried to chuckle. Then turning towards Dolke and standing more upright, he made a wide gesture of friendship and sharing.

Dolke laughed once – 'Hah!' – and lifted his right hand just above his eye; he seemed to examine an object supported in his fingers, which turned with his forearm to and fro. It was one of the most intimate gestures of his mind's sympathy, and spoke much to Kutten.

'A pupil of mine' (his regrettable words could not simply be shaken from his mind) 'accompanied me from the Tallow Gate.'

'Oh?'

'Friedrich von Fluorn. Very deft and observant.'

Kutten remained silent. After a moment, and with a perplexity or even distaste in his face, he said:

'Let's not disagree.'

'Do you know him? He's a boy!' exclaimed Dolke. He assumed that, if Kutten had a ground for complaint, it must be von Fluorn's well-known association with the gallant and blaspheming gentry.

'They are lascivious blasphemers.'

'What? Boys?' Dolke tried once again to laugh.

'All of them. Those . . . bravos.' His voice was hesitant and level, but his face was contracted with a flushed embarrassment that Dolke had not seen before. That Dolke had associated such people with *that* movement of his hand!

Nonetheless Dolke needed the last word.

'Well, he's very willing. You would have to approve his capacity for work.'

'You might ask Doctor Feucht. He has a considered opinion.' Attributing his view where it would be agreed was less painful. 'He puts it more kindly than I.' Kutten's voice became less husky. 'Young von Fluorn would be an "experimenter" he says, because of the fascinating shapes of the alembics and the excitement of the reactions. That is the real reason.'

For what? The reason for what, thought Dolke. For disapproving? Or for that outburst? What a puritan Kutten is! He has his narrow inch! Perhaps I am not so grey! He did not notice that Kutten's final, dismissive gesture was one quite alien to him. He was glad to be satisfied.

And there were always common enemies. He announced:

'I've already someone in mind for the masque. The Very Reverend Heysach is to personify the Liberal Arts.'

The Visitor to the university was an incubus on them both, with a malignant fascination for secular, indeed profane, judicial acts (as he was prone nonetheless to see the operation of human justice).

'And he has a name worthy of a Greek philosopher,' Kutten said, smiling distractedly.

'Well, we shall certainly have to choose. It won't be easy,' Kutten heard Dolke saying. He was appalled at his own behaviour. It had put everything in jeopardy.

He put aside explanations. His violence was almost bewildering. It had something dimly to do with a jealousy of Dolke's attention, teaching and right to discipline.

'I can't imagine how,' he replied, still not looking quite at Dolke. But the words, 'Lascivious blasphemers!' (he heard them again, and they almost filled his mind with joy). He looked straight at Dolke. His mind seemed washed clean and clear. His guilt was expunged. He would not surrender his sense of things;

he must, as he had meant, put before Dolke irrefutable evidence of their nature. He would evoke the old sense of investigation, of the imminence of greater knowledge. These, once revived, once recaptured, would without explicit reference and without debate pervade their portrayal of the university.

'How would you choose?' Dolke had asked.

'In the senators, seniority and dignity. In the students, grace, beauty, modesty and wit.'

He was now calmly serious; Dolke was smiling.

But to mention 'the masque' (with all its now clear implications of the problems of their collaboration) was only a matter of moments. They talked, circumspectly, of participants, then of help. Dolke had news of the Seneschal's assiduous ('not to say "devious"') financial negotiations, and Kutten nodded.

'And there are rumours. The King will come, if all has gone well.'

It was a note which could open and broaden both their imaginations. Kutten knew himself free to offer what was common to them.

'Then we must give scope to your taste for magnificence.'

'As I walked up I kept thinking of colour and fabrics. Much of the town is so drab.'

'"Colours speak", they say. You know so much about those slight distinctions . . . The legatus Arcute is besieged by his volumes on Imperial quarterings. Might not the colours of the oldest college . . . ?'

'Well!' interrupted Dolke, laughing; no, it was not time yet for precise agreement; to accept harmony is always to be swept along by it. Not yet.

'Why,' he said with a gasp, 'John of Mecklenburg beggared his court and a duchy with such an affair on his daughter's christening.'

It was not so easy for Kutten to abate the flow; emotion was bound up with it.

'Perhaps I would find it easy to be profligate. I had flattered myself . . . but here in this house. Or rather it is the house that fills my time. Not so many people come here, but then the house entertains me.'

Kutten was obviously excited. His words had been spoken with a suppressed agitation, a pressing together of the lips.

54

'It must be ancient.'

'The meal will not be ready yet. You remember how much we used to talk about history,' Dolke heard him say. He felt Kutten touch his arm and turn him towards the door. Dolke consented to come by raising his hand, as if enervated. He felt apologetic, to himself really, for having again failed to recognise sooner the strength of Kutten's feelings.

They went down through the house in silence. In silence Kutten took up two lamps and lit them. One he handed to Dolke.

The staircase was oak and stained very dark. On his arrival Dolke had moved up it absent-mindedly, thinking of von Fluorn, thinking of Kutten. Finding a blank between Kutten and himself, he concentrated on details. The walls were of white plaster, greying in places and with slight creases where the smooth surfaces of the uppermost of many layers had been cracked and pushed by the damp beneath into opposing inclines. These walls were hung with widely spaced portraits, painted on board and without frames. The pattern of the staircase flights through four storeys – ahead, down to the side, and on down – was broken by the vertical line of a massive beam set in the wall. It seemed to have burst through the plaster in which it was set, so closely did the plaster press against it on both sides, though an inch behind its outward surface. Its height and strength seemed to tie together the levels of the house; its insistent presence, as Dolke walked, and its central position gave the house the only form it possessed.

The staircase and the staircase well only seemed regular where their extent and direction could be wholly seen, from the very top or very bottom. From the middle of the flights a cramped little landing would stand back or an arched passage run off, railed across with turned balusters for perhaps half its width. Other spaces spread from the bottoms of flights; doors stood at curious angles to them. There was something in their atmosphere of the old buildings behind the Aula Senatus, the same suggestion of moods which could slide over one another like translucent layers, or dislodge one another in spite of the unchanging appearance of its features. Unaware of the uses of its various wings and suites, Dolke found the place even more confusing.

Passing the entrance to a passage, Kutten paused:

'I never go through there.' He pointed to a door at the end.

Dolke saw there was no joke; and Kutten would not have

talked in that way of something particularly private, even less of something sinister.

Kutten's face betrayed no motive. Indeed he asked inwardly why he had said this, though it was true.

Neither man saw how much this house thrust under the castle walls filled Kutten's world; that for him it remained the only unfailing source of mystery; formless, shifting and baffling, the only place that he allowed to encompass him.

A world needs its mystery, Kutten thought casually. Yet he was not aware, at least at that moment, of his need for such attributes of life itself. It was not what he had come to show Dolke. But Eberhard is intrigued, Kutten told himself.

They descended the last flight of stairs, whose walls were tinted with gold in fading arabesques. The air became cold. Kutten led the way to one side, at last walking quickly.

'You have an Aicha among your pupils,' he began abruptly, breaking the silence. 'I should like to know what he is like. He is a direct descendant of the great Aicha, is he not? We shall have to choose people. I should like to know what he is like.'

'He gets ten pounds a year from the university as "founder's kin".'

Von Fluorn has more talent, Dolke thought, remembering his pupils. Generations had passed since Ludwig Aicha. People simply didn't connect the two.

'Attention would be wasted on . . . on the squire.' Kutten was quite matter-of-fact (inside himself as if bodily compelled to dispel this clear irrelevance before they could begin to explore together). 'I can tell that he does not understand even the value of knowledge. He is incapable of recognising its beauty. He will never create anything.'

The cool, nervous, familiar voice was nonetheless startling. It was as if he had known Dolke's tactfully suppressed thoughts. Dolke did not reply.

They came to a metal-shod door. Kutten unlocked it. He raised his lamp before his face and entered first.

'And these are the most ancient parts of the house, the cellars.' He spoke proudly and as if continuing an earlier part of their conversation.

Dolke stooped to walk beneath the vault. Ahead of him Kutten's figure issued brisk words (that guests should see his house, he said, gave him more pleasure than that they should praise his work). They struck Dolke as quite uncharacteristic, almost sycophantic; perhaps it was the hollowness of words spoken into gloom, he told himself.

He bent lower than Kutten, to avoid the wet stamens of white mould. To allow his body to exert some upward, supporting thrust, he pressed against the ceiling plaster the tips of three fingers, all he could bear should touch its sweating surface. But he was somehow constrained not to protest or to give his host any other excuse for accusation.

They passed by the mighty butt of the wooden column which, standing in flagstones, seemed to thrust both up through the house – through the stair-well and the white plaster – and down, securing it all to earth. Kutten dragged forward into the light circles of their lamps curiously decorated chests, dispersing as he did so plumes of a strangely dry powder of fallen mould and stone. Some of the chests were rotten with neglect, some inlaid, and some with subtle locks were wrought from hammered iron.

'And yet,' said Kutten, as if Dolke had asserted some theory about them, 'they are nothing – except perhaps in the imagination of some of my visitors. What do you suppose? A draper's bill-boxes. And his father's and grandfather's. I searched all of them and found only one or two things.'

He laughed, then, after seeming to Dolke almost defeated for a moment, began with a new sense of purpose:

'These cellars – do you notice? – are far more extensive than the land on which the house stands. Had you noticed that?'

'I confess I'm totally confused.' It was the rough-hewn pillars and projecting walls and darkness.

'We are part of the castle.'

A trifle over-dramatic, Dolke thought, but he recognised, as Kutten drew him on, his companion's elation, of that kind that is an excitement of the imagination.

'It is no less, this house, than an extension, a fragment, of the castle.' It was part, he meant, of a system and pattern which had spread from its ancient, unsophisticated heart.

'It might be traced,' he went on, almost coaxingly, 'like any knowledge – by a sudden realisation and by feeling the way. With those same alternate sensations of enlightenment and suspense.'

He swung up his lamp and revealed two apertures in the wall.

'This passage was scarcely wide enough for one man. It is completely blocked now.'

He moved forward and touched the lip of one of the openings. Dolke too stepped closer; holding up his lamp, he gently spaced his fingers on the edge of the gap, like a surgeon examining a wound.

'I have tried . . .' Kutten began again, and broke off.

For a few moments the light of their lamps seemed to hold his long, white hand. A part of Dolke's mind noted its delicacy and softened his feelings about Kutten. Another, more assertive and leaping part was aware of the hand's continuous tremor and registered by contrast through his own arm the firm pressure of his own fingers on the stone. Kutten was afraid!

Nonetheless Dolke heard himself say, 'It's ancient masonry.'

Kutten was afraid! That leaping part of Dolke actually rejoiced at the idea. Kutten brought me here because he is frightened – by the draper's bill-boxes!

Dolke himself had been afraid. Even as he had entered and stooped into the darkness, he had thought, the madman's thought: perhaps Kutten is going to murder me. He had felt – the place had possessed a feeling – Vaslav may be about to murder me. Vaslav, whom he had known since boyhood!

Moreover his own fear was at once finally mastered. But Vaslav was still afraid. Perhaps he had hoped that by bringing Dolke here his fear would be dispelled.

Not only Dolke's aggression but the need of his confidence to be shored by every weakness of others that it could discover was struck by the blindness (was it dishonesty?) that failed to see or to admit the mystery of the place, of the whole house. Dolke's overt, speaking consciousness, deeply involved now in the stone, the passageway, merged with the crueller impetus. He was asking Kutten,

'Did you say you tried to explore this passage?'

Kutten was explaining, and one part, more and more, of Dolke was absorbed, listening. The inward voice of Dolke pursued its conclusions – yes, Vaslav is seeking this mystery. Without it he would not love the house. But he will not admit it is there; he will not learn what I taught him. An institution is a living thing. Fact, a known history, he will only bow down to these. He is an alchemist but convinces himself he is a scientific philosopher.

Dolke saw clearly, then, that, no matter how complex a synthesis Kutten might attempt, he could never achieve that place. He loved in it what was, in part, not amenable to analysis. In this flight of almost unconscious thought Dolke was also aware of a movement of his own fundamental attitudes. But did the life (mystery was an attribute of life) lie outside such eyes, as his and Vaslav's, that saw them – a hopeful life beneath the transient forms – or did the life, the mystery, only lie in some crazy, refractive quality which their eyes shared? Here was a source of continuing fear.

'But passages are known to have run from the alchemists' tower – the Crucible – and the tower of interrogation – of the Question,' Kutten was giving the known facts. 'Surely not to go out into the town, but to take *something – someone –* in.'

The theory pleased Dolke; it suggested more to the imagination.

'But there is little evidence of tyranny at that time.'

Kutten detected in his voice a desire to know, an expectant tone, as if Dolke were willing him to take the next step in the way forward.

'I have thought of re-reading the chronicles in the light . . . ,' Kutten paused. 'Of fact. It is rare to be given . . . I would ignore knowledge at my peril.'

His hand was now pressed firmly against the wall of one of the passages. Dolke began to cast round for some evidence or argument to set against their first theory. Why had this passage been maintained so long after the town had grown? Less ancient masonry – here – proved it. He was completely engrossed; more than Kutten had dared hope.

'But first of all, Vaslav, you will have to prove that these are the same passages – that they reach the castle.'

They would return together and with help, they promised – one day soon – and begin to dig.

Mrs Wimpfner's arrangements had been impeccable. In a small side room the turned limewood chairs stood somehow expectantly; the white linen made Dolke gasp. But they ate hurriedly and messily. Kutten got up while he ate and moved about. He was now certain enough of Dolke to put before his friend (to share with him, for Kutten was too generous to maintain a sole intention of convincing) his latest and most tentative investigations.

Dolke followed him into his inner library, infected with a similar, irritant sense that anything he saw – and in particular touched – might provoke or advance trains of thought. There was a broad circular table. On it lay a beautiful crystal sphere and a complex geometrical figure – a dodecahedron, also of crystal. He touched the sphere and turned the figure (wiping his fingers with instinctive vigour before doing so). Also there was an old 'Jupiter square'; its ranks of numbers always gave, by any process of calculation, a fortunate, cabalistic number.

'It wards off my Melancholy,' Kutten laughed, picking up the square and tapping it familiarly.

'"Friend and foe to the learned, Melancholy!"' Dolke quoted.

Kutten was alert to the presence in both men of that current of mental activity which, because it demands, believes possible, a fundamental, a total understanding.

'Here is a truly complete and lasting work,' he heard Dolke announce.

They had returned to eat, then strayed once more to the largest room. Above a writing table, in a polished case of shelves supported by carved consoles, were the volumes of the Code, Kutten's great contribution to the university and to the law. New and apparently unopened, the curves of their rounded spines ran as true as a wave.

A gesture very much Dolke, Kutten thought (but as if of another Dolke, a pedagogue of his youthful acquaintance). He made no perceptible response. He recollected one of those tutorial conversations of long ago on the Code, the great Code of the Roman civil law itself. Was a code, Dolke had offered – the Code – a petrification of the true glory, the subtle living body (though mortal) of centuries of jurisprudential and judicial hypotheses and applications? Was the Code the true glory? The faint partisan voices – his own voice – sounded in the crown of his head. But another occasion filled his memory and obliterated the moment of fervid self-assertion and resistance before final submission.

Dolke leaned forward. He took down the first volume of Kutten's Code with respectful care (though to extract it he had first to work it from side to side). He had meant his remark to express their refound intimacy. He turned the first pages of dedication. In clear Roman letters, a square formed in the centre of a page, was a declaration justly conscious of merit:

'The Civil Laws of the Realm are become by this work and the authority given thereto by His Majesty, John Christian by the Grace of God, a unified system of the Civil Law.'

Touched by the words, reminded also what at least some contemporaries had achieved, Dolke had read the passage half-aloud. In the volumes of the Code (he was, realising the magnitude of the work, momentarily astonished) had been set out under Kutten's design and inspiration, a just and efficient system of courts, of judicial appointments, of the law of all personal and commercial intercourse, and of property and its inheritance. Such near finality – such near perfection (in human terms) still touched him profoundly. Seven years had elapsed since it had acquired the force of law. Few changes had yet been found necessary.

'It is no Sir Thomas More Utopia, Eberhard,' Kutten murmured, but obviously moved by the compliment.

'You were the one who could do it,' Dolke said, but almost absently. 'I knew. No shifting sands; no treacherous Utopias.'

I accepted that from you, Kutten thought, with the pain of the reminders of that understanding which the work had demanded; and with a temptation to think, as absurdly he once had, that such cool scepticism of lasting achievement as Dolke's often saved a man from envy. Kutten's expression was impassive.

Dolke was still turning the pages of the volume.

'No,' he resumed, 'no Utopias, please! They change and our best efforts, our perfect laws, run with them. My boast – if I may – I think I taught you that.'

He did not intend sourness or unkindness, but he spoke with the complacency of one who has come to terms (for the moment) with his own inability to create perfectly and permanently or with the futility of any such attempts and of nagging desires to continue with them; perhaps in his own case even with that further aspect of himself which asserted his individuality when faced with what was said to be impervious to change.

'I didn't kill the old jurisprudence. The Code and the old law is the same life in a different form. The content, the fact, is the same. One can ignore the metaphysical difference.'

Dolke was again his clever, didactic instructor. Part of Kutten's mind was still in the past, fighting for the old Roman Code, exonerating his own future achievement. How willingly he would have acknowledged all Dolke had done for him! Above all, when some complex, hypothetical situation was posed, how to *know* which principle or legal concept was decisive. But there was the slight self-importance (too slight for grandeur or conviction). It had always been most pronounced when galled and probed; and his thin defence against the shock of petty outrage. Pedantry, or a blush.

'But indeed, Vaslav,' (Dolke seemed only now to have heard his reply.) 'At any one time there will be an eye made from the many eyes. And in your code you have delineated it.'

How he laboured that word – 'delineated'. Eberhard's charm, Kutten thought (and suddenly felt himself hot in the face); his charm is in his transparency and his inability to fathom his friends. With his eyes alone Kutten caught Dolke's attention, as mischievously as if he had resumed his old rôle, a provoking, favourite student:

'Even our Lord was not required to create perfection – just display it.'

'You are incorrigible,' Dolke said lamely, but, like Kutten, smiling.

'I have more to show you. Otherwise we shall have to sit in the past.'

They had to reach the roof.

'My belvedere, and my laboratory!' Kutten exclaimed, and stept out on to the shingles. There was a way between the slanting roofs and the parapet. Further along was a little platform of boards and on either side a primitive seat. Kutten went first:

'Have a care, Eberhard. Take care now,' he called, turning casually.

'I can still clamber.' But Dolke was reminded to steady himself; he held out his large left hand.

On an impulse Kutten turned again and with his right hand gripped the fleshy, hairy, orange-flecked back of Dolke's hand. In the same instant a momentary spasm of sexual awareness filled him, then a bewildering onset of directionless hatred. Never before had he given way to that prompting. Dolke's hand fell away from his. He scrambled over the platform and stood at the far side.

How nervously young he is, Dolke was thinking.

From under a heap of canvases at the end of the way Kutten swept up a broad mirror in one movement of his arms. As he returned with it, bravely, he could still feel his cheeks shining and a slight bodily shiver. He was not ready to look at Dolke.

When, though, he had set the mirror on the platform, its ingenious mechanism of catches and supports calmed him. Its face was beautifully ground and polished.

'You can release it,' he managed, and pointed without further words to the silver latches by which it could be freed from its position locked upright in its ebony frame to be swung by a touch to reflect upwards, down or to either side.

But first they must wait. They must be in light; the far walls of the city must be in the shadow of one of the slow, large clouds.

Below them, in warm and tremulous light, was the city. The glass returned the rays of the sun over the houses. Delicately, but with slightly trembling fingers, Kutten revolved the mirror.

The invisible beam struck, on the southernmost walls, on the edge of the conical cap of the University Gate, a faint burnished patch. Instantaneously he withdrew his finger-tips.

'Too quick to see! There you are!' He turned to Dolke: 'Do you think that a common-place? Doctor – well, a colleague of ours seeks to invalidate it. But you can witness . . .'

Yes, Dolke replied (but slightly surprised by Kutten's vehemence, as if Kutten had needed to excite himself, to dramatize), the beam had reached the tower roof and, yes, the moment it had come in contact with the edge of the target, the returning light had reached them.

'And you can witness that I maintained the pressure. How could I not, indeed? I could only know that it had reached the edge when I saw it return.' They had said, he explained more calmly (but did not say who 'they' were), that the light must have been returned from the roof, but from a point beyond the edge; the mirror would have been pressed round further before the light had time to return and tell Kutten to release the pressure. But there undeniably had been the dim glow on the very edge of the tower roof; though it was not easy to distinguish again, after the instant of change.

Kutten threw himself back into his makeshift seat, making soft sounds to himself, between laughter and contempt.

'A learned doctor at Bologna claims that the speed of these radiations is slow enough to be gauged. He suggests that once light from a mirror is seen returning, the expectant hand might in a sort of spasm turn back the mirror to align it with the edge of the target.'

His sardonic tone was almost sinister, but compelling. Dolke replied gently.

'We could devise a mechanism to turn it. The hand would only be ready to stop its motion. You particularly. Remember your ideas for stage machinery.'

'Perhaps you are not conversant, Eberhard,' Kutten began, abrupt but measured, clearly on a new track, 'with the papers of certain investigators of Leyden? The consistency of light, the colours in light – I say that advisedly – raise a thousand questions. These Dutch gentlemen ask some of them. But they also ask about the process of seeing this "light".'

He lowered his voice, and whispered of other experiments in other places – of the dissection of the eyes of a dog; of the dissection of a human eye. But what, he laughed, could a dead man's eye reveal? If light had ever come from, if light had ever played on it to give it sight, it did so no longer. He left unsaid that it was something he would never attempt.

'Vaslav, turn the mirror to play on the dome of Ulpian. The clouds are right.'

'You, Eberhard, you try. I have often done it.'

Simply and courteously he touched the rim of the mirror to relinquish it.

Dolke slowly revolved the mirror; the light struck.

'I can make out no difference,' he whispered with soft urgency, 'and the dome and the University Gate must both be a full thousand paces off. So it comes from copper as swiftly as from lead.'

'I agree – from the copper dome and the welts of the gate.' But an indifference affected him; it seemed to him somehow connected with the movement of the clouds and their thinning to greyness. He would lose Dolke.

He again touched the mirror, but without aim. The mirror turned. The beam moved, lost among the houses until, as it cut the walls of the transept of the Benedictines, it struck into the stained glass of the windows a scarlet and vermilion light.

64

'Colour!' he exclaimed (thinking, how beautiful my mirror is, how sudden its power!) 'As I said. Some of those Leyden gentlemen say that the colour is in – in the glass, and some say in the light. But . . .'

'And at night?' Dolke persisted, seeing Kutten falter. This, he thought kindly, is Kutten's new hope; and, for himself, he wanted to know. The mirror still illumined the windows of the Cathedral. A tissue of cloud, extending itself over the sun, transformed it into a diffuse glow and the colours were subdued.

They discussed intently but with few conclusions. Yet in their argument, Kutten believed, there was some advance, some observations made, or put more compellingly; these he must find again later and not forget. While they observed they pressed their knees uncomfortably against the timber parapet.

The sun curved gradually behind the palace hill. The shadows of the nearest towers of the Cathedral Church of the Benedictines spread enormously over the highest and the farthest of the beeches and limes of its close, over the irregular undulations of roofs beyond and a hipped-back church steeple of salmon-coloured brick with a silver vane. Both men counted the chimes of the hour: five o'clock. It was still delightfully warm.

'I could stay here all afternoon,' Dolke said.

'Then stay, Eberhard!'

Had Dolke been watching Kutten closely he would have noticed the return of a characteristic smile, no more than a raising of the cheekbones so that the eyes were narrowed and their gleam made prominent. The change in Dolke which over the last years had proceeded with insistent steps (and which Vaslav Kutten could only understand as loneliness and despair of achievement) had stopped. The years had turned back. Kutten was telling himself that he need no longer be afraid.

They decided on a supper of cold meats left over from their midday meal. (All sign of that had gone when they returned from the roof; which struck Kutten, with that surprise at and remembrance of the existence of things other than those in which he had been absorbed.)

Dolke left in time to walk back to his college in daylight. He left his thanks to Mrs Wimpfner and a penny for the girl. Kutten

65

showed him downstairs. At the door, with the late afternoon glow above the shadowed walls, they felt a sudden cold and parted with a short farewell.

Upstairs again, Kutten wrapped himself in a warm, quilted robe. For a moment it kept out something more than the cold that he had also felt in saying 'good-bye'. But the day had ended at the door.

As if also to maintain an impetus he turned to the library, opened a heavy atlas of the skies which lay out, and darted his eyes rapidly over the abstract designation of constellations (dark straight lines and pointed stars) and over the beasts and heroes with which they were associated and embellished. From those inky copper imprints the shadows of his love for Dolke began to emerge. He excised them with a homily of brittle honesty: he was a man of strong attachments, yes; but emotions (which could only be penetrated by God) endangered a relationship which required harmony but also policy; they would therefore be controlled.

He shut the book firmly. Walking, and trivial rhythmic movements of his hands and arms sustained the victory of his will. His mind began to touch other matters, so lightly that no question, perhaps only a phrase, was formulated. The masque. The afternoon. These gave hope. For himself and Dolke. The first half-formed recollections of the day left him confident. He had placed before Dolke a way of working and seeing and creating. He had (he was for the moment almost convinced), he had given to Dolke belief in the masque. But now he remembered a deep tiredness, which had seemed also to pervade his own purposes and render them trite. The obligation to Dolke of mind and body (a part of him confirmed; another at once refused to admit) was more potent, more genuine than his achievement.

Were not his experiments in any case tired? His observations, jotted in note-books, he had never seriously attempted to reduce to order and conclusion. What qualities of light, what historical clues in his home, he should recognise as lighting a way to great discoveries, he made no worthy attempt to say. Fascination for him lay (and this he could not see) largely in the mirror and the light and the moment of experiment, without commitment to conclusion or understanding of observation to inspire in him the further step. He loved the power and beauty of the glass and the cellar's alchemist shadows. They gave him the pleasure of which he accused von Fluorn, and the sensation of his own futility, though unconscious, made him bitter against whoever denigrated the little of value he gleaned.

That unconsciousness of failure was an aspect of self-deceit. He insisted on the erection of something perfect on an unshakable foundation of principle; he blamed the obstacles to obtaining the necessary knowledge. There were still moments of acute pleasure, but they were responses to the form or expression of a fact rather than (as he told himself) to the mastery of knowledge itself, to knowing a subject so that he could bring it before his imagination and see it there from any and every angle. Sometimes, in so exercising his knowledge, the refined form, the exceptional phrase, returned to him. Sometimes they brought with them a deeper understanding, but more often tempted him with their own qualities to believe that he had won a further insight. They seemed to promise a total understanding, such as would allow the perfect exposition. Kutten's dim sense of the gulf between the satisfaction he experienced and that which he might have found and held had he recognised his capacity to respond to more than dry truth, was what he called his Melancholy. He told Dolke that it was necessary, to drive men of talent to creative endeavour.

He now sat down at his writing table, drew a candle nearer and settled himself with his elbows on the desk and his fingers gently covering the crown of his forehead.

As he sat, he enjoyed a familiar day-dream; in a way he recited it. Dolke's early lesson, that even fundamental legal assumptions would change, returned to him. His sudden comprehension of it, its penetration of the bounded area of received thought, seemed once again to take effect and by a process quite outside his reason or the words of his old mentor. So exactly and acutely did his mind receive this revelation, however, that it instantly inspired a further realisation, one which instead compelled devotion to the effort to achieve something perfect and thereby permanent, quite contrary to what Dolke's lesson had taught. With that insight it became gloriously possible (during the span of his dream) to perceive in advance those elements of an excellent creation which would be immutable and, without compromising these its fundamental parts and principles, to foresee (could it be? – for the dream was in part obscure), and to anticipate in its structure, the evolution which external forces would demand.

Moreover (and this was new to his dream) this creation might be the masque, a model, as it were living, of the university itself. It was so rare to be given, rather than to labour and half-find, a purpose, and to have been promised a part of a lasting achievement. With wishful thinking, hope blossomed.

Chapter 3

Cloud spread in a platform over the city. Between brief, sharp gusts, which caught passers-by across the eyes or made them start at a slight whistling in their ears, it was possible to distinguish an interminable sound. It was the sound of a distant current of the air. Or was it, people asked, that of the stronger breezes of late autumn among the towers and roofs?

It was the middle of the afternoon. From the west-facing windows of Ulpian, where students worked, and where they took their exercise along the walls and gardens nearest the University Gate, the sun was seen to break through the deepening cloud-layer and diverge in clearly defined rays. It covered fitfully as wide an area of the fields as it was able, and turned patches of their grey earth from near white into brown, flecked with the shadows of hardened clods.

To the south, beyond the gate, and to the east, beyond the Benedictines, was a view of the unending, smoothly sinuous undulations of these hard-bleached fields. At their margins stood scattered copses of ash and birch, and in the farthest distance one looked for the marks of the forest. But that horizon had been indiscernible in the misty but motionless brilliance of the morning, and remained so, apparently dissolved with the pale sky into a diffuse glare.

To the west there was little space and no sense of emptiness. Below the palace its woods were a confusion of delicate lines, black or, against the sky, the colour of niello work. Their entanglements were almost oppressively close; those low down by the river bank seemed to wait like a trap for someone to plunge from the walls. Above them, and above their walking places on the fields, rooks rose hastily and fell forgetfully. As each climbed it seemed to draw itself up until it reached a limit beyond which it could not go, but always the next bird, also watchfully fixing its concentration on some small patch of the field, would rise a little higher. It was so cold that they had ceased their calls.

Men who, in the silence of a wide street of the city, passed others who stood talking on the farther side, heard their voices sound as clear and resonant as if all were together in a close room, or as if the words reflected and reverberated on the brittle earth and air. As the sun sank it tinted with coral and orange, and seemed to restore to life and motion, the ceiling of cloud. It caught, and broke from the monotony of shadow, all the pendants of the mass. It seemed to transform a smooth surface into a swirling turbulence. When, however, the sun had sunk behind the palace, darkness came almost at once.

Dolke had never felt the cold so before. With the approach of winter came fear, not of eventualities in which he might actively be involved, but of sights which might disturb his new balance, might with tumultuous clouds excite him incomprehensibly, might discover to him new perceptions which he would not wish to harbour. Winter twisted the faculties of perception. Winter lightly smashed confidence in the inevitability and significance of daily ritual – of regulated periods of academic accuracy.

For during the last months of collaboration with Vaslav Kutten they had established a delicate balance. There was the possibility of harmony. During some last bright still days they had walked in the royal gardens. In autumn they had paced the sixty paces of the white façade of the palace many times. They had sat, suddenly careless of ceremony, in its shade. They had admired the fragrance, the colour and the luxuriance of oranges, wisteria and pomegranates, the idyllic elegance and modesty of the arbours, fountains, water channels and cataracts, the subtlety of their geometry and the justice of their proportions.

He had found a revived delight in those forms. His life had been spent almost entirely in cities. His home-town on the Neckar had been close-walled and prosperous. In the formal and monumental gardens of great houses and colleges he had enjoyed his academic sense of approval, a sense sometimes of repose, and even a confidence of things lasting. Nature to him was largely domestic: roses and vines spilling over old walls and the Georgics. The strength of Nature had been the possibility of tendrils subduing mulberry-coloured brick and white coping stones (though an incomprehensibly potent source of horror to his childhood). It is true, that it could still sometimes disturb him,

70

with an idea, vivid enough to seem almost a memory, of cities ruined and overgrown. And the winter. For Nature's line and mass he had only had the greenwood crest of the nearest hills.

A yearning and a sense of mystery at the sight of distant mountains (seen as he travelled his rare journeys) he had kept pent in his imagination. He had suppressed the acute illusion of nostalgia which they could arouse.

In his new state of equilibrium, however, he remained capable of putting his faith in his personal response, in finding the whole truth there (as the Seneschal had seen). Kutten still required the assurance of received fact, whose prior selection by the chance of history and memory endowed rather than destroyed their significance.

But only Dolke was threatened with a rebirth of youth.

As he sat in his college rooms, though aware of the cold and dimly even of the desolation of the fields beyond the walls, he did not think about them. He was listening to a circle of students. The fire was broad-flamed and spirited; the materials of the room – for the most part wood – reflected the light where it lay against them. Even where they were in shadow, their surfaces seemed a source of warmth, in scattered, glowing points which the light discovered.

Firelight on their faces made him receptive. His imagination for once flattered his intelligence with the possibility that in this communion new ideas would be welcomed. The dim light made the young men lean towards one another. They needed to catch the expressions of the others' faces, so as not to mistake their true mood and emphasis.

Dolke put his head back into his chair and looked away. It was a partly conscious gesture. He felt the satisfaction of doing his duty. He had gathered half a dozen from their cold rooms and saved their wood. Beyond the walls men in winter would make a truce to huddle together and felt sometimes a sudden sympathy with strangers. Also he allowed himself a slight pre-eminence, and an evasion, leaving him free to listen to them or to his own thoughts.

To Holzhauer, the youngest there, a student of theology, Dolke's half-lit, silent form seemed to radiate a slight air of unforced restraint. That seemed to him an ideal of manners and of an openness, an unassertiveness, which it gave to the mind for the reception and invention of images. The tone was good-humoured – not frivolous. Dolke's age must approve this.

Dolke was thinking he had never felt so young.

Holzhauer himself was talking about music. Alderloh, usually reticent, found himself describing in response the winter services of the parishes of his home valley. Von Fluorn was there. He had brought along Gereon von Liss (a new recruit to his old companions) and Tassillo Aicha. Aicha was squatting close to the hearth. For most of the time he stared into the embers. He had said nothing but appeared attentive.

Dolke was used to the exaggeration and excitement generated by the sound of one's own voice. Another speaker – it was Geron von Liss – was pacing the room and indulging in rhetorical questions. He had jumped up, exclaiming that he too knew Alderloh's valley, but despite that enthusiasm he changed the subject as if compulsively towards another goal. Alderloh's valley. How he loved the land!

And not just its personal associations. He was explaining about the hunt. As he spoke, he felt the slight movement of the heavy oak boughs. In pursuit he squeezed the dry leaves soundlessly beneath his feet. He knew in himself an honest fury which left him not ashamed, made him worthy to take the life of the noble, savage boar. The slaughter of herded game sickened him.

Von Fluorn saw himself riding against an uncertain background. He saw himself as hurled over his horse's neck and smashed into fallen, thrusting branches, and felt a start of physical excitement. In him the association of sexuality with simple courage was not so strong as its related nexus with fear and pain. Cowardice was thus connected with an excitement rather than a sexual guilt. His father had warned him circumspectly of the disconcerting air of the country people were not their Lord's heir the last to lay by from the chase. They were perplexed, as if Nature had chosen to contradict itself. Von Fluorn was also remembering this.

But to the main part of von Fluorn's mind his fantasy possessed the same qualities as von Liss's account. He recognised only the motive compulsion and a fervour of the senses, which he and von Liss shared. He looked up with an almost startled excitement. He would evoke, express the same sensation. The whole room, he saw, was intent. He must emulate the achievement (as if von Liss had told a compelling tale – von Fluorn had almost no realisation of its truth). It was not in him to respond to von Liss's mystical idealism. (A part of his mind noted that von Liss's appearance – the tight musculature of his face, the cut of his hair – was ruled by that natural existence to whose principles, or dictates, his intelligence had surrendered.) Von Fluorn took up instead the element almost of unreality which, even for him in that room, had fascinatingly infected those distant scenes.

He left his seat and knelt on the floor, so that the others were closer, yet a sense of space was created. Von Liss had stopped and was listening to Holzhauer. Their eyes followed the movement; when he looked up again his eyes seemed to catch theirs. The lower level of his new position drew their bodies forward. But all this was more instinctive than otherwise; uncharacteristically, he had no plan.

'Once in Italy – when I had been hunting –' (Why, a small part of him was asking, talk about that? Italy. Was he about to make a fool of himself? What was the link with what had so far been said?) – 'I had left the others. And I reached the water meadows – frozen – of an old hamlet. The meadows were frozen as hard as those,' (he half-lifted an arm) 'by the University Gate here.'

Once or twice Dolke noticed Aicha's rodent features, caught in the firelight, raised towards von Fluorn with a shrewd glance. Was there also a twinge of contempt? Dolke saw with active dislike the highlights in the eyes and mouth.

'I trotted through them and came to a path under the walls. They were high and black – very old. Then I noticed a figure standing on the water meadows. She must have been there before.' (There had been something about that day, von Fluorn thought, but he must mark this, know this, to express its peculiarity. While he was speaking, the image sharpened. His confidence came.)

'It was a woman – a girl really, scarcely a woman, dressed in black. She stared at me. For a moment she was like that, completely still on the frozen ground. And it was bitterly cold. My horse could scarcely bear to stand. Then she moved, without any abruptness, and passed me. Her black clothes didn't tremble; and then she was gone beyond a buttress of the wall. I trotted up but –' (But what had really happened? It had been true; he had seen her in the cold Italian brilliance, and there had been something extraordinary. But what?) '– she was gone. And when I thought of her face staring at me I suddenly knew – there had been no features whatsoever to be remembered!'

He paused. 'I suppose she had gone through some little gate. Somehow I didn't see.'

His glance touched on Dolke's attentive frown. He knew without looking that they were all intent, though Aicha had given a little smile at the end. Was that why he had talked in this way, he asked himself? To impress them? Yes, and they were all listening now. He had appraised their responses even as he talked. To impress Dolke? Yes, him particularly.

Von Fluorn had talked also because that rare day had possessed a mystery and he an unaccountable, physical receptiveness. He would usually have laughed at von Liss; today he remembered in himself the mystery, a nervous presence. Also he loved to hear the words flow. From such days his youth preserved some hope of a sudden, an apparently accidental perceiving, on which a whole work might be elaborated. He would need to have taken; he would give, and would command. In such moments he did not regret the lack of any instinctive sympathy with the moral and religious foundation with which (and as if engraved on tablets of stone) he had been presented when a boy, and only by means of which (as he had been taught and as it sometimes seemed) he might measure the significance and profundity of his perception. The absence of that sympathy, appeared to him sometimes as a massive, looming obstacle, sometimes as a sudden unfathomable excavation, capriciously left in his soul. He turned to Dolke:

'I hope you will excuse, sir, a little exaggeration.'

'Imagination, Fluorn,' Dolke corrected him. 'That is only to be approved.'

'It really was something like that.'

Dolke had spoken with the certainty of someone going to sleep. He did in fact feel a tiredness like that which promises that in sleep dreams will sift and decide. He was surfeited. From von Liss he had received the type of an obstinately personal perception, but he had accepted the truth of its experiences. Its movement and crescendo appeared somehow a part of its truth. Von Fluorn's invention he still suspected, but he knew its force. Was it truth he wanted then, or originality? Unreality even? Common to

74

both their visions, and with a power close to absolute truth, was something too shifting to be fixed in a dry form. This elusive, undefined character seemed to him closer to truth than mandrawn abstractions. Those, which fact and grasp of rules assured him existed, seemed an illusion: that strange tower the university itself; but those intangible qualities not susceptible to proof (but which his mind, and von Fluorn's and von Liss's spoke of, or received, so forcefully) seemed so real as to be about to materialise.

Only the day before he had visited without Vaslav Kutten the library of the royal palace, and there had recurred from recent years past an occurrence that concerned and perplexed him. The King, most frequently at his capital or making his progress through some other of his provinces, welcomed the masters of the university nevertheless to his library and gardens, lest the place stand deserted. Gebhard Star, the porter, would willingly guide Dolke back through the wood if it were late. Anyway – and Dolke sniffed aloud – the idea that the journey might dismay him must be taken as absurd. The palace, its proportions and perspectives, met the ideal laid down by his reason. The forms of such structures pleased him and had seemed to possess a quite fixed and intended significance (if perhaps his imagination had never been taken by any closer sympathy). But when the time had come that the topmost leaves of the trees caught and broke the horizontal rays of the sun as they spread placidly through the windows, he had hurried away. Shadows touched, now here, now there, the resplendent columns. As he passed into the final archway, glancing back, he saw how they obscured and confused the regular and noble proportions of the arcades, and with a sensation akin to fear he had left the place to itself.

A few days later Doctor Feucht was running an errand for the Seneschal. As it happened, it required his carrying a slight reassurance to the Regent of Ulpian, who required for his continuing support of the masque the most considerate attention. Revenue for the masque, and so a levy, was necessary. It was reasonable that there should be reassurances. He was walking at speed (a habit when on any commission) and his whole body slightly charged with purpose. Among the colleges of Saint

Eadmundsburg Domitius Ulpianus was a financial colossus. A levy on Ulpian the college and a levy on Ulpian the greatest of colleges would be very different things.

He hoped to catch the Regent returning from the garden (the Regent took a customary seat in the gardens every day for an hour after breakfast, the gate-keeper had told him). Feucht preferred to avoid people on what seemed peculiarly their own ground – the Regent's lodgings or his customary seat. He found himself so easily on the defensive.

He dismissed that almost habitual discomfort of thought. He would approach no closer. It was pleasant to wait there in the blue early morning. The dome of the library of Ulpian may have struck a slightly incongruous note, he thought; it was nonetheless confident. This opinion was the product of a balance within himself. His glance was critical, but its necessary detachment was quite different from Dolke's. His was aware of his diminutive individuality but within the greater whole, within the living architecture which encompassed him. Devotion made an offering even of intemperate criticism, he thought.

There was no structure from Saint Eadmundsburg to Munich or Prague, so assured as the library. He noticed as a virtue how complex and mannered, how ceremonial, were the Corinthian capitals and Florentine windows of the rotunda, which was the body of the library and the base of the dome.

Rotunda, drum and dome, swelling from the middle of the cloistered range, had once struck him as might among men a new, prouder species, a bishop among monks. Its erect insensitivity to the subdued and attenuated dignity of its setting had been painful. Additions to each range of the court, of corner towers with cupolas and scroll-work, of roofs hipped to the height of the pilastered drum from which sprang the ribs of the dome, and lastly of squared windows and bold rounded arches, had achieved a degree of reconciliation. By no means an entire reconciliation, Feucht thought; one which raised the height of one building merely to diminish that of another. Sufficient of the magnificent, if almost monstrous, remained to provide something – alive. As he had entered the court he had left another, older and narrower, leading from the gateway and the street. It pleased him that in his university in all things the Gothic and the Renaissance were *alive* cheek by jowl.

As he dawdled, waiting, he made smaller, practical observations. The ivy seemed to have been cut back very high from the windows of the court. The work had surely been done late. It must be recent, and it was now the start of November.

He was delighted to see Dolke appear from the outer court. Professor Kutten and he were walking arm-in-arm. He should attract their attention? He hesitated; discretion prevailed. If he were to share his commission of trust from the Seneschal it would be in speaking with Dolke alone.

It was strangely exciting; his news should arouse Dolke's interest. Kutten, on the contrary, could not be approached. He was rigid – a theorist. His intellect sometimes seemed inhuman (you could not dismiss all tittle-tattle – his solitary rooms, his experiments), and his Code was inhuman, petrified, of stone or marble. It might be a monstrous classical tomb on which his gaunt corpse might lie.

Feucht had no theory of the nature or the operation of a university. Here it was around him in action and sound, glass, stone and copper. In his mind were the Seneschal's words for the Regent. He felt the co-ordinated motion of the university's machinery. Kutten had a vision but, he felt, it lacked everything spontaneous, musical. Though proud as might be permitted of his practicality (he often told himself that he could not expect perfection), and though he valued his curious critical detachment, there was no doubt in Feucht's mind even about the university's character; the university was somehow inherently 'good'.

This confidence, and his transparent pleasure in the university's working through his apologetically unworthy self were the springs of Dolke's contempt for him.

Dolke and Kutten were walking in the arcade of the library range. There was, Feucht told himself regretfully, a certain stiffness between them. The stiffness of Kutten, he thought, which stilted everything. Dolke would be talking straightforwardly; he could use the country idiom when he wanted. Though he attacked, and particularly one's motives, Dolke did not judge, he did not censure. Though they said he condemned all women out of hand, and that his talent for arousing hostility had baulked his career, he did so because, as he said, 'We are all for purgatory'. On the other hand Kutten's judgment of a man (Feucht inwardly confessed his own accusation) was handed down. It would be final.

'They will want re-assurance,' Kutten repeated to Dolke.

'Yes, their money's worth.'

'And a little flattery of ancient susceptibilities,' laughed Kutten. He put into Dolke's hands a complete list of scene changes for the drama; systems of stage machinery and how actors and chariots must be marshalled, displayed and concealed.

'May I add these to the totality? What we need for this evening are references. I do admit that there are only some which speak. You know them, Eberhard.'

'Some of the old constitutions had a ring to them. Some. In a masque there is room for fact and fiction.'

'We agreed they must ring true,' said Kutten coaxingly.

'An hour in the library and I shall have words that will make the Seneschal and all his committees eat out of our hands. Hallo, Doctor Feucht!'

He had glanced away as he spoke, supporting Kutten's papers almost distractedly with half-outstretched arms. Both men would in fact have considered themselves as very happy. They had worked together through breakfast. Dolke shivered now and then with cold. His greeting to Feucht was even kind.

'Professor Kutten here is showing me how to keep all my gilded carts at the masque out of the muck.'

There was often, when he spoke to Feucht at all, a little extra bluntness, for the sake of Feucht's prissiness, though Feucht seemed to like it.

'Good morning!' Feucht insisted. To Professor Kutten he gave a slight bow. Kutten was already making him nervous.

'Will it not be the crowds who will need the most careful attention?' Uncertainty often disguised in this way the point he was making.

'Let them do as they will for an evening,' laughed Dolke.

'Need that be said, Eberhard. The chariots will be well guarded, Doctor Feucht. And the people? Perhaps they may be caught up in better things.'

'Vice will not be tolerated.' Feucht's words, his voice, were those of the Visitor Heysach, used in his presence to the Seneschal. Feucht had not meant to dictate. Perhaps in his reply there was for him, before Kutten, a scarcely-admitted, reflected glory.

'Vice will have its hour,' drawled Dolke, as if tired.

And for an hour or more, thought Kutten, we have passed the time conjuring details which might evoke in an unresponsive body the eventual scene: where torchlight might illumine some solemn passage or the concourse process in silence past singing boys. He recovered himself:

'Well, I must be gone!' He made an inclination of the body and touched an edge of the tippet of grey fur which spread about his shoulders and down low over his coat. Dolke made a slight wave of the hand:

'Come early, Vaslav,' he said cheerfully, raising his voice as Kutten turned away. 'I shall have ready some hallowed epigrams.'

He and Feucht were alone.

'I must wait here for – someone.' Feucht could not grasp exactly enough the limits of a confidence. 'Please do not let me detain you.'

'Don't be concerned, Doctor Feucht. I have scarcely seen you in weeks.' Dolke was not quite ready to leave. The conversation had not in some way ended. Nor would he be dismissed for a confidence on his own ground.

For a few moments there was silence, in Dolke's mind strangely an almost blessed, clarifying silence. The two men were beneath the library rotunda. In summer, he remembered, this undercroft was a rendez-vous. Its massive piers, eight of them, formed a configuration which was neither quite a circle nor an ellipse. Three archways between the piers on one side gave access on to the lawn which filled the court. Three more balanced them on the opposite side; they opened through cool gates of ironwork on to a balustraded terrace and thence, by gradual stairs or sloping lawn, into the gardens. At either end of these bold, gracious curves, a restricted passage opened along the flagstoned and symmetrical corridors of the old range of the court.

Between his mind and Feucht the stonework, protruding, formed a barrier. Its solidity and its forms accorded to the newest ideal. They steadied him. He pressed his hand firmly against it. You cannot, he thought, press your hand against Gothic walls. With an effect totally detached from his present preoccupation with Feucht the elegant arrangement and complex lines of the pillars charmed him. While he looked towards Feucht he shifted his position, so that he could continue to enjoy and Feucht was obliged to follow. The lofty arches did not simply join the pillars but brought them into harmony with the gentle curve of the vault, so that its cream-coloured plaster shaded into the sepia of the stone supports.

None of this experience of architecture was sufficiently conscious to make an entry into Dolke's ideas.

When he had been standing in the broad dimness of the shadow, without reflection of any sun from the unpolished plaster and stone, it had dazzled and hurt his eyes to stare beyond into the cold sunlight of the garden. The light steamed about the iron foliage of the gates. Vaslav Kutten had observed that the sky over the dome might have been Italian. It was a pale but brilliant and even blue. The summer seemed scarcely over. But it was wearyingly cold. Feucht demanded his attention. For perhaps the first time in his life he felt that sense of old people of being caught in the open, of being taken advantage of unfairly. He ought not to be expected to wait on this intruder.

'At least I have some timely news – before your presentation.' He would share with Dolke something of his mission. That evening Dolke and Kutten must put to the committee of production and the Seneschal's own committee of finances their final proposals. Feucht could forearm him with what in any case he would learn then. He spread his arms with submissive jocularity, as if he did not expect his offering to be accepted. This habit had come to reduce the pain of a rebuff.

'The Seneschal has fixed, I gather, a limit to the financial burden of the masque on the university. Three thousand seven hundred and fifty gold marks.'

The Seneschal could weigh a matter, even his own ambitions, to within fifty gold marks, Feucht thought, and did not shirk the conclusions. And he had fixed Ulpian's contribution at not more than four hundred, but that he knew in stricter confidence, for the ear only of the Regent of Ulpian.

'Well, that is a princely enough sum. Kutten and I will not have to pare.'

'I may add that, at least until this evening, we are sharing something of a confidence.'

80

'I shall not forget.' There was another moment of irritation. There was no need, Dolke thought, for self-importance; nor (it was as if he suddenly remembered) were he and Kutten so green as not to have sounded the Seneschal in a general way. Then he saw that it was something else that gave Feucht his manner: not even caution – a sort of hope of intimacy, a need to belong. Dolke felt a moment of keen remorse. He said more kindly:

'Well! Like you I must be about our work for the Seneschal. I look forward to our meeting again this evening.'

'Tomorrow I hope, Doctor Dolke. Tonight – tonight there will not be sufficient duties for the Seneschal to insist on my presence. I will happily leave the work to the two committees – and yourselves.'

He was embarrassed. The skin on his broad forehead was white and smooth, and slightly damp along the rim of his felt cap.

Dolke remembered. Feucht had not been chosen for any of the posts.

But Feucht was still staring. Dolke turned. The Regent of Ulpian, the head of his college, was coming up from the garden. Dolke saw the tension of restrained movement through Feucht's body (preferring to the last possible second to avoid the explanation of an unnecessary concealment). He would be gentle with him. He said:

'I am for the library then,' and turned quickly away.

Dolke made his way by a modest staircase to the body of the rotunda. The stairs ended at cream-panelled doors with a pedimented door-case of an only slightly browner shade. Was he, he asked himself, as isolated, as lonely, as Feucht? To be detached was one thing. To be excluded was loneliness. He made a sound in his throat, perhaps sardonic. After standing briefly before the regular, doubled forms of the doors, he carefully gripped with his right hand the cool thin metal of the oviform handle.

Inside the chamber all sense of the ornamental, the splendid, was absent. The galleries and the desks standing in them were of smooth oak; its colour had already begun to darken. The book-cases, but for a narrow passageway, stretched from the outside wall to the inner, balustraded edge of each gallery, and seconded, as support for the gallery above, stout pillars which sprang at

81

intervals from the balustrades. Their colour contrasted only with parchment, some details tricked out with russet gilding and a mulberry grain of some of the books. These structures and the subtle variety of rich colours isolated each reader at his desk from the expectation of interference.

Dome and rotunda reflected the unity of the Ulpian library. Its many visitors saw it as a library of the civil law – that of Rome and the Roman Empire of Germany – and as a great building; some even as a universal library. They said, 'A jurist of Augustan Rome would have bestowed praise.'

Dolke, taking his customary seat in an upper gallery, was sensible of its qualities. But he asked himself whether those visiting noticed how easy it was to find a work there or how it was that, as they sought an answer, they found the next step, the next along each possible path, so close and easy to hand. That had been his contribution. It had been in him at least to arrange, to link, to catalogue.

'Down to work,' he said, breaking in on himself.

He was alone in the library.

Many references and quotations slipped his mind these days. He had decided to set down a summary of their programme, the orders of precedence to be observed and, as promised to Kutten, the quotations which would evoke the successive scenes and stages of their masque. The committee members, the Visitor Heysach particularly, would be alert to any infringement, however circumstantial, of hoary rights. As Dolke rose to seek a source he saw this.

He knew just where to find what he wanted. The history and government of the university were a part of the library which he had not only catalogued but augmented with a donation of twenty-five volumes. Twenty-five volumes! he allowed himself to think again, for thanks (and praise) were rare.

Ironically he was largely unconscious of the scheme of thought which to others clearly underlay and illuminated this his part, above all, of the library. In truth his learning was highly respected. It was Dolke who felt that their esteem might have found some worthier object in his work. Nonetheless the ordered volumes of statutes, tradition and symbolism struck the understanding inquirer with a clear image of the university. Indeed they reflected, and thus confirmed – perhaps even helped to create – the university's convinced image of itself. The names of the authors and the dates of volumes suggested by their lesser or greater familiarity what of this image had been transitory, what permanent. In Dolke's mind this assembly had been ordered by no more than simply familiarity, reputation and instinct. The works of Aicha had a place of honour.

Dolke's own awareness of his surroundings, of these books, was at that moment no more than of all those components, formal but organic as they were, cocooning him from others' importunities.

When Dolke drew a volume from the shelves and opened it on a nearby reading desk, he noticed for some moments only the intense whiteness of the opened pages. They were crisp, like newly pressed linen. Their horny edges were equally fascinating. The black lettering struck him as if they were purely meaningless marks, exciting against the white paper.

He moved as if guided by instinct among the most familiar shelves. He slid the chain and extracted that copy of Aicha's masterpiece he had considered so often. It was an early Augsburg printing, bound in Paris work of wide-grained goatskin, resilient to the touch. After a few moments spent casually turning the pages, Dolke returned the book to its shelf. He collected a small pile of clean paper and made it tidy, smoothing over the top sheet with a sweep of his sleeve.

'Colleges, religious houses and other foundations,' he wrote deliberately: 'Staufen'. He wrote the name without hesitation. To his mind it had pre-eminence. To his imagination it deserved first consideration.

Nevertheless he must strictly distinguish the romance, the sense of Staufen's royal greatness, from precedence. The summary was completed. Precedences were to be listed, and the due orders of procession determined. In due order each name was written: 'Electors', 'Empress', 'Fürstenau', 'Saint Lorenz', 'Saint John the Divine' – and so on until he had written 'Domitius Ulpianus', the least ancient but not the least significant of a list of sixteen.

Whatever he had intended by this list, it exerted a strange influence. Did it have a music, a poetry, which would not be possessed by the same names written in another order? He could not say. Von Fluorn had told him to his face that such rhymes

83

were still to him like the litany.

Were the names themselves coming to mean as much to him as the colleges they denoted? When he uttered, even in this context, the word 'Staufen' it was not merely the name of a college. It evoked the lost and alien court of that Emperor, the Staufen called 'The Wonder of the World', who had achieved at Saint Eadmundsburg the white façade of a new kind of residence and the foundation of the most ancient college of its university. And with that word his exotic kingdom of Italians, Byzantines and Moors – humanists, mystics and astrologers – was at once admirable – wonderful. In memory of him the students familiarly named the palace and its gardens 'Sicily'. Dolke approved the name.

History, precedence still had some impact; sounds had sometimes a terrible, almost physical impact.

Suddenly Dolke laughed.

Most of those names, which refused to ring more distant, rang clearly from another world. The overtones of 'Staufen' were of things lost, of the romance and tragedy of inevitable change, which he had long known to be in the character of all things. Change, that was all that was certain. That was all there was to the music of these names, these archaic formulae, and all other manifestations. For him they would never again present the architectural illusion of a whole. It almost seemed to him that they had never displayed the idea, the certainties of an edifice, to have been the bricks of which a great tower was made.

Kutten would expect to see displayed all the hallowed banners. Their inscriptions were of a sublime ambiguity: 'The King by God and under the Law'; 'To our Sovereign proceeding by Right'. Ancient frauds! Legal poetry! For Kutten they were of the fabric of the whole. He could not conceive of government and freedoms distinct from the truth of their ancient establishment or the grandeur and conviction of their epitomes. Of what else could freedoms be built so that they might not be taken away?

He is very proud of the privileges of the university, Dolke said to himself, and he knows less about them than I do.

Dolke turned a page and looked again. Yes, he loved books, but what did the words say? They recited a long-spent privilege – for the levy of a toll on flour and corn at the University Gate. There were pages and pages of them. Annotations set out the authorities. Here was fact for Kutten.

Even the great men of the past had ceased to embody purposes and conclusions. The truth of their names remained to Dolke, but they filled only a ceremonial and serpentine procession, filed in gilded chariots of their own contrivance, and metamorphosed into the varied images of other men's perceptions.

A presence interrupted his thought: a sound, 'switch-switch' on the library tables. It was as someone seeking something in an unfamiliar room; after a hesitant pause objects were lifted. The old man who dusted the desks. Each day he dusted them and set out supplies of ink and paper.

He appeared before Dolke's table.

'I have ink of my own, thank you.'

'There are a lot of people who will want to get on with work today, sir,' the man said, his voice grudging Dolke an explanation but knowing that it was expected.

Dolke gave way to the duster with manifest pain.

'I'm sorry about the disturbance, sir; I got to get it ready for them and be out of their way.'

The man moved on. He thinks the place his, Dolke thought irritably. He picks up the dust from one table, and deposits it on the next. He thinks he's essential. Lurching along with a dirty cloth and piles of paper, that's all a university is to him.'

Others would soon claim their due of the library. It was their silence, Dolke told himself, that was important, reassuring, as were the numbers and feel of the books and the unblemished surfaces of their pages. When he had arranged and listed these, he must have been doing them honour. He could scarcely abide the thought of his own intrusive footsteps here and their echoes in the vaulted ceiling.

It was no mere chance that what was becoming of sole significance to Dolke was his own image of the university. He disapproved; he marvelled. He remembered, and he felt the power of associations peculiar to himself; but he was no longer a part of it and could no longer possess its sense of identity. He might only seek to understand it and its components as he might a person. And in observing, in trying to understand someone, he was bound to see the inconsistencies and the gradual transformation of that person. We cannot, he would have said, share another person's sense of something essential to himself which does not change, his conviction of personal identity.

Outside, the brilliant October light had been diffused and dimmed by a moist suspension, such that drops of water seemed to coalesce and hang in the air. It rose from the river. From inside the library the drops seemed almost the sudden creatures of the windows down which they started.

Dolke brushed clear a small space of condensation. The court, the University Gate and the tower of Saint Lorenz were all half-obscured. Everything beyond them seemed tenuous. Where Kutten and he had aimed their beams of light on the leads of the gateway tower, was the same metallic sheen. Voices and figures were muffled. The elusiveness of words spoken, and their uncertain origin, fascinated him.

How irrational was this insistent pleasure! His pride should be undiminished: in his administration of the library, in which the man with cloth, paper and quills and the diligent souls who would soon huddle at its shelves were part of a scheme; and in his scholarship, in his industrious researches and in what they could surely produce.

For a moment he congratulated Kutten for his austerity, for Kutten surely would have overcome such folly.

There was scarcely a sign of movement in the court. The ground below him lay concealed under an almost opaque white inundation. Above it loomed gates and bell-towers, solid and grey. The sounds from below were totally lost, but from over the roofs periodically the successive blows of clock-hammers struck. Dolke could not resist the infection of its mood. It seemed the towers reigned over a harsh land, in which the life of subjugated creatures was both concealed and blind.

And in an hour he would see von Fluorn. It was von Fluorn who had brought him not to disdain mystery and to accept a sense that his reason, his knowledge and his investigations were narrow. He remembered that he had asked von Fluorn to stay for a quarter of an hour after instruction (it was to be the law of the constitution). He had hoped that, if his summary and his chosen phrases provoked the compliments of the young man, he might expect those of the committees that evening. The irrationality of a sudden, anxious excitement suddenly possessed him. He was perplexed by a sense that the work might be of little moment, but that it should be his and should be judged. There was an urgent need to write. Kutten and he had conceived a masque of symbol

and drama. Now there must be dissolution as well as achievement, the passing of a serpentine procession.

He was reborn. With an air, but with a tremor of defiance, he
picked up the pages of his notes and tore them in pieces.

They were waiting for Doctor Dolke. Von Fluorn was lounging
against a door-post to his rooms. Aicha was listening.

'We've a week of bright weather left, I should think – if you care
to make the effort, Mouse.'

There *was* something rodent-like in Tassillo Aicha's long clerical face. Yet he was also like a young saint in an old Flemish altar,
not one of those agonised with physical or spiritual arrows, but
one of those academic saints, cleanly tonsured, with a cowl laid
back in careful folds from a shaved and attenuated neck. They
were often portrayed concentrating intently, almost short-
sightedly, on an illuminated book.

Von Fluorn had invented the name 'Mouse'; Aicha accepted it.
He stood in front of von Fluorn, gazing down at the floor-boards.

'I should like to climb the Alchemists' Tower some day, that's
true.'

That day when he had climbed up to the castle von Fluorn had
somehow lodged close to the heart of their friendship. Sometimes
Aicha almost believed that only by some slight ill chance had he
failed to take part in the adventure.

That day was central, or the image of that day – for von Fluorn
only a few incidents of his climb remained exact – the four towers
first seen from the paltry houses, the scraping edges of the rock,
the height. Sometimes he remembered the moments of fear.
Gradually the facts and the immediate reactions of the time had
grown less vital. The events had become a frame on which his
imagination built. First it found in him facts (were they facts?) and
more intense reactions of which he had been unconscious at the
time: the precarious feel under the finger-tips of broken yet firmly
mortared stone; the dizzying effect of great distances. The remembrance was as that of a dream, which during its occurrence
had possessed convincing sequence and even significance; the
dreamer, recounting it, must provide from his waking imagination whatever must in it (so it appears to him) have reconciled its
now obvious inconsistencies, and have given, to details which

now seem trivial, form and meaning.

The sensations, actual and discovered within himself, assumed an intensity, a purity of all that had been incongruous – an appropriateness – which they had never possessed. The day, opportunely brought to mind, saw in von Fluorn's memory the birth (or was it the pinnacle?) of his sensitivity, the promise of great achievement. He often told Aicha about that day.

'The Alchemists'! Don't you remember? I could see from the Crucible a great crack . . . You'd need some practice first.'

Here was the other impact of those familiar incidents. They suggested arduous, almost athletic activity. Aicha shied at it; so that von Fluorn returned to them sometimes to exercise a confidence of physical superiority (though indeed selective, creative memory had made him, and continued to make him, braver). He felt it with Aicha alone among his friends.

Von Fluorn did not intend Aicha's giving in to his suggestions; Aicha was necessarily half aware that such a response would have no part in their scheme. And somehow Aicha was still successfully reminded of his inferiority.

Aicha's hands were closely pressed flat along his thighs. His back was arched forward slightly (he could look away without feeling that he was too obviously averting his eyes). At von Fluorn's banter his lips darted, formed a line or a pout, as if he were whispering rejoinders in a tone as bold and light as von Fluorn's.

It was the nervousness of his stance, nervous and quick-witted, tense but primed, that had inspired his nickname, Mouse.

'Though it's largely a matter of putting one's weight on each step, but keeping one's balance . . .'

'He's late.' Aicha had interrupted; he glanced abruptly to his right as if he expected Doctor Dolke to arrive through the window.

Von Fluorn was not insistent in his flippancy. There was a restraint, today as always. It was born in his sense that, if he pursued too closely, the fabric would suddenly be torn; his dominance would in an instant be deflated. A retort would thrust impatiently through his words to some complexity they were intended to evade, some gap in himself which should not be made explicit. Aicha half saw both their needs. Von Fluorn was aware only of the danger to himself. That acted on his conduct without calculation, like a taboo. Even while he was standing, talking, before a silent Aicha, he felt the danger.

Today it had been particularly difficult to maintain a manner. Aicha was bound to learn that Dolke wished to see him after instruction. He was flattered to have Dolke's ear. Yet with Aicha he must put himself at a distance from Dolke, he could not say why. Recognition of Aicha's secrecy had given him advantage to take Aicha up; but that secrecy had unforeseen depths, sudden caverns from which a muffled mockery sometimes sounded.

'He's a bit of an old maid, Dolke. Don't you think?'

Aicha stood exasperatingly inscrutable.

'He wants me to stay afterwards and hear the latest on the Seneschal's masque.'

'Will *he* listen?'

'I suppose I have at least seen these things before. In Italy and England. I daresay I could surprise him with one or two things.'

Italy. Having taken much, Aicha had recently begun to show him some drawings, accomplished pieces, which he had done. In fact von Fluorn had judged things nicely and had asked to see them. Aicha had introduced each with a dismissive remark. 'This one I might give some credit for a certain accomplishment.' 'Accomplishment', that had been his word; so that von Fluorn had not been sure how enthusiastic to be. And Aicha, when he chose to, could make von Fluorn so long to see famous paintings as Aicha did. When he spoke, von Fluorn understood. But when they explored together the treasures of the city and the university, von Fluorn's serviceable safety device was a remark that he simply had not found the artistic spirit to which he could really respond. Aicha asked him about Italy, difficult questions. Once von Fluorn had blurted out that in the frescoes (decorative and erotic in fact, he remembered) of a palace of the Dukes of Mantua he had found 'something essential'. Memory of the wilful assumption of a risk of discovery made him feel sick and wicked; the risk itself seemed almost real. Since then he had made references to the heady effects of a ducal court. In need, Aicha might discreetly derive an excuse, and even believe it.

In his inability to read deeply of Aicha's thoughts a timid sympathy drew von Fluorn again towards his old friends. Did Aicha indulge him? Surely he had social pretensions, von Fluorn would reassure himself.

'Friedrich, I think you could.'

For Aicha there was something, an air of expectation, about von Fluorn's descriptions. He was happy to hear von Fluorn's story of the climb to the castle and the dizzy effects of the high and broken parapet of the Crucible. For him von Fluorn was a close friend, his closest friend. Both had set out to charm, to meet the other. He was disposed to see at the wider moments of von Fluorn's imaginings a great sensibility. Von Fluorn's raillery, if thin, had the ring of worldly experience. Von Fluorn's possession of wordly experience gave him hope.

'Really you could. You could surprise Dolke.'

Is Aicha laughing at me, von Fluorn wondered. He *must* put Dolke further off. Aicha would never discuss him, as if that were bad taste. In the same breath he delivered an impression that perhaps their tutor's opinion, on anything but the law, was not worth consideration. It was worse to be despised by a friend than to be disloyal to an acquaintance. Denigration was the clearest dissociation.

'One doesn't like to be too involved. He and Kutten. Do you suppose he's – vicious?'

He knew he had succeeded. He had spoken as casually as possible. Aicha stood and frowned, as if stunned. For once he was without his elusive, flexible replies. Aicha could not think such thoughts, even less speak them. But without any doubt in the world he was impressed.

During instruction Aicha played faithfully his rôle of foil to von Fluorn. His incisive questions (he nearly always made his points in the form of questions) had an underlying consistency, as if he were pursuing some theory of his own on the question in hand. This self-effacement touched Dolke; it also irritated him. He expected the enthusiasm with which von Fluorn would take things up. Aicha probed for details to construct a line of thought, private, Dolke said to himself, but no doubt very profound, very complete in the amalgamation of those floating little points. Von Fluorn was adroit at the art of inventing situations, distinctly but indefinably contrasted, which one was forced to accept fell to either side of the boundary of application of a principle. He convinced the intuition.

When it was over and Aicha hesitated at the door, von Fluorn excused himself from across the room with a wave of the hand:

'I shall see you to eat. The usual hour.'

Aicha smiled and left.

Von Fluorn had ready a point he would make about the masque. In return for Dolke's confidence he must earn its continuation. He should impress, otherwise he must charm. Italy had given him a generous store of observations and contrasts. Since receiving Dolke's note he had thought hard. No-one, not even Aicha, could say he was not observant; he had trained himself to notice things, and he had a good memory. He had thought secretly.

'Fluorn, I am afraid I have nothing to show you.'

Dolke put down heavily a sheaf of Kutten's writings.

'Just detail.'

Von Fluorn stared at the pile of pages. He did not want silence. His mind still possessed the motion of the previous hour. He knew better than almost anyone the details of the masque. As he stared now he put from his mind the assumptions which made sense of Dolke's and Kutten's melodrama. He heard Dolke say, 'Tell me about Italy' and in a moment was standing, describing the approach to Mantua of the Triumph of a Gonzaga.

The excitement of the populace under a capricious duke was depressed by a curious tension. From the distance had come closer a most bizarre sound; and he had suddenly known it was laughter and delirious enthusiasm for the philosopher-ruler who could precede his march with his dwarf dressed as a herald riding backwards on a donkey. It was the Duke's anti-masque!

'This is not to be Lupercalia, Fluorn,' said Dolke, with the curt paternal wit of superior learning. But von Fluorn's delighted shout, his leaping energy, conjured up a different world. Dolke smiled with one side of his mouth.

'The university is scarcely a Duke of Mantua, needing to be laughed at while it continues to misgovern. Is it?' Dolke went on, with the same arch gravity.

'I wouldn't want either ridicule or farce,' exclaimed von Fluorn, with an authority of taste which made Dolke pause.

'Self-display then.'

'Do you think perhaps a lively mind needs that, sir?'

'And you are just looking for an opportunity . . .'

But as soon as Dolke had heard von Fluorn's first shout, he had known that his pupil's imagination was far – wonderfully remote – from the desert scheme in which he had been wandering.

'In England – in their new drama – it is the anti-masque, the comedy, which points the history – the tragedy.'

'Sophistry!' Dolke interrupted (but this was nearer to something emergent in his own mind). He fell silent at once. His masque, and Kutten's had had meaning. It could, and should, be read and understood like a book, he told himself; the culminating scenes would celebrate like a poem. He had remembered Kutten, and was a little afraid.

To propose an anti-masque was only an excuse, a device, to bring him far from restraint, form and established purpose. Was this not what he had expected when he had asked von Fluorn to stay? When von Fluorn had cried out, he had begun to see instead of the structure, the analysis, that he and Kutten designed (instead then of the paraphrase, the lecture), something of individuals, of himself, and of understanding beyond the stone and crystal of the form. In such a case the whole must be personal to *himself*, and surely no more true than that. Though he mistrusted his personal response, he possessed nothing else (and he *must* write soon! He heard the imperative instruction). The old ideal, the accepted truth, no longer inspired. Only its formal beauty, like that of gardens or of the purest architecture, retained its effect and commanded his unbelieving reverence. Von Fluorn had presented him an image, but it was not quite compelling; it was not quite attuned to his need. Dolke hesitated, like a man expecting the moments in which his thoughts will coalesce into what may be written.

Von Fluorn was still alert to the uncertain tone of Dolke's last exclamation; he retained a vestige of a smile. His tutor was sitting upright, breathing regularly and noisily. Sometimes Dolke pursed his lips as if to display his attention to some inward process of reason, as if to prove to gods and onlookers that he had made his choice under the rule of cool reflection and deliberate perception.

Soon, Dolke was thinking, I must write – I should perhaps postpone . . .

What made von Fluorn go on at that moment is obscure. As he noticed Dolke's expression ease and prepare itself to look up, he began to talk. His words were fortuitous. His ideas and with them his voice had without premeditation modulated.

'In England once – it was at Richmond. There was a grotesque. By night, and by the light of flambeaux, he brought a sudden – contagious – mystery. Dejected dwarfs, filing before a choir of singing boys; they aroused a quite bitter sympathy. All the confusion of one's real feelings for things – all the glory of that is just movement, procession.'

Again and finally Dolke admitted to his mind the image of a gilded train. In von Fluorn's words were a consonance, a corroboration.

'A brilliant train!' Dolke burst out. 'A subtle serpent.'

There was little more. While Dolke sat with his head heavily against the back of his chair, von Fluorn expounded a dream-masque. Experience of the wealth, elegance and invention of Italy was fluently mingled with the sensuous majesty of England. In his scenario each participant displayed a personality (a mood, at least, and a taste). The university, subject of their opinions, seemed to appear with a more complete identity. The design and form of masque and anti-masque were left unsaid but given the delusive enchantment of the memory of incidents without chronology, which seem capable of having always had an existence isolated from all other circumstance.

His voice, Dolke thought, is surprisingly musical. Though his gait was almost awkward when he hurried, his gestures were gracious and interested – not the least urgent or insistent; and his voice was so expressive. Even Kutten could not repulse such eloquence; though (and Dolke asked himself why) he so irrationally disliked von Fluorn. That, and not the power of the Seneschal, was the only cause for fear – the putting of all this (or a part of this, a voice urged already) to Vaslav Kutten.

Von Fluorn too, even in the outflowing of his words to someone who would listen, was troubled. An instinct of self-preservation made him end abruptly.

'Well, that's a student's eye. For the rest I have no ideas.'

'Forgive me. "The rest"?'

'The drama. All that side of a masque I know very little. And the variety you permit to make up the whole – the themes.'

'The committee, that is, have their expectations?'

'Surely they must, sir. And rank and precedent.'

'I contrive the scheme. I might let it contrive itself. Others hold the purse-strings.'

Again a prickling of fear: Kutten. His words did not reflect his thoughts; they reflected only a revived sense of practicalities.

'You will wish to be going, Fluorn. Do not forget Aicha. Perhaps I did not quite explain. I must put the final scheme, complete, to the Seneschal and his committees this evening.'

'Thank you, sir.'

'Thank you, Fluorn. You have given me "food for thought". And pleasure – I daresay "pleasure"; and I must write.'

But when Dolke heard the clocks strike he was amazed. He had sat alone in his rooms for over an hour. An almost physical sensation of the need to write possessed him before any other idea could do so. To talk to Kutten was somehow, again almost physically, less imperative. And he was without hunger.

He began a preface. It fell uneasily between assertion and policy, and almost jarred him free from the impetus of his need. He tried again. Abbreviated ideas would not smooth out. Then came quick flights of words. Writing, he glanced up, many times it seemed subsequently, marking the achievement of the lengthening time of unbroken concentration. But another level of his mind was fixed on Kutten. A sound startled him. He found that, quite irrationally, he expected Kutten to appear. He expected and wanted Kutten to come.

The vividness of von Fluorn's conjurings was modulated by knowledge and by reduction to writing. Images which had been almost too radiant with figures and emotions to be scrutinised, proved, as they were transposed into forms for his masque, to add only a dab of colour. Dolke struggled to identify changes and new incidents which would help him to identify his own new sense. Thereby he was drawn into an attempt at synthesis, of traditions and great men, of past and present disputes and architectures. Names of colleges, fragments of speeches seemed of themselves to present truly an aspect of the whole, to suggest meaning.

Then the anti-masque; its elusive and assertive beasts and men remained vivid in his mind. Procession, drama and anti-masque. And the obscurity, common spirit and subtlety of the human

94

element would be presented in the ancient tradition of Solemn Dances. His plan was at last before him.

He looked up finally. He was very happy, almost light-headed. The images seemed very clear (thus in a sense were very clear). His only discomfort was in their pressing thickly about him, and in his head even.

The papers for the evening had become hopelessly muddled. Gathering them up casually, he pushed them under his arm. He would hurry to the Barschgasse. Kutten was bound to go there before the evening. His own thoughts would cool as he walked (he saw himself and Kutten walking back together for the meeting); he would know what to say. Before leaving he had first to satisfy a compulsion, perhaps a genuflexion of a part of him to order, to set neat and square the things on his table.

As he stepped out into the court, his attention was held by the familiar shadow of the opposite range, lying as if immobile, parallel to the buildings and square across his gaze. The sunlight had that brilliance as sometimes at that time of year, so clear as to make him blink. Time did not seem to be passing.

As Dolke walked up Tenth Day Street this immediacy of beauty made him less willing to compromise. His responses were so clearly of value. The masque was his own. His and von Fluorn's perhaps?

At the opening, where he saw the palace, he stopped. To stop brought relief; but relief in turn dealt a slight shock. There was no doubt that he would get to Mrs Wimpfner's. He must inform Kutten; it was their custom. But his habit of obligation, of duty, had faltered. Moreover his guilt must be obvious. Anyone seeing him would know: he did not even want to tell Vaslav Kutten. As he walked away, more heavily he felt, towards the Upper Town and the Barschgasse, Dolke began to excuse his feelings. The work was his; he was impatient even now to be working at it. Yet he moved on. By habit he was soon walking almost quickly.

Catching sight above the roofs of the travelling pinnacles of Saints Ulrich and Afra, he noted his speed. New propositions shifted his attitude. Kutten would not be susceptible to reason in this matter. What point then in putting to him the truth, that their old approach was, not wrong, but empty, arid? His own powers and Kutten's failure were present and certain. The painful, the less than perfect, statement of his new ideas stood in the background; a curious, attendant sense of frustration appeared only as a crossness with Kutten.

As he entered the Barschgasse he felt also (more for the first time a reaction of his body, his stomach, than a process of his brain) a disquiet, a sudden melancholy: of being vulnerable and being wounded but unable – no, unwilling – to defend himself. This suffocated other consideration. He stared at, he made himself notice, the buildings as if he might suddenly be deprived of their sight and memory for ever.

Mrs Wimpfner answered the door.

'Good afternoon, Mrs Wimpfner. Is the professor in?'

'I am afraid not, Doctor. But you might wait.'

The details of the staircase struck him with the clearer impact of something familiar. Yet he had last come in June, the day of their shared searches and experiment. That was the last time, but he knew the place. A visit lasts one for months, for ages, Dolke thought; it might almost have been yesterday. By reference only to such points, things can seem unchanged; but all is changing.

Something in Mrs Wimpfner's hand, still on the door, or in the angle of her head seemed to celebrate a small victory. She was standing aside to introduce Dolke into Professor Kutten's sitting room. As she had declared, he was not there. Perhaps then he would not come.

She left him alone. The slow mechanisms of a clock intruded on her behalf. He waited and time passed. He counted its regular sound to a ridiculous total. Did he intend to see Kutten? Yes; but if he returned to Ulpian now there would still be time to clarify his new ideas, to make them compelling. He could not write them at Kutten's table. But if he could himself grasp them exactly, set them down, it would be almost painless for Kutten's reason to accept what must be accepted.

The minutes were too full. He fixed the ultimate moment of his delay to the striking of the next quarter. At last he stood up, and standing wrote (in Kutten's ink, where Kutten wrote), 'Please come early'. He added his signature, 'Eberhard Dolke'. Might he add 'I came to see you'? Superfluous. As at Ulpian, however, he spent moments re-reading and replacing in an exact position dictated by his brain, but this time only to increase beyond reasonable expectation the ridiculous mass of seconds wasted.

Outside, Mrs Wimpfner was standing on the staircase.

'You are welcome to stay, Doctor. It will not be long now before he returns.'

'Unfortunately I have to be again at Ulpian. I have left a note for him. Can you be sure . . . ?'

'I shall, of course, Doctor. Goodbye.'

Dolke wished his excuse had not been so specific. Elaborateness of speech only half excused a lie, because it did not properly conceal it. He had waited at most half an hour.

He walked and rested in his rooms. If Kutten came, he would convince him. But no-one came. A nervousness prevented his rest. He owned a Turkish sofa, his only luxurious furniture but his favourite piece. He had lain on it with a sound of expectation, a sort of nervous invocation, of rest. But a draught seemed to slip under the door. People called hoarsely in the distant street. Birds twittered from the eaves, which made their songs uncertain and unmusical.

Then it was time to leave for the meeting. He realised he was hungry. As he left Ulpian he said, half-aloud:

'What will she say to him? I was a fool not to have waited.'

A comfortable apartment in Staufen College had been set aside for the meeting. It stood at the head of a flight of stone steps which led out of an ancient hall, known always as the Examination Chamber. When the porter brought keys with him Dolke knew that he would be alone.

He stood inside waiting. Despite his preoccupation, the dark, high walls of the Examination Chamber arrested his attention. Though it was infamously cold and damp, he lingered, because the height and the near invisibility of the squared, black beams of its ceiling infected him with a new anxiety. There was no need, moreover, to await from the single entrance to the upstairs rooms the footsteps and nonetheless sudden entrance of Kutten.

For more than the height of a tall man the walls were clothed with a revetment of variegated marbles. Above this, black stonework rose for three times that amount. It was into this stone that there were cut slender windows. These, though reaching upwards, cast no reassuring light into the dark recesses between the walls and the ceiling.

At this time of day the three windows of the western wall, and only these, caught the light. When Dolke entered, he was facing them. Through the whole length of each the light sloped towards him like sails, or like a staircase descending from a brilliantly lit vault. Above, the gloom hung loosely below the ceiling. Dolke's dazzled eyes found this impossible to penetrate. He was thinking:

'Kutten must come early. Mrs Wimpfner saw how I looked. She will have told him. She is sharp; she guards him like a watch-dog. It is my work, damn her.'

With three quick strides he crossed that line beyond which the sunlight completely bathed his face. He put his hands to his eyes, spread them over his cheeks. Never (as it were another part of him was thinking) had he felt such joy at a room. It soothed and exhorted him; it exhilarated and frightened him. It was unrelated to his concerns. This shifting of moods seemed to him subtlety, further evidence of his percipience. These were the oldest walls of the university. So it was said. He turned to right and left, nodding his approval.

Between the simple moulding of the windows the sole decoration was a single, elegant shaft. Each stretched from the marble revetment to a capital supporting a bracket, on which a ceiling timber rested. The capitals were in every place eaten away by damp. It had smoothed away their carved detail, or whitened them into a skin which in the dim light seemed to exude its own cold luminescence. The effect was at once of space, permanence, royalty even, and decay. In Dolke it reduced a receptiveness close to worship. The Emperor of North and South, the Emperor Frederick, had indeed been here, he assured himself. In the northern light the marble panels had lost their brilliance, but their subdued colours – blue-black, porphyry and white – were illuminated here and there with their old richness by the chance effects of the light, as if they merely concealed their splendour.

In this stillness, Dolke's response, a change in himself, seemed almost physical. It was like the bristling of the skin when, during a meditative theme, slight but distinct chords lure the attention, and excite the expectation of a new theme and a new mood. He braced himself to receive some hopeful impulse that the building might exert, and which he was beginning to crave. The only sound of the room was that of a delicate mountain ash, which began to brush the windows of the south wall.

Kutten entered. Dolke saw his smile.

'You found my note?' Dolke may have sounded off-hand; but he had been taken unawares.

'Yes. Mrs Wimpfner showed – Are they all coming?' Kutten looked round the empty room. Even as he had entered it and seen Dolke's loved form deep in thought, the still hall had seemed to him, as to Dolke (but to himself, he thought, from long, lonely familiarity and the inventing of associations) – had seemed possessed of a music. From its recesses and in his mind came, half-aloud echoes of the long whisperings and haunting resonance of the German language.

'Yes. It's not that,' said Dolke hesitantly. For once he was aware of the impatience of his embarrassed voice. Mrs Wimpfner, he was thinking – nothing more specific. He heard Kutten say, 'Oh good, good. No doubt the Seneschal will be here soon.'

Their conversation seemed to be escaping his control. Yet Kutten must know. He could so easily ask about the note. Somehow it was inevitable that they come to that subject. As for himself, nothing else could be expected.

He stepped up to Kutten and stared into his face. Kutten shrank as if accused.

'Here are your papers, Vaslav.'

'I came early,' said Kutten, receiving them carefully with both hands: At the same time his bowels contracted with unease.

'I have had to make additions.' To speak the fact was for Dolke to come close to guilt, to losing command, but the directness of the words sustained him.

'All to the good,' Kutten said, with a cheerful intonation, but softly. 'You always find the Ulpian library – harmonious.'

Of course, Dolke remembered, he had been expected to produce refinements.

It seemed in that moment to justify everything. He almost laughed.

'I have had to make some changes. I had to consult you, but I knew you would see. . . .' There was another moment's hesitation. 'There have to be changes, Vaslav. I have kept our scholarship. I have found precedents . . .'

He knew Kutten had caught the cadence and the implication. He indicated with a decisive movement of his hand the sheaf of papers. Kutten was turning the pages; he made a slight sound like a gasp.

'We have done all this. But, as you say, there must be "harmony". There has to be more than one note, one line, to music.'

'An eye made from many eyes. That is your theory.'

Even hesitant condescension gave momentary relief. He pushed out his hand and the papers to Dolke. He began thinking, I have been punished quite enough. He wanted to speak again, but he faltered. He wanted instead to see Dolke's expression, to push his face close to Dolke's.

His fingers, Dolke noticed, marked the pages with their pressure and a little sweat; his face scarcely quivered.

Dolke took the papers. The first was boldly, repulsively scarred with his fresh jottings. It was hard to grasp Kutten's feelings. Despite his own new zeal he would have found it hard to accept that a scholar as rational, as austere, as Kutten could so devote himself to a masque. Without a little scepticism!

Kutten had fixed an impassive expression:

'I shall see those properly when you put them before us.'

Turning away, Dolke saw the Seneschal standing with the King's Marshal.

Chapter 4

Dolke wanted reassurance. The events of the meeting at Staufen required no apology. The fact of it, he repeated to himself, did not allow apology. The fact was his having been unleashed from Kutten. There had been moments (though Kutten's near self-abasement had made difficulties) when his thoughts had soared. His ideas had surely been vindicated. It had been almost a triumph. Circumstances, however, had not allowed his reason to confront and answer Kutten, to do them both justice. They had denied Kutten the last word. The guilt of manners irritated a more profound uncertainty. Without triumph, without finality, doubts about his vision, about his new right to assert himself, would linger. Dolke had not seen Kutten since that day.

He had confided in no-one his feelings. Von Fluorn was now sitting on his prized Turkish sofa and conversing rather cautiously. He was telling himself, silently but very distinctly while von Fluorn talked, that he confessed some fault. In some dark way expiation and his new belief in his work were linked. For several days Dolke had played with a sense that he must tell von Fluorn the details of that meeting.

So he was expecting reassurance, and relief. He talked in his turn, and brought the subject round.

'Well, Fluorn, my evening with the Seneschal was a good lesson in the number of different ways a group of doctors can see the same body.'

'Is all settled then, sir, or . . . ?'

'Professor Kutten is a man of austere perception, and taste. He stood rooted to the spot when he saw my notes for the anti-masque. Your anti-masque, Fluorn, but I wouldn't advise you to dine with too many on that story. The idea does not meet Professor Kutten's standards.'

He found himself slipping past the exact words he and Kutten had used alone. He skated past and pared off their edge. To have met them would have put at risk his strengthening equilibrium.

In response to their proximity, he inwardly analysed Kutten's wound and bewilderment, and in his speech he took the opportunity of being generous.

When he used an euphemism or evasion – that there had been no time to explain to Kutten what he proposed; that he had felt bound to take sole responsibility and put his scheme to the committees – his remembrance of the occasion did shift, imperceptibly but significantly. Things were reassembled. To his own and to Kutten's attitude to the merits of each other's view of the masque he attached awareness and a remarkable detachment. Thus he might suppose that even their emotions had not contradicted their understanding.

He described the Seneschal – alert, tense and on his dignity. To be almost indiscreet helped to give release. His speech, still with its small formalities, was confidential.

A young man, he continued, was talking deferentially to the Seneschal. It was the King's man, his Marshal: with a face old for his age – a proud forehead and pronounced and determined nose and cheek-bones. His manner was not unlike Fluorn's. The power of the Benedictines was personified in their 'Visitor' to the university (and in whom a lawyer's orthodoxy blended curiously with benevolence). The Very Reverend Sulpizius Heysach.

'They say the legatus, Arcute, enjoys his conversation. And certainly they are both of them impressive. You know Arcute's face – Saint Libori's Day.'

'Forgive me. I have an ungrateful tendency to forget faces.'

'He was just before you on last Saint Libori's Day. Indeed I think so. Well, he is Public Orator. Advocate to the university brings its obligations.'

'Such occasions are a little too terrifying,' von Fluorn said, with a slightly nervous laugh.

'And he is a not unimportant man. He will have listened to *you.*'

'And you think he will be more important, sir?'

'He has a habit of whispering. Even while the Seneschal was speaking . . . He has a pleasing, musical voice, if rather high.'

'I doubt whether he would have listened to me,' said von Fluorn with only a slight betrayal of his attention.

'And he is a man of greater moment in the university than might be expected of a lawyer. A practising lawyer, that is to say (which one might have expected to impose a degree of distance in his dealings). But – as we were saying – he will have listened to *you*. He is a man inclined to make judgments. I observed carefully his demeanour that evening, and it gave me hope.'

He paused, and drew himself up slightly:

'This can all be cut short,' he announced, as if acknowledging a reasonable impatience of an interested audience. He uttered a sort of laugh, a loud sound. All at once the moments he was about to describe no longer seemed to him the climax, the almost inevitable conclusion, of a subtle interplay of precedence, character, influence and persuasion. It no longer seemed something which he might have calculated and might now analyse. Everything had turned on one moment.

'There came a moment,' he began afresh, in a low tone which marked the change. 'I suppose it was a period of five or six minutes. Suddenly it was clear that the Seneschal and I were *ad idem* – a lawyer may be permitted the phrase. His imagination had caught; I knew it – as if I had seen it written in the Code. He stood over the table and flounced out his robes. I could see him conjuring with images – some of them mine, I suppose. But I shall never know whether he would have had the courage – alone that is. Then the Regent – just as Feucht said (he almost gave an undertaking, but that was another occasion); the Regent of Ulpian saw just as clearly as I (and the honour of the college weighed too, I dare say). He stepped forward with a jerk (as he does) and simply said to the Seneschal, and to us all, "Sir, if you approve this plan, I shall support it to the utmost of my resources". It was over.'

Von Fluorn was enthusiastic. For him, the moment, the crisis, always contained the whole truth. Other details had served to suggest what he might have felt had he been there to see. His sense of a scene highly charged with suppressed emotions and in which the actors (for so he saw them) were aware of the importance of their own actions was intense and immediate. Dolke, unable to control his own excitement, had not intended to convey this.

'Of course,' Dolke continued after a moment to collect himself, 'that was not absolutely all there was to it.'

He remembered his own part and, wanting to share the moment, said with a smile:

103

'My own forcefulness surprised *me*.'

'They were not even doubtful about the anti-masque, sir?'

'Not in the least. And to think I only had time to give them a sketch of our ideas – after all, they were transformed by your contribution, Fluorn, transformed. And indeed I had not clarified things to myself.'

Both of them laughed at the irony; von Fluorn laughed at a little refinement which struck him; for he could not imagine Dolke in his present, slight pompousness inspiring enthusiasm.

'They must have been stirred by something, sir; those at least whose voices counted.'

When Dolke spoke again, it was in a tone in which recognition both of his modest part and the extent of his triumph seemed to be mingled:

'Yes. Even at the end there must have been many views held in that room – as many as there were people, no doubt. Professor Kutten had slipped out during the meeting.' Dolke added this suddenly, apparently without satisfaction or disquiet. The flow of his words had carried him up to it and he overcame the last obstacle without audible discomfort. As he spoke, he was almost convinced that he was no more than politely obliged to Kutten for his decency in having said nothing.

He was aware what Kutten might have achieved had he opposed. Yet, as he remembered his own exposition of half-formed ideas, it seemed to him that there had been no rationality that Kutten could have relied on. It would be dishonest to pretend that his own ideas could ever have been justified by reason. Their claim on him was not that they represented the truth any more than a thousand other, different observations might have done. Indeed, there were no certainties against which they could be judged. But they pleased him; his mood, and to some extent his reason and knowledge, responded to them. They inspired some feeling in him, but his own mood and view of things equally determined his response to them – derisive, sceptical or exalted. That afternoon seemed in a flash to exemplify von Fluorn's understanding (unconscious as it largely was) and to match the variety and contradictions of his own reactions to certain familiar scenes and places. This variety even seemed for a moment to appear before his eyes. It could be represented by no structure, but had sufficient of form to appear like an open fan, spread horizontally and tremulous with uncertainty, and each element stretching away along its own course, further and further apart from the others.

To escape this uncertain vision he turned to von Fluorn; resumed a didactic, paternal air, which of late he had only rarely adopted consciously. And he turned to defend his own fading assumptions.

'I heard your gibe at poor Holzhauer, Fluorn, when he accused Liss of bad taste. "Leave good taste to those who need it!" You must be careful about remarks like that. I thought you would offend.'

'But I added that I had good taste myself,' von Fluorn said and smiled engagingly.

Dolke, however, was scarcely listening. The character of the masque seemed curiously a matter of chance, almost of caprice. His imagination was in tumult. With an increasing intensity of excitement, he seemed to himself to stand on dangerous ground.

As the coldness of the weather increased, a curious euphoria seemed to infect the people of Saint Eadmundsburg. They sensed the imminence of a great frost. During the first weeks of November it had begun to snow. Coronas of ice spread at the bases of the bridges' numerous piers. Shiftless groups had watched almost regretfully from the river-banks the floes which other men dislodged into the stream by the blows and pressure of barbed poles. Ice already covered so solidly the channels which crossed the meadows beyond the Benedictines and the University Gate that it seemed to clutch the rushes, whose slender tubes pivoted awkwardly from their exact point of juncture with the frozen surface.

At about this time the townspeople began to give up the struggle to defeat the cold at every point, and began in stealthy and curious ways to adapt to it. The roads were no longer kept clear of snow; only Tenth Day Street, the Forum, the markets and one or two others. Indeed such openness itself began to seem unnatural: its colour and surface seemed brash by contrast with the even white, and it was the sleds fixed to carts and carriages, the raised walks of timber and the other compromises with persistent cold which began to be seen as part of normal life.

At a congregation of doctors in the Gallery of the old university buildings on the Forum, in which winter was dispelled by hung fabrics of crimson, pink and all the colours of warmth, and by tapestry scenes of feasts and gardens, the King's Marshal presented to its library on behalf of his Lord an ancient *Book of Pericopes* illuminated in gold on grounds of purple. For the collection of paintings which the King was in process of establishing, and in expectation of his arrival, the Marshal received in return a Deposition from the Cross of van der Weyden, held in esteem by the university second only to their Madonna Enthroned by that same master. The King, thirty leagues away, would be well pleased; his Marshal had considerable authority, and sufficient discernment, to bestow praise. The King would approve the gift, the Court would approve the masque; and for himself he delighted in the sombre gallery and the sophisms of the discourse of Andreas Arcute.

Vaslav Kutten stood among the foremost of a respectful press of academics. At first he noticed only their compacted shuffling. To do so was to remain detached from them.

Detached, he welcomed nostalgia and its blows into the heart. Dolke had cut him off from the university – from his Seneschal; all (he almost enjoyed repeating) to which he wished to belong. Remembering their last meeting, Kutten formulated Dolke's offence. He and Dolke had walked arm-in-arm. They had been expected to achieve excellent things. How could Dolke have made him so alone? Then later, how could he have made him hold those pages and made his movements clumsy?

Kutten did not want to exhaust loneliness, but to indulge it; and by seeking to enhance his dependence.

There were gliding movements – and stooping, and wonderfully beautiful objects. White hands lay along fur-trimmed robes; a hem was deftly shifted to allow a courtly gesture. Bowing and gold on purple parchment must, something insisted, have meaning. In his ecstasy he became kind; 'If only Eberhard were here!' he thought. 'He too would feel the presence – the greater whole.' He turned expectantly to left and right, glancing over the heads of the other doctors. In the hope of something lasting and greater than himself there returned paradoxically something of his strength, his individuality, his desire to create.

Afterwards he began to talk to others. The Visitor proved in conversation incapable of any response (greater than an epigram) to the mystery at which they had been present together and seemed thereby strangely diminished. Kutten's vision and expectation began the process of adapting themselves to smaller virtues, which did not aspire to achieve in himself the whole high nature of the university, but which could be touched and satisfied. By such mechanisms of compromise a void was not left, or was bridged to any reasonable expectation. Kutten's empty time had been spent in excavations in the cellars of the house in the Barschgasse. He began to consider what he might do for the university.

By mid-November the river was under unbreakable ice from the bridges below the castle south as far as the white bridge leading to the palace, and even beyond. The languor with which people had observed the scene remained, and was sometimes mingled with gaiety. By night lights glowed on the river, swelling from a distance to take a definite place in the pattern of fire. Broad paths for the carriage of burdens were marked on the ice by braziers, while safe and elegant avenues of flambeaux and torchères night after night criss-crossed and extended.

The nights, people observed lightly, were of a brilliant transparency; the days like dusk. Fire blazed on the surface of ice; water was dear. People had time to notice these pleasant ironies. Periods of such coldness were not rare; warehouses and cellars were well stocked. They had but to be patient.

At about this time Kutten heard more frequently the association of von Fluorn's name with that of Doctor Dolke. He sensed again the uneasy suspicion of a deception. The idea of anti-masque was not Eberhard Dolke's. He would not have conceived such a defilement. It was the vulgarity of a mountebank.

Then his reason reasserted itself. He put completely from his mind – for the moment – the question of deception, and whether von Fluorn might have played a part . . .

During the past Kutten had studied with fascination the decisions of the great judges. He admired (when he remembered) with almost uncomfortable intensity their extraordinary ability, facility almost, to put from their minds a matter which might prejudice an issue. Perhaps sometimes they, as he, put out the distraction by placing it, he surmised, on a height or in a certain chiaroscuro, which gave it the appearance of such virtue or complexity or individuality as convinced the mind of its need for exclusive consideration when lesser problems had been closed. Von Fluorn was incapable of ideas. Yet Kutten was now aware of an insistent mental image of him. Moreover, something told him that this image was insufficient, and unworthy of his own capacity. Did he really know what Friedrich von Fluorn looked like? he asked himself. From that moment he thought about von Fluorn more and more frequently.

One morning people awoke to be called by friends, who spoke in hushed voices, to come to the walls. The deer were come down from the woods and even, their numbers declared, from the forests far to the north. Along the river-bank below the palace, where the trees left a precarious space, some threaded their placid, indefatigable way. Others must have crossed the river; the river must also be blocked above the city, people reasoned. Those animals that had reached the other side were filing through the fields, across the snow. Their movements made no sound. Now and again, however, a stag would throw back its head, and its sudden bell struck the hearts of the listeners with awe. Most curious and disquieting was it when one, or a line, of the beasts at the river-bank or one of the channels below the walls turned as if with some secret and concerted purpose towards the city. It seemed to people that their southward march was like that of an army. Their approach and passage were curiously bold, as if the animals were aware that their implacable pursuers were held fast by some paralysis of the spirit. To some people they suggested the silent circumvallation of a town by a subtle enemy. Others gazed in sympathy, as it were on a beautiful but defeated army, whose way was no longer led by anything but instinct, and who perhaps were pursued by something far more menacing. It was in either case a response of fear.

Not only was it the sudden aspect of these animals which inspired foreboding. People reasoned – and confirmed their alerted fears – that to give rise to such a migration the area under the sway of this hideous cold must be enormous. Some stood and reckoned the numbers of the animals that passed, seemingly in review, during the whole of that day – as if they might by such knowledge come to some important determination. The vision and thought of others led them to other fears. Nothing was certain any longer. What use was reason without knowledge and certainty? Who knew what cruel people might not come out of the white hills?

In various parts of the town, one and then another, was heard with a growing sense of its inevitability the sound of the passing bell. It came at last even in the night. Dolke heard it from his rooms, a repetition which on any day of any year might be expected from some quarter or another; it now seemed interminable. He turned from his work and set himself to listen, as if he expected that by confronting the sound he might shame it into silence.

Von Fluorn, in his own rooms, like all awake at that time in and about that district of the city, also heard the bell. 'The sonorous passing bell,' he quoted to himself from a familiar writer. He turned away with a certain sense of irritation; he might have left the city before winter, with Aicha and the others. In their absence, he reminded himself, a chance to settle down to some work had presented itself and he had little enough desire to return home much before his duty required him there for Christmas. To think, he reproved himself mockingly, to think he chose Death rather than his family as a neighbour.

He stood up to take a turn round his sitting room. The reverberations were uncomfortable.

'They're quite close,' he whispered to himself, as if to a confidential friend. He was slightly alarmed by a vague image, the approach of gentle Death, which was somehow associated with the closeness of the ringing. And he was slightly expectant at his heightened realisation of the purpose of the sound.

He sat down again, settling the chair into its correct position at his table with an elaboration which could distract and soothe his mind. He focused his eyes far beyond the reflections of his face and room, both mirrored in his unshuttered window, and with this distant expression seemed to be trying by a conscious effort to free his imagination from restraint. He felt almost that this mental power was one to receive images; that he had the power to do this but was prevented from doing so to the full extent of his abilities. As he sat, he repeated to himself, just aloud, a phrase, 'The Dead! The Dead!', as if he might conjure them up, or make their image pass before him.

But the thought, or image, was no more than a suggestion of the solemn clangour of the bell. Its sound, even the danger with which it was associated, had an allure. It was this, the enjoyment of his own fear, which aroused his imagination. His train of thought again seemed to be deflected, but it was by memories of a similar excitement – of himself scaling the rock plinth on which the castle stood, seen in the same shifting images as if from a vantage point and again as he had seen himself, the palm of his hand over a swelling of rock, or his foot on the narrow ledge. Then he saw himself again, perched on the towers, above the city.

He awoke to realistic associations of death, all that he had experienced – funerals, hunts – detached from him, having left him unscathed. He felt the same remoteness in this mood from the news of the town. What were people dying of in Saint Eadmundsburg? He did not even know that for certain. It was said that people were dying because the water was impure; because of the shortage of clean, wholesome food. Some people blamed the direct effect of the cold, whose like had not been known for twenty years.

When Dolke, some days before, had sought his company so that he might venture on to the ice, von Fluorn, oppressed by lassitude, had evaded the request. He decided to take the first opportunity of accepting. If necessary he would remind his tutor of his proposal. The tolling of the bell, now over, still summoned him to escape from a suffocating existence.

The city was now isolated; but it had happened before, and, while the funeral processions gathered first in the main about the drab or tawdry churches of the crowded market streets and later at college chapels and even at the Cathedral Church of the Benedictines, strollers still made their way out on to the ice. By day they slid and skated; by night they met, close to the warmth and motion of a leaping fire.

Dolke eagerly took up von Fluorn's renewal of his suggestion. On the day agreed for their expedition, von Fluorn awoke with the light (an obligation of childhood that he had neglected recently). He walked, and from the walls which overlooked the eastern fields he observed a man struggling with the burden of a dead buck. He supposed the man had killed it, probably in the oak copse which stood on Abbey land about half a mile off. On his back, von Fluorn suspected, was strapped a cross-bow; its horn and wood protrusions seemed somehow, as much as his efforts to draw backwards the creature at his feet, to press the man down, and to give him the appearance of being bent in the frame of some sort of halter.

Perhaps, von Fluorn told himself indulgently – for he was surprised and slightly ashamed that his first thoughts had tended to lead him to judge the likely illegality of the act – perhaps the man has been up half the night to get it.

All four hooves of the animal were tied together on to a pole so that, with one hand to either side, the man was able to pull it along. He stumbled. Von Fluorn tensed, and when the hunter staggered again, found himself gripping the ledge of the embrasure from which he watched.

When he had relaxed he smiled at his concern, but knew then that he would have liked to be that man. It was not the criminality, probable as that was, which excited him, but that in the clutching, jerking heaves of the man's progress across the centre of the exposed, grey landscape, there seemed to him proof that the action was the result of feelings which were compelling. His own feelings were never so strong. He was almost envious.

The hunter was again within two hundred paces of the frozen water channels. He floundered in deeper snow and paused; von Fluorn recognised with distaste that the long neck and delicate head of the animal, despite their extended and sinuous curvature, were no longer supple. They were frozen, and, as the man hauled, gashed constantly against any protrusion from the snow which opposed their rigidity. Scarcely any blood ran from each new wound before the opened veins were hardened by the cold. The hunter turned his eyes away from the city, on which he had seemed to try to keep them, and looked down at the animal. He jerked upwards on the pole; as von Fluorn thought, a futile gesture, a waste of strength. Von Fluorn decided that it was no huntsman, no forester, he was watching; he knew more about what should be done himself. As the figure again began to move closer, von Fluorn saw what he had already suspected. It was a boy, an apprentice or some such – a town boy. A man approaching von Fluorn along the wall paused only to glance and to give only a brief and significant snort.

Of course the effort deserved disdain. The decisive, inarticulate sound confirmed the rectitude of his own contempt. It also reminded him that he wanted the boy to succeed. His own hands within his supple, tanned gloves were cramped with tension. He continued to wait.

On the far bank of the main channel, he was suddenly aware, three men were standing. They moved forward without gesture, and apparently without a word. Von Fluorn realised, with a tension in his stomach almost like excitement and with an instant of regret, that they were not coming to help. The boy turned away and held fast to the buck's legs. He was somewhat, von Fluorn thought, like a small bird who turns away from its predatory fellows when they are about to seize the food it keeps tightly in its beak. He made no attempt to touch the cross-bow strapped to his back. He did put up one arm to fend them off (von Fluorn found himself raising a little his own right arm, bent), and then threw down his burden. They moved him to one side without apparent roughness.

Their task also was hard. They had to pause several times, addressing meanwhile a few words to the boy, then at last falling to busily until they had hacked away what they could manage and had left the boy to drag the befouled remnants into the town. Von Fluorn turned away, satisfied that he should not pass judgment; those men had, after all, simply felt the same compulsion. He grasped this. He could see himself doing as they, almost gently, almost kindly, had done. His power, a voice began to say, his genius perhaps, was one of understanding. Its source was perhaps the vitality of his instincts, the sympathy of which his senses (rather than his sentiments) were capable? And perhaps a higher element, a tension of the senses close to compulsion, which could be excited.

At the corner of a quiet street, as he walked back briskly through the town, he found himself face to face with Vaslav Kutten.

'Out of doors,' said Kutten, not quite forming a question. They had never been so close. A brightness in von Fluorn's eyes confused him. 'You are a pupil of Doctor Dolke.'

'Yes, sir. Friedrich von Fluorn,' he said firmly. He sensed, without suspicion, that the professor had been waiting for him.

Kutten caught the tone correctly. His guilt gathered facts which were true; for he must defend now.

'I saw you walking. This is scarcely an area for a young gentleman of the university. The people here are desperate, some of them, with cold and hunger. Is anything the matter?'

The last question was spoken almost tenderly. His first words had been meant to carry his mood from defence into examination. Instead he paused.

'A boy there, in the cold.' Von Fluorn turned from the waist. His arm, it seemed to Kutten, found an habitually elegant line.

'He killed a buck.'

'A poacher or a boy?'

'Deft' was how Dolke had described him, Kutten remembered. That was how he could lead Dolke on (in the same instant Kutten was struck by the stupidity and ugliness of all evasive but suggestive idioms).

'A boy. And then men took it from him,' said von Fluorn in a soft voice, and twitched.

That movement communicated itself to Kutten with a piercing shock and excitement. He knew himself to be nervous with desire. Nothing was clear but a desire to reach and touch.

'Crimes. But in winter one tries to be merciful.' Meanwhile those mechanisms in Kutten alert to conceal the nature of his sexual impulse clamoured about the instinct to reassure of the power of life in a dead time. From the almost unbearable noise in his mind he extracted a genuine desire (to which even a few moments earlier a part of him had kept), to reject cruelty.

In a few moments the shouting was silenced and von Fluorn – his clothes, his voice – was again distasteful.

'The others took it from him,' von Fluorn said more emphatically.

'They may have been the King's men. They sometimes only take the deer now, and spare the poacher.'

'They were all equally hungry.'

There was a light still, Kutten saw, in von Fluorn's eyes. The careless movements of von Fluorn's body displayed no distress.

'The penalty for stealing the deer is death,' Kutten said in a cold voice, and passed on, trembling slightly as if he had uttered a threat. He prayed never to see von Fluorn again.

In the last light of that day von Fluorn found himself with Doctor Dolke at the curve in Tenth Day Street where Dolke liked to pause, and which is the summit of the winding path into that extraordinary view towards the palace. The smooth declivity lay covered in a patchwork of cobbled ways and outer walls, the abrupt tower of the College of the Three Archbishops (called Electors' College), gardens and orchards. Long shadows confused them. Beyond, the spreading curve of the river made its course, and there was no need for a city wall.

What was presented (by chance), von Fluorn observed, was such a vista as gardeners now sought to create at great houses and pleasaunces by immense pain of invention and labour.

In spite of a patchwork of kitchen gardens without geometry (indeed in summer its harmony of brick brown, maroon and red, greens and grey pleased Dolke rather than otherwise, though for what reason he could not quite be sure), here essentially was such a *coup d'oeil*. He gazed between the pilastered façades of the wings of two of the finest of scholarly new courts, as if they were the piers of some framing and ornamental gateway, towards the white bridge and so across the river. Along the breast of the swelling undulation of land which rose beyond, covered in beech and oak, lay the royal palace. The serenity and strength of this façade were in its simplicity. It was a smooth wall of marble. On it sunlight made its whiteness sometimes dazzling, sometimes lactic, and lent an illusion of greater solidity wherever shadow was cast from those few embellishments that the wall possessed. Dolke knew well how the space of gently terraced gardens allowed the range which opposed him to appear to ride above the nearest trees.

As the sun descended from an icy, empty sky, the river of white and steel, the black intricacies of the trees and the intruding black geometry of the silhouetted palace in turn to the unaccustomed eye disappeared.

With night the lost view presented to von Fluorn's eyes a scene from the romances. For as far as he and Dolke could see, on the right of the white bridge as far as the two bridges below the castle's bluff, where indeed over those slower waters the smoothest and most massive ice extended, spread avenues of light. These connected, and in great numbers radiated from every part of wide places of resort. In the centre of each of these openings,

114

circled by the flaring entrances to the different walks, was the splash of light, and sense of air in motion above, of a gigantic bonfire magnified in its natural mirror of black ice. Dotted everywhere were the numberless flames of smaller fires, and many of these gave some faint illumination to a shelter or a stall.

As Dolke and Von Fluorn walked down, around them was a constant flow, a formless sound, of people pursuing their way forward as if in common, with deliberate but unhurried steps. Among them there was little loud talk or laughter. It was this absence, Dolke realised, which suggested so forcefully an urgency and the current of some shared determination. Both men, moreover, began to feel themselves infected with the common impulse.

'Look, Fluorn!' cried Dolke; and before them the tower of Electors' College jutted among the distant lights. Where the mass of stone lay over the fires, was a clearly defined space, its blackness intensified by the contrast. Higher, against the impenetrable darkness of the woods, some solidity was suggested in its grey surfaces.

From Electors' a noisier, more impetuous element was injected into the stream of people. Students appeared from the low gates which led from the gardens of lodging houses. Some seemed even to rise from the shadows of walls, as if at a signal, or with the sudden sense that the time was now right for them to go on.

It was now that hour at which the custodian of the palace responded to the proliferation of lights over the river. So peculiar were the qualities of the white façade of the palace that on all nights but those of the most profound blackness it appeared, to the gradually accustomed eyes of those at least who knew where to look, as an unshaped luminosity along the hill. To others it appeared strangely as an intrusion blacker than the surrounding darkness. From flambeaux ranged along all its façades there was suddenly thrown over these surfaces fluid patches of light, which leapt as the night breeze scattered and splayed the exposed flames. Thus from the distance there seemed to be white flames bursting among the trees on the convulsions of spontaneous, hidden fires.

Already hastening as they searched the way over the last stretches of the path, the crowd about Dolke and von Fluorn – bellowing, pointing with outstretched arms, transforming themselves as they paused into angular and dramatic silhouettes – dashed forward. They slipped between one another like elusive animals, and at last scattered over the ice.

The crowd were congregated all along the neat bank and out, following the rays of torches, towards the centre of the river. The whole was given an apparent order by the ranks and files of light; its extension and attenuation were almost imperceptible, except when a new line of lights was quickly illuminated and ran out alone deep into the dark. Amid this slightly shifting multitude could be seen, now and then, compact swirls and stirrings of physical activity. Beyond, in either direction towards the bridges, whose piers might have given shelter and a setting against which to play, there was a void.

Once on the ice, Dolke and von Fluorn were abandoned momentarily by their sense of purpose. The flames to either side, the perspectives and vistas of flames, fascinated and bewildered them. Their sense also of place was threatened, by all around them that was leaping and two-dimensional. As they walked, people beyond the consistent light of their avenue were at one moment visible and then lost, returning either to intense darkness or to the concealment of some dazzling light; so suddenly that these others seemed, instead of strolling, to glide at speed or to flit like shy creatures.

Again and again von Fluorn would exclaim, 'This is exquisite' or 'Look, sir, there!' but he always wanted, Dolke felt, to push on to see something else.

Nonetheless, as the two of them cooled, the sights around them became more intelligible. The various incidents on the ice distracted them pleasantly. The sale of things – food, drink and fripperies – was conducted with an unusual intensity. There were parties skating, or dining off tables, and there was the curious familiarity and even intimacy of manners in common experience of something strange. Around many of the fires stood knots of people, men and women, some of them boisterous. Some sat on chests, boxes or stools close in at the flame. Some sang and seemed cheerful, talking and keeping their eyes fixed on the light.

Faces were here more varied, or more deserving of his notice, von Fluorn thought. At least he did notice them more; more curious, more ugly, more indiscreet of their feelings, as if he had

116

come upon them stealthily in their own homes. There was curiously little conversation, he thought; or perhaps their voices were lost over the ice.

In front of the two men was the white bridge. No-one was near it, or seemed to have any regard for it. It might have been the flimsy backdrop to a stage-play. Indeed it looked just as flat and two-dimensional. Its nearer side reflected only dimly the light of the distant braziers and torches. At the bases of its piers there was some slight crackling glow from the light thrown by reflection from the ice – a thin imitation of the sunlight which the stone caught in summer from the smoothly moving river. Everything beyond this façade, all the vaults of its arches and its recesses, was indistinguishable in blackness. The absence of any grada-tions of shadow or of focus poised the masonry on the water, apparently hanging washed white like canvas, yet mysterious in its scale and rhythmic regularity, which insisted that it must be an object not merely solid but immense. Where Dolke and von Fluorn loitered, almost at its mid-point and before the keystone of its central span, it was the latter effect which predominated; the light, though like smears of paint, accentuated, rather than hid the texture and intricate pattern of the hewn stone.

They had come first to the heaped and broken ice about the piers of the bridge and seen the snow still soft and powdered on the topmost angles of ice and flotsam. They heard, as they passed beyond the façade, the higher, penetrating note of the funnelled air, and smelt the river smell; the cold had not totally exting-uished it where it smeared the ribs of the bridge. So strong was the association of smell and running water that both Dolke and von Fluorn started, for a moment expecting, without reason, a treacherous fissure of the ice. Sound, stone and smell had cut them off from the society of the crowd.

They were now past what had seemed, though it had never been, a boundary or even an obstacle, Before, the whole city had seemed to be around them. Though they had seen no familiar faces, there seemed to have been there the people, the castle, the palace and the university. Even now they could see, if they cared to turn, the skein of light diminished in the perspective of the arches, and now and then they caught gusts of sound. From this farther side the course of the river presented its unhinderable sweep, until its broad expanse disappeared before them. The river seemed, as they stood almost midway between the more intense darkness of its banks, to fall away from them gradually to either side, into a certain convexity exaggerated by the inscrutable blackness into which it shaded. Ahead of the two men, the only sound was that of the passing bell.

Von Fluorn knew that he wished Dolke gone.

It was von Fluorn who stopped first. It was as if he was in sympathy with what was about to happen, and thereby prescient of it. Perhaps he felt some crepitation of the ice beneath his feet. With a courteous gesture he led Dolke slightly into the shadow. Looking towards the city, straining slightly towards the sound, he remarked, 'The bell of Saint Ursula,' as if the identification of the sound (small and clear but with a certain thinness) explained his conduct. His irritation with Dolke (so he considered his earlier, vehement desire), that was gone. Indeed his awareness of Dolke was very slight. He was instead possessed by unease, by a prickling, animal alertness. His attention had fixed on the bell as the only certain presence besides themselves. There was more comfort in its identification than pleasure in the sound.

Then there emerged from the darkness ahead a great column of people. At first its appearance only existed in contrast with the ice over which it spread like an extension of the shadow of the bank. Its head having reached the ice, it paused for a moment. Then, contracting with the action of a muscle, to concentrate its strength, to give it a resilient and compacted firmness, it marched out over the surface.

It extended itself with the ease of extension of a man's arm. It directed itself towards the farther end of the white bridge. As they trod softly over the ice, its members raised a low music, a steady and rhythmic murmur.

Dolke was listening. Their sounds conveyed nothing to him. The fact of the presence of so many people (when all the world had seemed gathered in the fire-light) was momentarily bewildering. He could not tell whether this sound (this sigh, this reverberation) was for the attention of those like himself, outside, or was instead instinctive – a mere cry, or that sound made by every member of a herd to support its own and its neighbours' confidence in their continuing presence.

'What do they say?' he repeated, turning to von Fluorn.

The head of the column stood out of the darkness. The figures of men – men and women – formed individually. As they did so and Dolke thought he could make out the motions of their faces as they formed sounds, he distinguished the word, endlessly and inarticulately repeated – 'Down! Down!' In the same moment that he saw faces (eyes and mouths in particular) and clothing (head coverings and face cloths to keep out the cold) both his fear and his fascination vanished in a sickening despair.

Which were men, he tried to tell, and which women. They were so muffled. In holding close by one another, those on the fringes of the mass fell into a short, lurching step which brought them back close among the rest. The head of the column was so near that they must see him and von Fluorn. The column must take account of them or choose to pass by; for only the first ranks seemed to him capable of decision.

In a few moments they had crossed the invisible line, marching distractedly, with heads slightly lowered as if to sustain some effort of will towards something far away. All fear left Dolke.

All sense of tragedy (so vivid and dramatic as the crowd approached) had passed from Von Fluorn's mind. He observed their course towards the far end of the white bridge. An ascent, a smear of mud, tapering towards the junction between the bank and the white parapet, had long been trodden into a place of landing and embarking. Though slippery, it would not be difficult to scale the bank here and gain the paths which led from the bridge and through the forest. The mass of figures spread, mounted in part, struggled, and succeeded. The way forward, though covered in snow, he thought to himself, would be distressing.

As for the sound they made, he thought (turning from an unpleasantly vivid impression of the frustration with which they would grapple with every fold of smooth mud and its elusive, treacherous hardness), as for their sound, he could not decide, even now as he turned to hear them repeat it, whether it was an expression of despair, an imprecation, or a call to action. It communicated nothing. It seemed no conscious articulation of their feelings as humans. It was an instinctive sound, expressed in common.

Nonetheless, for another part of him, it possessed an arresting music. The mass possessed a force. He could see the buck jerked

119

bloodily over the ground, as if it were his own body, or by his own hands.

Dolke was still subdued by the unseeing crowd. He felt so exposed before them, though not to danger so much as to scrutiny, or perhaps to some unanswerable accusation. He turned cautiously, gently, to look at von Fluorn. The head of the crowd was lost among the trees. The last of it was still filing by. Von Fluorn was watching intently. He did not move, Dolke noticed. His hands, held close to the collars of his coat, were clenched into fists. Dolke leaned closer: there was nothing in them of hostility. Indeed von Fluorn's face was empty of emotion. Dolke had leaned closer. With a spasm of guilt at his own intrusiveness, he pulled back. The rhythmic voices and the soft shuddering of the ice seemed to have lulled von Fluorn away. There was no trace in him of sorrow or sympathy. The two men had been watching quite different events.

'Did you hear that?'

'That . . . ?'

'Down! Down!'

There was a movement of excitement under the drawn skin of von Fluorn's face. When he had caught its rhythm, von Fluorn had longed to be among the crowd.

'And they moved as if the lower part of their bodies were cramped together.'

'That cry is the cry of despair, Fluorn.'

'Despair of inaction. But not of feeling.'

Their sudden presence, the painful press of bodies, their disgusting appearance, and the tautness of apprehension were exalting. Their anonymity and unknown purposes invested them with a mystery and drama. Their desolate appearance on the ice, he told himself, was almost beautiful. He wondered what it would smell like, to be massed among them. He had never been in a dense crowd.

'I think it is absence of feeling and action,' he heard Dolke saying, 'except in the last sin of Judas.'

'It is compulsion, and that is close to inspiration.'

Dolke emitted a harsh sound (like the man on the city walls, von Fluorn thought). He wanted to be angry, but somehow had scarcely any strength. He shook his head.

'Despair is the absence of restraints; of everything that

deadens,' von Fluorn insisted, but almost softly, feeling the duty not to hurt over such a feeling. 'The feelings compel, I know, and compulsion is a sort of restraint, but – well, at last one knows what one is capable of.'

'That is not despair.' Dolke spoke, and caught at von Fluorn, who was turning away. 'This is not pedantry. Those people will do nothing. Perhaps they will hurt themselves.'

Dolke at once regretted the malice of his final words.

'We shall see.'

'They say the King's Steward is a kind man, Fluorn.'

But von Fluorn had already begun to follow. Turning back only for a moment, von Fluorn lifted his head, almost as if it might in that dimness have been lit to advantage:

'Times are hard. He would be well advised to be.'

Dolke watched his first, swift steps into the gloom.

Von Fluorn's failure – his simple failure to see the truth of – of poverty and despair – hurt Dolke more than he could have expected. Logic compelled the view that the fact that had been before them, transitory in itself, possessed innumerable facets, some only visible to one eye, some only to another. The suspicion came into his mind for the first time, that, despite theory, he looked to von Fluorn for a shared understanding, a corroboration of the importance of his often lonely perception. He fixed his eyes fiercely on the darkness. He could make out a figure – von Fluorn certainly, following circumspectly the distant, black presence. The obstacle of the final steps – fear and alert proximity – would surely teach his power to see that he had not been at one with them.

'It is well enough to speak of total stocks of food. Over what time must they last?'

'Some might say, "Let them last so many weeks. If the cold outlasts it, then that must be the will of God."'

'That we suffer?'

'That we suffer dearly, Professor Kutten,' the Visitor insisted.

'And you will tell us how many weeks to choose?'

'I suppose it is theologically impossible,' the legatus Arcute asked gently, 'that God may not wish us to suffer, and the cold may end, but the King may come with little?'

121

'If we can get a messenger to His Majesty' (it was the King's Steward who spoke) 'we can at least meanwhile vouchsafe something for four weeks. We have wood for four weeks – and some food for that long.'

'But should you,' asked the Visitor, 'give in response to demand?'

His concern came from his belief that the whole of the city had gathered at night about the fires on the ice. Not himself, of course; nor of course his bishop; but the whole city – rich and poor, university and town – all who were not cloistered. Who then had marched on the palace? It was as if there had been revealed the existence of a secret population, whose minds were not open to his scrutiny.

The Visitor always wished to know the reality – of a single word, of a gesture; of the unseen motives and characters of men. Perhaps for this reason he found himself attuned to the inquisitorial aptitude of the legatus Arcute. As for the townspeople (those who had gone to the palace), his inclinations were not uncharitable (he was uncommonly aware of the duty to do good), but he found their conduct incomprehensible. When faced with something whose significance or explanation was not apparent, he tended to confuse (and almost to believe that no distinction could be drawn between) the originator's actual intentions and the most reasonable explanation of them. To find the most reasonable, the most likely explanation, he fell back on his experience. The necessity of making his decision in the light of circumstances with whose force and nature he was unfamiliar continued to exercise his mind.

'There is another aspect,' Arcute pointed out. 'You have described the mob at the white palace as a procession. Might it not be better considered a march on the palace?'

'I had those words in my mind this very instant.'

'No violence was offered,' said the Steward, looking down with a sort of embarrassment. 'They spoke of deaths in the city. They left respectfully.'

The Steward had been seeking help. He looked up abruptly, and caught the eyes of the Seneschal.

'You give us four weeks in which to plan and act, sir. Gentlemen, each to our houses and make return within the day what – by separate reckoning – what to each of us is superfluous.'

122

The meeting, after just one hour, was effectively at an end.

There was in the Seneschal the same artificiality, Kutten was thinking, the same difficult resonance. The effect somehow filled him with enthusiasm.

'Professor Kutten!' A movement forward had reminded the Seneschal of his presence. 'You have been considering the public distribution?'

'The food will be transported under guard. The guard will distribute the provisions. Nothing will go to a mob. The Steward and I have looked into it.'

Kutten could hear the briskness of his own voice. He was convinced by its strength and purpose. Still he wanted to thank the Seneschal, to make an obeisance to him (the Steward withdrew with the bow of a soldier). To his pleasure he found himself walking with the Seneschal.

'I must thank you, Professor, for all your arrangements.'

'They will distract the townspeople from fear.'

'And prepare for the thaw – your work on the water meadow embankments.'

Kutten loved the townspeople. Connected with this, with his new purpose and science, his clarity, was to rescue Dolke from isolation; but they were discussing the more efficient use of water in the colleges.

The Seneschal had been studying, discreetly, the cold exultation in Kutten's expression. He approved of it rather. Both of them had been indefatigable. Under his own persuasion, colleges saved fuel by the sharing of chapels and halls. He had exercised all his influence. He had hinted, and perhaps more, at preferments. Why should a man not be preferred who responded for the common good? Kutten, he thought, could understand this.

And the good to come, the realisation that gave life to his belief in this goodness, was that it was the year of the masque; that it would soon be spring. The city must have the time and will to recover for the summer. And the winter had somehow separated Doctor Dolke from them. Dolke denied them, and seemed lost in the pursuit of some surely cold, lonely image. Sometimes his silence seemed itself the spell which held in abeyance the building of chariots and triumphal arches.

Kutten, looking at the Seneschal, knew he could speak as he would.

'I wish Dolke had been here.'

'I confess I am a little stung by Doctor Dolke's attitude.'

He was entitled to retain in his voice an echo of the condescension he was prepared to show in greeting Dolke and which veiled the intimacy of the confession. 'Indeed he has lost touch with all of us; but it would not be excessive to call his recent conduct high-handed.'

The incident in his mind needed no explicit reference. Within the past fortnight he had received report of an alteration to his own rôle in the masque – not a reduction, but nonetheless an alteration – made by Dolke without explanation or previous intimation.

'I know he feels the importance of the work, the honour of his position.'

The Seneschal turned sharply; but he must keep in perspective Dolke's separation from them (since the break with Kutten, unfortunately so apparent to all, or perhaps since the cold, Dolke had gradually moved among them less and less). It all made more difficult, more anxious, his task to keep also in perspective the space of the cold. (He had had attacks recently of a disorder of the bowels, appallingly violent, cold and degrading. They almost caused him to cease believing either in his right or in God) He clung to the image of the summer, the only certainty.

'If Doctor Dolke understands degree, if his work respects it, why does he leave us to doubt?'

'In a man of free mind a sense of the imperfection of worldly things (of their transience) is a reflection of his sense of individuality.'

Kutten had never understood Dolke so well; yet he spoke in a way dishonestly. As he spoke he opened painfully to himself (but instantaneously reburied) a new awareness that that sense of imperfection and the desire to create anew, the individuality he had spoken of (his own as well as Dolke's) were also reflections of a distance, of an end to the sense of belonging, of a loss of faith. Even in his new happiness Kutten half-admitted the impossibility of perfection.

In thinking of Dolke, magnanimity and loneliness almost overwhelmed him, though he knew, and Dolke did not, the identity of the university and the authority of the office of Seneschal; which made levers to be exerted, shattered ice and hunger, and looked beyond the inevitable end of the cold to the time when the King would come.

'I bear the misfortune of the certainties of rank, Professor Kutten; and I am patient – or tactful – enough to see whether Doctor Dolke is blind to the university, in all its imperfections.'

'He is not blind to its power, or to its unity.'

The force of Kutten's expression and its humility (though he was lying) touched the Seneschal. For a few steps, however, he merely seemed to form under his breath the word 'stung'.

'A part of him already knows . . .' Kutten began, slightly opening his arms towards him.

'I shall send Doctor Feucht to him.'

Dolke greeted Feucht courteously. Indeed there was a warmth which was unusual and gratifying. But Dolke began:

'How are you, Doctor Feucht? And your family?' and Feucht had decided that his own first words should be:

'Doctor Dolke, the Seneschal has asked me to see you.'

This might be trivial, and Doctor Feucht was not incapable of responding to the unexpected, but the carefully chosen words remained obstinately in his mind. Until at last uttered, they stilted his sentences and prevented his collecting those words needed to put his points justly.

Without those words, moreover, his remarks were without virtue and without strength, because they were without status.

When the Seneschal had approached him, and asked him, Feucht had undertaken the task eagerly. His idealism tended towards cheerfulness. He remained placid, not given to demonstrations of joy, but he surprised himself how often after disappointment a sense of belonging to what was virtuous made him pause and stare, or made his heart clutch. That morning there had been a fissure through the cloud; a brisk light reflected from the snow. As he had made his way towards Ulpian, along the awkward wooden pavement raised along the kerb of Tenth Day Street, he had enjoyed a slight tremor of adventure.

Without those words he could scarcely see himself, could even less act, as the effective instrument of the university. In his prayers he would sometimes come as a suppliant to God; but that he dared pray for intercession was no indication of pride. There was in him an almost complete absence of the common egoism (the boast of some that they tested God with prayer he held the greatest blasphemy). Even as he prayed, or prayed to the university for the vanity of a greater rôle, he did not expect to receive. He did not imagine, as some did, that circumstances which affected his happiness had been directed by God, whether to chastise or endow, towards him. Even less would he have presumed to see himself as God's instrument. Yet today, by operation of those words, he was the university's.

As he spoke he did his duty; but the assertion of his individuality (an insistent suspicion that the Seneschal should not have chosen him) undermined his authority and his ability. At first he could add nothing to what he believed the Seneschal wished him to say. Once he had spoken (with pedantic emphasis and without conviction), his argument might be ignored without shame to him.

Dolke was looking at Feucht's grey felt cap. No wonder in committees he put people off. There was something more than touching about Feucht, pacing the room and embodying the university. Dolke noticed too a gentler weakness. In the Seneschal's presence, Dolke thought, he is heart and soul behind him; but it's too painful for him to prod and cajole me back to the fold. Partly kindness, partly timidity. Feucht needed to belong. The nearest he can hope for in friendship is when he and another are in agreement.

As they spoke, Dolke was tempted again to malice. To maintain the illusion of friendship Feucht would surrender for the shared time any opinion which he would have maintained obstinately against another man. In the absence of disagreement, he almost convinced himself, at times, that there was harmony. His own opinions he resumed later in lonely privacy.

'I would not suggest, Doctor Dolke, that anyone cultivate the friendship of the Seneschal.' The skin of his face was cold and drawn, irritating to Dolke.

'I have no doubt. But you see the value of . . . how would you put it?'

'I would say that the masque would benefit from co-operation.'

'But Doctor Feucht, tell me. Is the Seneschal really interested in the details of his masque?'

Dolke lingered as carefully over 'details' as Feucht had paused before 'cultivate'. 'His' masque was a slight prompting of malice.

Dolke sat with his knees raised and his feet resting on a cross-bar between the front legs of his chair. Concentrating, he had set in that attitude. It was not exactly comfortable, but to have moved must have threatened concentration.

Feucht's grey cap moving about the room was suddenly imperative. Dolke stood and gazed out of the window over the gabled roofs covered in snow. They were like the frozen river with its jutting ice floes and the abrupt piers of the white bridge.

'The Seneschal has a right to know.'

Feucht belongs, Dolke thought (and at once had to suppress something by biting his lip hard). He is part of the scheme, of the building. Dolke had always been alone. Vaslav Kutten had not the strength to think alone. Kutten was lonely.

'Perhaps a word will help, I agree.'

'The Seneschal does rely on you; but you might also be prepared to hear him.'

'If he is concerned, he will let me know.' Dolke paused and smiled foolishly. 'But of course he *is* letting me know.'

'It is not easy to ignore whispers that you are uninterested in the opinions of doctors.' Feucht was flustered and offended. Dolke would not even turn towards him (though perhaps Feucht would not have wanted that). 'It is not easy for me, when I hear it said that you value the opinion of your bright pupils more than the erudition of your peers.'

'At last you are speaking for yourself.'

Did he value von Fluorn's opinions? It was vital to accept – to believe – on the contrary that not only was his own image or understanding of what he saw true, but also that for him there could be no further truth.

The blank courtyard outside was as silent as the solitary river. Von Fluorn had seen and been exultant (no other word was possible). As for himself the tragedy on the frozen river had scarcely touched him. His understanding, his sympathy had been inadequate. His mind had been on von Fluorn. Remembering this, Dolke was afraid.

He believed in a personal truth, but he did not want a truth which was poverty-stricken and unconsidered. He was afraid of Kutten's self-frustrating devotion to knowledge, and of the temptation to escape by finding importance, when the sun struck vermilion from his mirror of fine-ground glass and into the windows of the Benedictines, in what was meaningless. Then there was no pleasure in knowledge but the pleasure of the sense of knowing and for some the effect of the forms of facts to entertain the brain with shapes. Dolke could not quite be sure whether von Fluorn's power to imagine – to make an image – did not tend to the meaningless, to the excitement of his sensations. He doubted also his own powers; and it was not so easy now to be alone.

Suddenly turning, Dolke went quickly over to his sofa and almost threw himself on to it.

'My bed of indulgence,' he interrupted Feucht.

'No indeed, Doctor Dolke. I always find somewhere comfortable the best for thought. Your sofa is an excellent piece.'

The moment had passed in which they might have come closer to friendship. Feucht could do nothing for Dolke. He spoke genially, but he had failed, as he always failed, to exclude the unacceptable hint of an inner intensity. He had betrayed his uncertainty to a man seeking help.

'Perhaps this is the most important thing,' said Dolke, and ran his fingers over the sofa's fabric. He was determined to shake Feucht's sense of belonging to its foundations. 'The Seneschal knows its value; and the masque shall be sumptuous!'

'Have we not had five years' peace to celebrate?'

'Then it only remains to decide what is best to be celebrated.'

'The university. Please do not think me trite.'

'Then should I look to my own understanding of it, or have all decide? Or rely on the virtues set out in the Foundation Charter?'

'I would listen to the Seneschal. I would decide, but I would open my ears.'

'But what good, my dear Doctor Feucht, would it do if I were to listen to all the doctors. I should just have to allow each of them to write one scene.'

'While you are confident that your perception will evoke the whole.'

'More at least than would the recitation of charters. What I am asking is, what document contains the truth of what this place is, or has become . . . ?'

'More than would its history and buildings and hierarchy?'

'The masque will culminate in a drama. Kutten and I designed it. It is taken from Ludwig Aicha. Its ideals and values are fixed. They are almost eternal. My new small contributions suggest what is transient – personal, what is peripheral. Our buildings, new and old, will be part of the scene. I will not give a history lesson, but I will present Ludwig Aicha to speak for himself through allegory. If the doctors respond to him then his truth about the university will still be true.'

'Will you allow him to remind us of our place in a greater whole?'

His face, Dolke saw, was radiant in its anger.

'To what end?' Dolke asked softly, half afraid. 'What does the university achieve beyond what you and I achieve?'

'That must be your last word,' Feucht said when he spoke at last.

He had done more than his duty; he had become angry. His sense of failure was so great that he would not further expose his ideas to such cynicism. As he spoke he had begun to make out in his mind's eye, for the first time clearly, a university which was more than the sum of its members. It was a continuing achievement, which for those who were part of the constant process of its creation was the highest form of both service and pleasure. Whatever he achieved was magnified in that it formed part of a greater and more valuable whole. His delight in his achievements would be magnified in proportion. His feelings, he told himself, were not without inspiration. His imagination and Dolke's shared nothing.

Dolke too was angry, but his anger was as contemptuous as Feucht's was indignant. After *his* effort, his achievement was proposed to be lost in some figment of a small man's inflamed imagination. To achieve the 'eye from many eyes' his contribution must be sacrificed. That was it. His work, he was being told, should become indistinguishable, merged with the orthodox, deprived of existence. They would have this from him, or they would ask him to identify the whole truth from the views of everyone. The 'eye made from many eyes'. Yet his work represented the truth as he could see it. How could he find more truth from other attitudes?

Dolke moved quickly across the room, hugging his house-coat

about him to avoid brushing things to the floor. On the shelf was his copy of Marsilius. The book, lying in his hands, smoothed out his anger. Which then was more important, his small work or many component eyes? Might he not yet build a greater whole around his own limited observations? The words of Marsilius had been his watch words. They would be on his tomb. But, though they might be true of the way laws come to last and change, and even of the nature of laws, the truth of other things, more elusive things, no longer seemed to be governed by them.

Feucht, after all, had begun by thinking of the university as a high, invulnerable tower. He was soon forced to see that it was more complex, more shifting. When he left he had adopted the tone of Marsilius – truth lying in the understandings of many. Had Feucht even been aware of that? He had left behind the precepts of Ludwig Aicha. Yet in his eyes, even at the end, there had still been the conviction that he belonged to something distinct from, something greater than its parts.

Gently and accurately, minding the sharp, exposed edges of its vellum binding, Dolke laid the book back in its place, and left the room.

Since the snow – no, since the break with Kutten (he forced himself to acknowledge the connection, and did so with surprising ease), he had not visited Master Michael at his carver's workshop in the close of the Benedictines. He had not been to the chapel to supervise (as he had liked to see it) the construction of the sepulchre in which he would eventually lie beneath his stone effigy.

The chapel stood in the older of the two courtyards of Ulpian. Its choir had been enlarged only recently, and in Gothic. Despite the swelling new dome in their second court, the college had had no difficulty in choosing. It was the achievement of Master Michael and his workmen, as was his own monument.

Dolke was still in awe of their curious powers. In his sense of their achievement lay such hope as he had, little stronger than a feeling of curiosity. He approached more with an awareness of duty; to them, who had devoted so much skill to his work. Otherwise he thought of what he was about to see with a remoteness from excitement, a mere curiosity, as if he had learnt that the college were erecting a monument to Marsilius of Padua, or Ludwig Aicha.

The chapel door had an undeniable charm in its effect of symmetry. Its flanking pinnacles and central gable were topped with statuettes in a variety of gestures and holding staffs or books. The smoothness of their tapering sides ran with interlacing tendrils of flambuoyant, freehand carving, among which saints, cut in low relief, were hopelessly lost or even intertwined. Below this were set older figures dressed in stiff folds, wearing crowns or swords, and standing with the sunlight on them. They were protected and their majesty pronounced by their canopies of openwork stone, which jutted forward like small blocks of richest honeycomb. Beneath their feet was the snow. Their charm, so undeniable and yet so inexplicable – so far perhaps from their sculptor's intention – only made Dolke anxious. Averting his eyes from any further sight of them, he pushed open the door.

By this time the sun was already low. It streamed in from behind Dolke between the pillars of the old grey nave with the peculiar brilliance of winter. The flagstones were patched with a pale, luminous wash of light, which drew Dolke's eyes from the nave to the choir-screen.

The pillars which rose from behind this bewildered him. An elevation higher than that of the nave seemed to suggest some alchemistic defiance of the laws of strength and structure. Far above its ceiling, each of the four pillars of a lofty enclosure tapered and seemed then to resolve into its components, with the appearance of the muscles which splay from the top of a taut and elegant neck. A confusion of soaring, slightly curving lines, turning out as well as up, passed over the surfaces of a vault and reduced themselves harmoniously into each of the other pillars of the choir. While a hesitant stream of light passed into the nave, the topmost lights of the choir windows were radiant with shifting, glinting colours; and on the alternate smoothness and ribs of its vault these colours were cast like the patterns of some translucent fabric.

Dolke could not deny the present beauty of the scene; an effect, he felt, which must be recognised by all with the minimum of sensibility. He could not deny its placid intricacy, and there might be expected from its luminosity even a certain sense of exhilaration. Devoid of meaning, he remembered, it entertained his brain with shapes. It made his mind wish to dance, he concluded, and to be set, now in one configuration, now in another. The confident but subtle splendours of the choir drew him towards it.

Yet in its meaninglessness (for Dolke could not associate the images at which he looked – the patriarchal and humble saints – with the faith with which they were portrayed; the forms of this hall could not communicate to him any confidence but that of the architect in his craft) its sublime optimism could lightly be dispelled or perverted by the shadows of the night. The beliefs which were exalted there were not made more certainly true, and he suspected that, as men searched the place at different times, they would gradually recognise in it the reflections of the weaknesses and sins, as well as the virtues, of the architect. They would also find the presence at times of a mood created but never intended. Did it ever convey – did he, Dolke, ever see exactly what the artist had hoped for?

True nature, then, lay here, as in all things, in the mind of the observer, if it lay anywhere. Dolke now saw the danger of understanding too well what was put before him. He could build nothing round his own glimpses, because he was isolated. He responded to the shapes and lines, but they communicated nothing. Yet he could no more cease to believe that his truth might not contain something of a deeper, fixed truth, than he could cease to believe that his own work might be understood by someone at least, whether or not his sight had been deceived by light, or had failed even to be moved by the crowd moving over the white river, or had fallen in with the fantasy of von Fluorn's ghost-girl. Von Fluorn.

It was a moment in which Dolke saw himself more clearly, and more mercilessly, than ever again. What was impossible for him to accept – yet for that moment he was convinced of it – was that he had nothing to say. He was convinced in fact of the poverty of his achievement and of the narrowness and unoriginality of his mind. Von Fluorn was guilty of having crumbled away his belief in the power of things to evoke some understanding of themselves; of leaving Dolke with only his personal response. Dolke was guilty himself. In any event he had surrendered to his imagination.

With an uncharacteristically feline movement he slipped through a small doorway in the choir-screen which led from the south aisle. Beneath the light which seemed to suffuse the whole of the upper levels of the choir Dolke continued to move sidelong; softly, rather as if feeling his way at night. His own broad body, his pendulous robe and his thick beard seemed to him cumbersome and properly relegated to the shadows. His glance, having surveyed the heights, was inevitably drawn to the framework of his tomb, a neat, large construction of rectangles and triangles. So Dolke saw it (and saw it also almost with surprise), beneath a glittering and insubstantial canopy.

This was to be his monument to the creativity of the individual, and the resting place above all of that part of himself. There seemed no possibility of divining his meaning from the emptiness and pretentiousness of its stone.

Should he pray? That he be reassured that his work contained truth? That he surrender happily his image of the university? He stood for a moment but did not kneel. For him there was no purpose in imploring divine intercession. Even in despair the God of Dolke's perception matched exactly in His detachment from worldly affairs Dolke's own detachment.

The skeleton form of the tomb, which in the last moments had somehow disappeared from his vision, was suddenly again insistent on his attention. Indeed its orders and its geometrical aspiration to the eternal were pretentious! And its attempt to make his face eternal through stone. Yet it recognised, he thought, its inevitable demise, his body's decay and people's ultimate forgetfulness of what he had ever thought. In this it served a purpose; had a value; celebrated what he still valued in himself.

Here lay the only escape of which Dolke was temperamentally capable – to find value in his achievement, to support it defiantly – perhaps sometimes with a curious, querulous stoicism. From Marsilius, he told himself, he had been able to extract a justification for attaching to his own mediocre productions a temporary usefulness. The value of his new work was in its individuality; in so far as it found no response in the minds of others, its value was in its value to him. His truth would rarely be shared.

Even as he half-accused himself, and stared at the stone configuration, it echoed in his mind that these conclusions had not been unjust. The monument still spoke to him, if ambiguously. It would never say anything, he supposed, to anyone else. As for von Fluorn – he shook off the creeping return of uncertainty and loneliness.

He accepted too – he almost spoke aloud – the necessary conclusion, that he must accept what he was told both by his rational perception and his imagination. That was only to admit the fact. As for the university then – he repeated the word quite aloud with phrases he had heard somewhere – it was a social web; a serpentine procession. In this mood he turned from his memorial and his sepulchre. His imagination (though it adopted the forms of reason) was dominant.

As he withdrew from the choir, he kept again to the shadow. The nave was now in a sort of twilight, without the presence of any direct ray. Ironically it was the atmosphere of the chapel which sustained his imagination. He remained expectant, with, like a Roman, neither fear of the failure of his works, nor hope of knowing a greater truth, a greater achievement, than he would be able to judge for himself. The university was a figment; it could provide comfort and diversion for those, like Feucht, who could not trust themselves to be alone.

In the distance, confused by the thickness of the walls and the height of the windows into an incoherent resonance, was the sound of a strident human voice. Dolke, startled, caught the sound and those, he thought, of mingled, accompanying voices. In the pressure and echo of that first voice, he detected, he thought, an urgency and a gradual approach. What did it say? He could not hear.

He reached the south door and drew its weight back. When he had placed the door fully at rest his mind, only then, was struck by the force of the commotion.

'The King,' he heard, and the roar of voices. But they were beyond the walls and it was difficult. He paused.

No-one was in the court. The crowd, as if by common consent, or common instinct, was silent. Once more the hoarse, strident voice cried, perfectly distinct, carrying into all the recesses of the old buildings.

'The King is coming! Only two days more!'

There were answering calls: 'The King!' and 'One more effort! One more sacrifice!'

Only two days more! The sudden bitterness which moved Dolke appalled him. It was as if he had stumbled in flight. The

134

mob, the voices of students and citizens seemed already to be celebrating their delivery and their victory. Dolke thought he heard calls for the Seneschal. In two days more, then, he would be completely alone. He slipped away, back to his rooms.

Chapter 5

By Easter, which fell towards the middle of April, the roads were once more white and firm. The King had been as certain as his word. Two days after his messenger had reached the city, he had arrived with an immense train of engineers and supplies. A passage along the river had been cleared, gunpowder used with tremendous effect, and a service of messengers and posts established to exchange news with military encampments and the nearest towns. Above all, the King revived belief in the rational certainty of eventual, complete deliverance: that the snow must melt and that the apparently impenetrable fabric of clouds must dissolve. The distribution of the supplies (little enough for a city, but something), the ceremonial demonstrations of joy and greeting, his own thanks for loyalty, and the might which was night after night proved by the distant and thunderous reverberations of the joy-fires of his ordnance over the surface of the frozen river, recharged and diverted the pent energies of the people.

Secret fears possessed the Seneschal that such self-indulgence of emotions might leave the townspeople enervated for the task of expecting, and preparing for, Saint Libori's Day. He told no-one. They passed quickly as he again immersed himself in university government and his own revived attentions to the masque.

The university had foreseen the dangers of the thaw. Vaslav Kutten was the most active of its members. He was to be seen (thinner still now, more sudden and angular in his gestures, so that he always seemed to break a horizon) on the banks above the water channels, directing men who carried fascines and timbers to heighten and strengthen. For the river banks he had the almost frozen mud cut from under the shallowest snow on the river margins. The courage and energy of these people, he found, could still be made to flow; for himself, he felt at times as he worked that day of ceremony, of the giving of presents and of warmth of colours, of the university asserting its power of unity, as incapable of death as royal succession itself. So warmed, he could put from himself von Fluorn and the hurt of Eberhard Dolke's coldness.

In the early hours of the morning on which the ice revealed by its translucency the imminence of its thaw, Kutten stood directing with the point of his stick, and perched on a haphazard platform of building materials. Old colleagues thought him as during his work on the Code itself. Some, though, detected something frenetic in his activity. It was agreed that his manner of speech was changed. The careful, formal sentences were rare. When he produced a sketch, of buttresses of wood and wattle, say, to keep water from walls and gates, Kutten would say, 'That's done. It has its purpose, and then is done with – that's complete in itself.'

When the thaw came, then, its tragedies were divorced for the people from memories of the cold, were not accumulated on them, and so could be faced.

On the roads outside the city the sunlight was brilliant with fine, white dust. Friedrich von Fluorn and Tassillo Aicha had never felt so much at ease in each other's company. They had leave of absence for the whole of this first week of May, so that they might visit Aicha's family. Since the time of the famous Ludwig the Aichas had lived at no great distance from Saint Eadmundsburg, though their origins lay far to the south-east, near impenetrable forests and the Marches of the Bohemians. Their home now was Trelle, a small town two days' easy journey away.

Despite the spring dust, the two young men noticed a clarity of the air; Saint Eadmundsburg, close to the river or lying low by water meadows, seemed at that season by comparison dank and close, for their way ran to the south-west, and had by now gradually but perceptibly begun to rise.

The leaves, particularly those of the fruit trees, were everywhere a bright, unpolished yellow-green, and still tightly curled so that, rather than conceal, they set off the farm buildings that stood among them; nor did they as yet conceal their own branches, or the lines of the tree and black intricacies of its structure.

Greater trees disclosed church towers and fine residences. All seemed ideal. The winter could be forgotten; yet because of a barrenness neither Aicha nor von Fluorn compared the scene with previous years', or otherwise made himself too aware of the ravages of the cold. Even the stern tower of Waldshelm, of the severe House of Hohenring, seemed above its copses of oak and aspen, as the two men rode past, sleepy and inviting. To their right the blades of the young corn were yellow, bright and matt; to their left, as they glanced across their extent into the afternoon sun, they were pale grey-green and almost translucent.

Aicha pulled up his horse sharply.

'The dust. My eyes refuse to tolerate it.'

'They'll run clear.'

'I've got to – touch them.'

It was irritating to be aware of Aicha's hesitation, despite his running eyes, about releasing a hand from the reins. Von Fluorn had been surprised how uncertainly Aicha rode. That reassured his serenity. Aicha had also been making some veiled, rather unkind remarks about his mother. He used little, formal euphemisms, and pet-names which sounded like accusations. Yet it was a sort of confiding. It had made von Fluorn want to respond, to explain about his own father. But it had also given him another advantage.

His father, von Fluorn told himself watching Aicha fidget in his saddle, would never condescend to stay with an Aicha. To recognise that only heightened his own achievement. He was buoyant, confident; almost excited.

The Aichas' house at Trelle was poised, sheer-faced, at a point on the high street where the single curve of the road, gentle but immense, was almost totally balanced by the enormous width of its cartways. From this position the house enjoyed – most of all from its fifth and topmost floor – a proud view over the street; but moreover a proximity, and a municipal eminence second only to the Town Hall itself. Indeed they were joined on their ground floor by an arcade, so massive in its vaulting and pillars as to appear low, and almost treacherously dark even in early morning, when the sun could not reach them over the opposite house-tops. The flagged path under these vaults and the passage of people seemed to thread the two buildings together. The

Aichas, like the previous occupants of their house, were of substance and influence in the town.

No door, however, led from these public arcades directly into the house. Beyond it, however – on the side, that is, furthest from the Town Hall – was an arched entrance. It was this, indeed, which broke the serried façades of the street and interrupted the arcade, which then continued, to link and compose its other houses. Behind this gated entrance was a passageway. It was of grey stone, with neither plaster nor the bright coating of yellow wash of the steep Gothic front of the house. At its end was an irregular courtyard with an ash tree whose spread of branches and dry, deeply cracked bark, gave an impression of even greater age and rigid strength than it actually possessed. Over the earth and flagstones beneath in warm weather were scattered fragments of this bark, flaky outside, and softer inside than people expected. It fell from high in the tree with no more then a sound of tumbling. Twigs, some of them large, dropped from time to time with a sudden dry snap. These scattered pieces and the soft familiar sounds of their fall on hot days confirmed, rather than disturbed, an air of age and peace.

Just by the entrance from the passage into the courtyard, and of the same grey stone as the walls, was the doorway of the house. As a frame the same stone had been carved in an academic and archaic fantasy. Two columns, wrapped with the vigorous spiral in stone of a vine, supported a curved canopy which projected from the wall. Behind these columns, and framing the door more closely, were tall narrow panels and a narrow lintel, of the same material but carved with Italian masks and the staring faces of old men. Pierced above all this, almost capriciously it seemed, was a circular window, compartmented by a trellis of leads and set deep within the embossed circle of its scrolled frame. Late in life Ludwig Aicha had made a journey to Italy, and this had been his last contribution to what was already by then the home of the Aichas.

To von Fluorn the lemon-yellow front over the street and its pink, ochre and blue neighbours became at once quite detached from all this that lay behind it. Inside, the house maintained the austerity of the passage, the peace of the courtyard, and even something, subdued, of the insistent individuality of the door. From the circular window a pale sunlight lay on the neat black and white lozenges of a cool, high entrance hall. Ahead of him rose a staircase whose dark brown mouldings and turned balusters made their way in a configuration of complex and mannered geometry upwards into shadow. His impression of the courtyard had been of a harmony of greys and near greys spanning all the shades which lay between the two extremes represented in the smooth blocks of the hall floor, and every texture from stone to the fluid shadows of the leaves. Then he saw that Mrs Aicha was standing on the stairs. She was dressed in the black of a widow, and was wearing earrings, each of a single pearl.

She stepped forward to welcome them.

To Aicha that interior, his own home, was entirely a reflection of his mother's personality. Herself and her reflection were the ideal of taste, both for his everyday world and more profoundly (though he forgot the place or denied it) when he was lost in others. At the effect on von Fluorn of the courtyard and the hall and of his mother's sudden presence (her movements were liquid and harmonious, Aicha thought), Aicha had been overjoyed. Von Fluorn had passed a first test.

That evening there were moments of anxiety, almost of pain. Von Fluorn was at his most attentive. Mrs Aicha was charmed. His description of their lessons together was in terms more flattering to Tassillo than she had ever heard. He called Aicha 'Mouse', but it was without an inkling of condescension; it somehow associated Aicha with another circle of whose existence von Fluorn casually gave unaffected glimpses: days in the saddle, or among the alleys of a garden near Saint Eadmundsburg. To such others he attributed, Aicha suspected, his own wit.

For Aicha it was at sudden moments as if a gulf would split the ground between himself and these two: a sense of dishonesty or, when he found von Fluorn's new intimacy acceptable, of a superiority of von Fluorn's position. Worse was when his mother submitted herself to that pretence, and a fear of discovery of his own passive dishonesty. She wanted for him what she heard and would not keep herself from nodding her approval as she listened . . .

That, he suddenly decided, was indeed a fault (he was not blind to her faults, he told himself). A fault that was bound to

140

come out, he told himself. Just to do that, and laugh when von Fluorn came close to banter; that betrayed her dignity, and perhaps indeed was evidence of inferiority. For a moment he was silent, bewildered that she could not see and react as he did.

Von Fluorn saw the danger.

'I should prefer – though it be an abrupt change – to let Mouse – Tassillo – talk about pictures. But he has a circle to hear him in Saint Eadmundsburg.'

That was a clumsy enough leap, Aicha thought (perhaps a leap to safety, for it was his house they were in). Von Fluorn had polish, but he had need of more. Aicha thought this, and in the rapidity of thought one part of him was amused by his own ability to stand apart, to raise or lower the expectations on which he based his criticism.

Moreover he found himself, his speaking self, disarmed, in spite of everything. He liked the way von Fluorn set off his praise with the forms of mockery. He began, 'Well, engraving . . .', and made confidences. They both listened to him – he had a week ago made his first impression from his first attempt. A Saint John. Yes, he had brought it, would show it later.

During that night, while von Fluorn slept, Aicha made his way to a small room he called his 'study', slipping along the passage with his usual side-long tread. For him there could, as usual, only be a few moments of safety. He was aware of his candle flickering as he worked. It even sounded loud. He had chosen in his mind his best work, but as he took each hastily from its shallow drawer, its merit seemed hesitant. He came to new decisions, no more certain. He arranged what he could where perhaps they would show well in the next day's light.

Early next morning Friedrich von Fluorn, presuming on his unfamiliarity with the house, wandered into an upstairs sitting-room. He found there Mrs Aicha, leaning heavy-bosomed on crossed forearms at a window, gazing up and down the wide street.

How uncharacteristic, he thought? So heavy and so intent. Or was it? How easy it was to be convinced that someone does not do – so many things, simply because one has not yet seen him . . . because one trusts others more than oneself.

141

She turned sharply. Then she was herself (as he expected, that is), lofty but kind. She belonged, in her short, black, satin house-coat with its heavy collar of undyed wool, to the room for example. It had cool panelling of bleached wood up to the ceiling. On each panel was a shallow decoration of applied, carved wood: a central fluted pillar, pilaster perhaps, from whose almost awkwardly distinct capital sprang two equal round arches. Their slight irregularity avoided monotony; and was somehow a home for this woman's love of restrained, harmonious pattern. Von Fluorn admired her deeply at that moment.

He expected to talk about the town. A question came to him: to ask what she had seen. When he had arrived at Trelle its sweep and raucous colours had excited him. He had wanted to spur his horse into the clamour and interweaving of the carts. He had checked himself, he remembered, for Aicha's sake: Aicha's expectations!

'I was thinking about you and Tassillo.'

Von Fluorn, slightly taken aback, only smiled and made a polite inclination of the head.

'I was thinking that it was easy for me – a widow, as you see – to convince myself that an acquaintance of Tassillo is a friend of his.'

'Mouse and I?' These words were a form of reassurance instinctive to von Fluorn.

'You and – Mouse, as you say. This house, the town, has its limitations. He thinks of you as a friend. His letters. A close friend.'

She was moving towards him, but suddenly passed by him very close, so that she almost brushed against him. Her eyes had moved from him to fix on the distance. To von Fluorn she was a smaller, shy woman.

He turned round to her. His stance (he felt it, but could not adjust it) was confident; not, he hoped, overbearing. He knew he was being offered a rôle, almost humbly. There had been no trace of accusation in her voice. His own, again irresistibly, had the easy softness and resonance of his father's:

'We are scarcely out of each other's lodgings. One or other of us always has some plan . . .'

'You will excuse my saying it. You *can* do much for him. I think you will be friends.'

She smiled again, gently, and left the room.

It was a momentous occasion for von Fluorn. Never before, except from servants, had he received such acknowledgment.

Aicha was agitated. Of course he had asked von Fluorn's judgment on this or that (Aicha would even have used that word, 'judgment'); but now von Fluorn was to be the judge of final instance. And in judging the whole he must judge also its purpose. Von Fluorn's father's name was synonymous with cultured magnificence. He did not fear von Fluorn's opinions; yet von Fluorn might, with the better opportunity, have a better achievement, more discreetly disguised.

For a moment as he climbed Aicha felt weak with the surrounding motions of uncertainty. His distaste and fascination for von Fluorn were finally balanced. Yet somehow von Fluorn had passed his tests.

'Please don't be restrained,' Aicha muttered, pulling himself up at a door, 'by politeness.'

He stood with his thin legs apart and his elbows close into his narrow back, managing the door handle with both hands. Von Fluorn (still generous perhaps with the memory of Mrs Aicha) felt for him for the first time genuine warmth. Aicha seemed almost lame, far more awkward in all the lines of his body than von Fluorn had ever felt himself to be. He almost expected Aicha's legs to drag behind him like a cripple's.

The light of the room for the first moments distracted von Fluorn. His first impression was simply of daylight. It was fine, half-shuttered light, and yet filled the room evenly; it slipped between the two long windows.

Aicha's stringent expectations, Aicha's presence, distracted him. He concentrated on the table. Outlines were formed amid white, powdery chaos; which seemed to beset them as rubble does the remaining monuments of a ruined city. Before his eyes, in most exact and exquisite details, stood the Pantheon and the Colosseum.

These assumed in his mind over the surrounding turmoil their just and unchallengeable scale. Where his eyes turned, weals of a perfect smoothness cut through the surrounding confusion in every direction from these focal points. Von Fluorn's examination followed now one route, now another, and though they imposed no form on the bare spaces of white, it was with a sense of dismay that he saw them walled by a sudden barrier of wood which retained and protected the whole model.

Aicha pointed. 'The Via Flaminia. Of course it is only a very small area of the city.'

'Tassillo, I am overwhelmingly impressed.'

'Tassillo' was clearly more suitable than 'Mouse'; and von Fluorn was impressed. He knew his voice expressed it.

Plaster, Aicha explained, was the basis of his model; left white and dusty in some parts, but the buildings painted by him with a transparent glaze of his own invention. It transformed plaster into marble. Bronze details too he painted. The art of applying gold leaf (he pointed out the doors of the Pantheon) had taken him months of his spare time to learn. He still, he added (in the required moment of self-belittlement), only knew its rudiments. He had minute drills and lathes for turning and cutting chips of marble and stone. He had prised tools from possessive and secretive old men in the street of carpenters and the close of the Benedictines.

'The detail is so important,' von Fluorn began, and at once began to suspect that it might be all-important.

'To fix the image. To be certain,' he added, wanting to reassure, for he could see that there were in Aicha imperatives.

'Some days – you will understand me if I say – I can enjoy this piece of Rome as if I were there.'

'You did go . . .'

'Once. Though I don't mean that. And a friend writes to me about the new discoveries. So often. Statues, mosaics. Whole buildings.'

'It is difficult to omit anything.'

'I sketched the Arch of Titus. Here, there is none of that disgusting incrustation of buildings. You can see . . .'

Aicha darted forward towards the model. He could feel himself move down among the monuments which, with such intensity of concentration, he had re-erected in his own mind, had made concrete again, and was trying to fix for ever on this table. Only the insistent laws of Time foiled his imperative wish for the certainties of achieving in one life span (which might have been his) and in one place (where he might have lived) all of those beauties; foiled him and demanded self-deception.

Was von Fluorn admiring? Did he sympathise? Aicha heard himself wondering.

'You could consider this the beginning of a new science.'

'It is scientific; though I could not bear to leave any of them aside. The Pantheon. The temple of Antoninus and Faustina. Can one allow that Augustus lived but never saw them?'

'Call it Rome of the Antonines.' Von Fluorn did not intend any irony. For the moment he hoped an honest compromise could be reached between science and Aicha's needs, whatever they were. The needs of his imagination? There seemed to him very little. There was just the piling up of facts into an unassailable mass. A city which had not existed when Aicha insisted. Had never existed.

He had attempted the same operation himself, he remembered; in Mantua, in Rome, at the castle, trying to build a marvellous, exciting whole out of dry bits. At least his brain had not been entertained by the game.

'You see I have to have them.' Aicha exclaimed, with almost rasping enthusiasm. He pointed dramatically towards domes and pediments.

Almost fiercely. Well then, the accumulation did touch something deeper. There was the desperation of a desire to see a thing complete in itself. Aicha's eyes were filled with the bewildering irreconcilability which faced him where one beauty had obliterated another. There was too the tormenting certainty that to have seen it all he must have outlived it. How absurd, such pain, von Fluorn thought. And this effort.

And the exquisite water colours of carved capitals and ruins (some with languid Romanish figures). And the superb copperplate impressions of plans and elevations. The Rome of good taste. That was Aicha's dream. Did he have no pleasure from reality, from change? If it did not admit change, it was dead or a lie. . . .

Himself, von Fluorn needed the streets peeling and changing, changing as smells rose and dispersed and people passed. He could do better than Aicha, he thought, and his confidence, his deep hope of achievement, began again to well up. He would go away and do something. . . .

Aicha was watching. Von Fluorn glanced away between the

shutters, over the wide street and somehow into the distant jangling of the traffic.

Aicha. Von Fluorn drew up his concentration and passed along the row of pictures close together to allow the greatest number. At each he paused, took it in (or seemed to himself to) and without comment took another sideways step. It was then, however, that he became more observant. Either the subdued richness of the colours began to assert itself, or he forgot Aicha's demanding silence so close behind him. Choosing to keep silent rather than commit himself irrevocably in what he praised, he felt the handles of the low drawers of the cabinets, and began to slide them out firmly one after another, extracting now a drawing, a Roman or Venetian engraving, or a watercolour, as if he had expected each as the logical successor to the earlier.

Aicha stepped up behind him. There was a tight expression about his mouth. His air was modest but insistent, expecting praise; which von Fluorn gave.

'Tassillo, this deserves the daylight.' (So he had pleasure from a sort of reality.) He laughed. 'They are like reflections in water. An Italian boy would dive into such luminosity.'

It was suddenly easy and pleasing to praise; but the pictures could still hold him. He withdrew another, and he was absorbed. First he was thinking: this is what I would have expected of him; then, at new evidence, how strange, how disturbing such discoveries were. Did Aicha intend *that*?

Did these discoveries hold together with the watery luminosity, the representation of precious materials and the soft resilience of the paper? Von Fluorn had come to the first work of Aicha's imagination. He knew them by their hesitancy, though of the now familiar cups and intaglios. Here was a kneeling girl, as if a relief, her thighs suggested through her enveloping robe. At her waist there was a turn, so that her body faced forwards, while the lines of her sides and the roundness of her shoulders suggested – though her face was raised and stared out – how she leaned over or shrank. Above her back were just visible the folds of her robe. Behind her was the standing figure of a young man, whose hands, arms and chest, all naked, were visible. Like the girl he was slightly stooped and tense. With uncertainty and fascination the tips of his fingers gently raised the folds of material on her back.

146

He, von Fluorn, possessed Aicha's friendship, and was entitled to benefit from it; and compete with it, he thought.
He could, as Mrs Aicha hoped, help his friend. As he handed
the picture to Aicha and awaited his words, these attitudes
assumed a place in his mind. They were, he said to himself, a part of
friendship.

The bedroom which Tassillo Aicha had long settled on as his own
was small. It was high up on the fourth floor at the back of the
house and some way therefore from the room von Fluorn was
using. Despite its size it gave a first impression of space, almost of
bareness. It was very neat. Aicha's bed, a high-backed chair with
arms, a chest covered with a quilt and a small table on which he
kept his candlestick and some books were arranged as if locking
into a square in one quarter of the room. Each of the other pieces
seemed to refer in some way to the bed, which was exactly in the
corner.

There was little else: shelves of books and a larger chest for
clothes. On one wall was hung a piece of fine Turkey rug. It was
said to have been brought from Bokhara or Samarkhand, and was
most intricately patterned.

The clothes Aicha had been wearing that day were now folded
carefully on top of the larger chest. He was in bed, under only a
sheet. As he lay he had an oblique view through his window of
the placid night sky. The casement was open; it was the first of the
expected, really warm spring nights.

Lying quite flat he gazed up at the window. He loved the
narrow view, as much on clear nights as on brilliant mornings. It
was the window, white-framed and cheerful and with this view,
that had caused him to choose this corner for his bed. An hour
ago, nonetheless, he had been sitting, naked, in his chair, watching through the leaded glass; until, that is, his mind had seemed
to open, and to release in the air his extraneous thoughts and a
certain expectancy. He had sat with his hands flat over his thighs,
and rather stiffly upright. But his mind remained alert to anything that might happen. Once in bed his mental activity again
began to intensify, and only briefly with less sense of tiredness
than before. The warmth of the night both made his receptiveness delicious and aggravated the sense that his tiredness was

itself preventing sleep. The day had changed him, had almost exchanged elements of himself and Friedrich. He could call him Friedrich; the name had a seriousness. But he could no longer say why he had chosen – quite deliberately – to bring all this about. It was also impossible to understand the anxiety that he had known was in his face when Friedrich had taken out his painting of the kneeling girl. Except that he had put himself through an ordeal, proved himself, revealed himself worthy of admiration. A sexuality (which he identified not by any word but only by a mental presence and an immediate awareness of his whole body) was closely connected with this achievement; with the colours, the stiff cream paper, the monuments rising from dust.

The whole sensation of his mind struck him suddenly as sordid. He looked up. Surely he heard a woman's voice. Sordid but insistent. He stretched out his hand, as if compulsively, towards the books on his table. Thinking of his own image, of the crouching woman and the expectant man, woke his mind to full activity. The sound, penetrating him, was repeated. The books could no longer give him their customary reassurance. He pushed away the sheet and stood on the floor. He strained to hear; his legs and body were pitched and held forward, and his jaw was tensed open. Unaware of the roughness of the floorboards, but with his habitual softness and quietness of step, he trod to the window.

The nearest branch of the ash tree was just beyond his reach. Its primary boughs reached above the height of his room, spread wide apart. The spaces between their branches were scarcely clouded by the closed brown points of early buds. Beyond were the backs of buildings. The distance was no more than the width of the little courtyard, but those houses and tenements overlooked, not the High Street, but the narrow Joppengasse; they were the homes, not of merchants or dignitaries, but of lesser artisans and their apprentices. Some were now lodgings for itinerant workmen. From different levels of the house immediately behind the Aichas' lights shone so that the shape, the order of the whole was lost, and a jumble, a maze perhaps of rooms and passages, was substituted. The lights lit the branches of the ash tree curiously.

Aicha asked himself who lived there. His family name was sufficient to have allowed his mother to ensure the maintenance

148

of its respectability; but (so far as he knew) there had been no occasion for her to exert that influence. There were apprentices there with others, he suspected, or was disposed to think. The suddenness rather than the loudness of sounds, and the late lights which flickered to and fro sometimes, suggested to him young and vigorous men.

There was the sound again! His mind placed it at the longest of the bright windows. He was standing stock still, as if to take someone by surprise. Figures moved. There should be a prostitute there, gross and smothering; that was his expectation. He expected the revelation of an immorality with a tense pleasure. At the first recrudescence of this fantasy a stab of fear, a moment of regret, had hurt him, but was gone.

On the first inkling of eventual disappointment, after perhaps one instant of almost panic-stricken anger, his fear and revulsion were resurgent; and, unlike on other occasions, were both of a clarity that gave him no pleasure. His reason too reasserted itself, leaving as guilty delusions his fantasy and imagination. A part of himself admired – indeed almost worshipped – the most beautiful of women: those virginal creatures (somehow more virginal than himself) whose gliding steps took them sometimes with other members of the Court through the galleries and gardens of the white palace of Saint Eadmundsburg. But this memory proved the guilt and cheated his uncertainty, that they were no more exciting to him than the bodies of the grossest women of the town.

He was dizzied, but he brought no verdict of guilt, except against his fantasy's ability to trick him into knowing its power. There came a calm, almost a euphoria, but with still some fear: an awareness of physical weakness, as if he were already punished, or defenceless against punishments, deprivation and sleep. In this helplessness the image of being smothered caught at him, like a splashing of the deep water, and a sense of some elusive but certain deprivation recurred. Both disposed him to find guilt, and confess it.

He remembered a casual boast of Friedrich's; when, during their early friendship, Aicha had been (he admitted it) pedantic, Friedrich would revert to the language of his old circle, or at least of his dominance of it, and his banter would be coloured with the conventional phrases of sexual licence. His boast was the gradual

149

reduction to a series of formulae of what had once been his compulsive, almost spasmodic, pleas for help and mercy to God and Christ. The formulae had all the virtue of an anodyne. They relieved him without any sense of expiation, and without any of the old sense of belief in his own repentance (he no longer desired it), which he had once craved and feared to be without.

Aicha secretly resented God. This required, of course, that he believed in Him; he felt His oppressive imminence, and His invasive percipience. But propitiation might get easier.

There was no moral brake on this course, but von Fluorn's conduct would always be – could only be – calculated. The power of his conscience – the power, then, of his imagination – would never inspire his actions. Both had always lacked something or had been atrophied. They had never convinced, or tricked, him. The desires of his body would never pain him irresistibly. Aicha still clung to the penetration and vehemence of his long-hidden imagination.

Nor could Aicha imagine his own reason and instincts balanced so nicely as von Fluorn's. Yet von Fluorn, on their ride together to Trelle, had insisted on dissecting Doctor Dolke; laughing and saying he was scarcely human: 'To be human there has to be inclination, either to the male or to the female.' To have said that in the sunlight! (It had been his only moment of fear. Why had Friedrich said it?) There had been nothing spontaneous in it. Von Fluorn was scarcely human; von Fluorn might teach him not to be a coward to his imagination.

When the motion of Aicha's mind slowed, however, imagination again made conscience out of instinct fear. It fixed the fear with specious reasoning and refined it into a sort of pleasure. Yet something had already come to insist as he prayed, sometimes to his irritation, first on an extraordinary fullness of description, later on a curious exactitude of phrase in those silent pleas, in order to ensure, in effect almost to produce, expiation and forgiveness. Each and every element of the sinful thought had once been necessary in order to make the precarious all at once automatic. Something still insisted, then, that the words of his promises be precise and unvarying. Might they not otherwise evidence an intention to make ambiguous the obligations he undertook? Then, at the end he won release. He repeated these operations now, like slow breathing after exertion. When he had finished he listened once, as if to prove that there was nothing that with an unsinful mind he might risk hearing. There was no sound. He returned to bed, and slept.

Chapter 6

Over the door was a mask of Comedy. It was painted in blue-grey. Yellow heightened the bulging, intelligent forehead and the mischievous nose, cheeks and lips, and glowed through its empty eye sockets. This was the first thing that struck Doctor Dolke as he stood in von Fluorn's main room. It was his first visit. He felt slightly awed, slightly honoured. It was a month since he had seen von Fluorn. Approaching the door he had been fearful.

For three years now von Fluorn had lived here, just close enough to the college to meet necessity. The street, of recent houses some of them tall and painted, was the home of many of his old, sociable friends. It was said he eagerly exercised and consistently enjoyed what he found the civilised life of comfortable lodgings. The gaiety of Alt-Albertusstrasse remained perhaps a stronger link with them than he was inclined to admit . . .

But above the door was an expression not merely of youthful enthusiasm, but also of imagination. It laughed not at things but at any attempt to fix the nature of things. Being an expression, it was elusive, yet more significant, Dolke thought to himself, than purely physical resemblances. Von Fluorn had seen a ghost. Or a water sprite, was it? He had been trotting through the water meadows and come on to a path under the walls. . . .

Dolke again became aware of the mannered, sprightly piece of embellishment. The room was light. From it was a good view of all that went on in the street. Perhaps that was why he liked its proportion better than the amusing but intransient angles of older houses.

Von Fluorn had delivered his invitation ('to come simply to see the place, and perhaps to eat a little should he care to stay') with his usual overt charm and deft hesitancy. For Dolke it was not only the first invitation to these rooms but the first such from any of his students: an unlooked for absence, for he had never stood on ceremony. So he too had hesitated. A blank space suddenly existed in their acquaintance. Dolke had chosen not to expect too exactly what he might see.

The mask was painted on the case of an inner door. What Dolke observed, however, were eyes and wings (which grew life-like out of either brittle edge of the mask), and leaves, among which the whole design seemed to rest. Indeed the eyes – the glowing sockets – did not stare boldly or inquisitively. They gazed outwards and up at, or through, the ceiling. It was as if the mask were settled in the tenuous web of leaves, whose tendrils sprawled and spun into a frieze along the wall.

'Delightful, Fluorn!'

'I had little enough to do with it, I'm afraid.' (He was standing behind him wondering when Dolke would speak.)

'I had a colleague, Doctor Michel . . . dead sadly, though a good age. You would not remember him . . . he drew in grisaille' (he searched for a word that would not devalue with flattery) 'with quite unusual fluency. And even when I was young I –' (again a pause, for a word or an incident which did not exaggerate, yet which would indicate, his own ability) 'I studied the matter for some years quite diligently. It was an unusual accomplishment in those days.'

'It was almost frowned on, I have heard?' Von Fluorn was polite but brief. He wished to keep reminiscence within bounds today.

' "A past-time for monks" – the gentler people said that.'

'And now, sir?' asked von Fluorn, indicating the wall somehow.

'Well, I approve. But what was your hand in it?'

'Aicha did it for me.'

Von Fluorn saw him start, very slightly, as if he had come to an unfamiliar path.

'I did not know you and he were such friends.'

Dolke had never associated them, beyond their presence in one of his classes. It was a gap. And he had to be sure that he *knew* von Fluorn. He noted this new fact, but he formed no observation or further image. He took in the name – Aicha – and immediately after continued to set the two young men quite apart.

'Tassillo Aicha, indeed?' Dolke continued, as if Aicha were certainly a stranger to them both, and then to von Fluorn, 'I approve the colours. They seem very confident and bold to me. And usually, if you will allow me to say it, I am not struck by such effects.'

'Well sir – yellow, blue, violet – I chose those. I can take either the credit or the blame for them.'

The furniture in the room was masculine and excellent. There was vigour in the turning of it and in the sparing gilt: the arms of a chair that ended in blackamoors' heads in gold; and the piece, von Fluorn said, had been brought from Venice. Dolke inspected, and praised liberally. The room was comparable in some ways with his own, he told himself: nothing mean or close in it; but with a necessary distinction of civil rank. He smoothed the palm of his large hand over a carved, gilt head; then he returned to the walls.

'The solidity here – the eye is quite deceived.'

He pointed to a ram's skull whose painted dimensions, bone and horn seemed to fill a corner. He raised a hand as if to check that he was not the victim of some double deception. But the painted leaves writhed up to it, and wreathed and trailed over it.

'Tassillo – Tassillo Aicha – underestimates his talent.' Von Fluorn remembered what he had seen in Aicha's room at Trelle. He was tempted to mention it, but there was no strong enough reason to . . . betray, for it had been a confidence, really. In thinking this von Fluorn remembered a phrase which had occurred to him while examining the model or those drawings . . . yes, one of those exquisite inventions of a temple interior, or baths. He had not used it. Even if just, and half-meant to please, it might have hurt. Unconsciously he had stored it for a better occasion. Nor would it make himself foolish for having worked here tirelessly with Aicha for weeks: designing together, Aicha executing. It had decision, and for Dolke truth perhaps. Von Fluorn used his phrase:

'And all quite meaningless!'

'A serpentine procession, Fluorn?'

'Yes, sir, if you like.' He had forgotten the phrase.

'Like the masque? My masque, I mean. You see that in the same way, Fluorn?'

Von Fluorn was taken by surprise. The tone of the question was not quite abrupt. It was almost without accent. There was no time for tact.

'Yes, sir, I do see the masque like that. I want illusion and intricacy for their own sake, I suppose; but there is something more to it than that, as I hope there is to Aicha's work here.'

'Some scholarship? Some art – should I say "design"?'

'A contribution to my sense of the place.'

'Not wholly meaningless then.'

'But not as meaning is laid down – sometimes.'

Von Fluorn led him over to look at another mask, a ram's skull, a garland of autumn oak and ivy. He had never been so proud as today of what he had done, perhaps almost never been so fluent:

'I enjoy colour and these surfaces. I love illusion even more. All meaningless but – effective. I give moods to them' (the blue-white skulls and the flowers) 'and my moods, or theirs, give them a significance. Sometimes – when I sit late in the evenings, it is they which seem to hold the mood – curious high feelings – since they were completed.'

He had retrieved the situation; as he (and Mrs Aicha) knew he could. (And what he said was even true and at every moment, he thought, increasingly perceptive. In the evening how delicate, how mocking, how disturbing, how libidinous these colours had been.) There was no anger in Dolke to be feared; perhaps only a sort of envy, a desire to be freed.

They turned to the details of the masque.

'Yes, the concourse will – wind its way, I may say – from the University Gate to the Forum Academicum. And what you say about colour, Fluorn, is true. Gilding . . .'

As he meandered, now one way, now along another, Dolke's voice modulated and revived.

'But when under way, sir, will there be room for it to move as a whole?'

'A living whole. Expanding and contracting, no doubt, like musculature; or like a skin of scales, disjointing and re-interconnecting. There will be in it as many indistinguishable, yet distinct parts, ready as if to pursue separate ways (and as many permutations of choices and collisions) as there are from moment to moment in the university.'

'Shapeless but not meaningless, sir?'

'Shapeless and meaninglessness enough, but, as they will have it, it will have order and meaning.' He smiled grimly. 'It will have due order; it will have its whole order and purpose. It will have serpentine and ceremonial purpose and meaning. Others might wish to present the university as a pyramid, or a tower, and Professor Kutten may prefer to see it as a dodecahedron or perhaps as an object possessing a certain elastic roundness. My form has the slight merit of reminding them of the presence of inner living organisms. And there will be colour, gilding . . .'

'And the anti-masque will follow, and infest the track of the masque?' (For a moment, before Dolke's bitterness had subsided, von Fluorn had been afraid.)

'Yes, it must follow. They said it would mock what was sedate and magnificent, hierarchy and opulence. I told the Seneschal it would be a foil! But I never thanked you properly for the idea; though I have my own conceit of it now: the sense of finding new ways and works and men, by a flickering light. And the variety of forms. And perhaps if *they* are right, the triumph of something – magnanimous – over empty and contradictory things and perverse shapes.'

It was growing dark in the room. The pale spring sky glowed blue against the darkening gables and shadows of the street. The paintwork, wood and fabrics among which the two men sat began to dissolve. Of Aicha's invention only the yellow highlights on the darker wood stood out.

There was a pause. Dolke was looking away; nor could he prevent his face forming (his lips and jaw perhaps, von Fluorn wondered) as if to comment on something apart on which his mind was now running. His head was twisted to look over one shoulder, and he had leaned his body forward to permit the strain. His glance fell on a broad hat that lay on a chair and then on a simple crucifix of horn, hanging on the wall.

Von Fluorn rose and excused himself softly to the motionless figure. He hesitated at this lapse of attention, at Dolke drifting towards sleep. Yet he was confident that *he* was the corroboration Dolke had been seeking in his last sardonic assertion of the value of his views, and that he must take the opportunity. Examination of his own motives began and ended as he crossed the room. He could not even say whether he had always intended what he would now do; but in a moment it would be too late.

When he returned from his bedroom, clicking the catch firmly and clearly as he closed the door, Dolke opened his eyes and saw von Fluorn in front of him, holding a manuscript.

'When the players of the anti-masque speak to the crowds

about the university . . .' Von Fluorn faltered. At any public occasion there was always some licence, always invectives and eulogies; but Dolke had not actually said . . . 'I confess I hoped this might interest you, sir.'

'Always "the university", Fluorn? Might they not talk about men?'

'Well, I could not resist a personal effort.' He was relieved, even happy, at his own – honesty.

'Something entirely your own for the masque, eh?'

'Men persist, they say, sir. Institutions fail.'

Dolke took the pages, smiling.

Von Fluorn sat, and then, almost motionless, watched him and rehearsed the question to which he had reduced his conscience. Was this his *main* reason for inviting Dolke? Answering it satisfactorily. No.

'You chose your moment,' said Dolke, without looking up and without condemning. Indeed he felt receptive even while for the first moments he turned the pages sightlessly. In spite of many things he remained enough of a pedagogue (he told himself) and with enough sense of position to be put at a remove by this submission. In a space of time, he knew, his focus would adjust. He was strangely expectant.

The first words of the title became apparent:

'One of a Number of Satires to be performed by the anti-masque between the arrival of the masque at the Forum Academicum and . . .'

'I shall take it to the library with me. I have some work to do. There are some commentaries, you will remember, that the King's Custodian keeps in his hands.'

'On the Supreme Court of the Empire, sir?' asked von Fluorn, acknowledging that his own part in the conversation was over but for courtesies.

'It will not take long. No doubt you will have comments on your essay before noon tomorrow. Thank you, Fluorn, for submitting it to my approval. Discreet supervision. It was the right thing to do.'

His speech was almost terse. In speaking, however, his mind completed its adjustment to the manuscript. The motives for its submission were known and put on one side. Words and even part of its intent took on a shape. He glimpsed the extent of von

Fluorn's effort, and here and there he took the effect of a phrase. Others, seen but not taken, returned and fitted into a place.

And he did not want to leave. The welcome had touched him. He could not afford to leave such hospitality early. When he was alone his imagination must rely upon itself; but here there was sustenance for it.

'I wonder I can examine this so hard. The final drama of the masque is Professor Kutten's. The chariots are the Seneschal's. The music is not my sphere. How I could reject a single statement of how an individual sees the fact . . .'

How then could he approach this new work critically? He knew that he should no longer look for evidence that he possessed – that they shared – the whole and undivided truth, but he might hope perhaps for some comfort, a species of corroboration, that what he saw existed for others.

For this work mirrored something in his own masque. Did it flatter him? It really did seem to trace his masque's illusion, to bare its trick. Did it say, did it point, what he did not dare? The characters were apt. In place of abstracts – the virtues, history, religion perhaps – were disputants in the costume of anti-masque – a statue, a monkey, a great crow's head. What were they saying?

'A debate, is it? A dance?'

Looking up, he saw von Fluorn waiting patiently, almost stoically, with arms unfolded and eyes unfocused, with an uncharacteristic confidence perhaps. His own coat was as if suddenly ready on a nearby chair.

'Well, Fluorn, indeed this all looks very interesting.'

Von Fluorn lowered his arms respectfully. Dolke struggled with the sleeves of the coat.

'I shall take it to the library,' he repeated urgently, while von Fluorn helped him with his sleeves. 'A glance suggests you have made a very praiseworthy mockery of my masque!'

'And of the university, then, sir,' said von Fluorn with a slight laugh.

Dolke strode towards Electors' College and the white bridge. There had been an eager shower as he left von Fluorn's rooms, a sudden douche typical of the month. Dolke enjoyed it. Its nature was neutral, was nothing, he laughed to himself. What mattered, what characterised it, was that he liked it. And that somebody else did not! He laughed this time aloud, an almost emphatic sequence of sounds. The rain appeared, and disappeared as quickly, in a pale blue sky. Spring, for that matter, was his favourite season for visiting the palace, though he would have preferred the morning to the afternoon, which became dusk so easily.

His head and shoulders were spotted with rain but, as he observed, the points of wetness on his face and beard only increased, for no explicable reason (he thanked God!) his growing sense of excitement, and purpose. What mattered was his response, his *sight*. In so far as there was truth it was the sum of these imaginings. No, not the sum; that was what he had once believed from Marsilius. There were many eyes, but no final eye. His mind tried to distinguish a real difference in these attitudes; felt uncomfortable in his heavy tread; half admitted that this elation of his was the fruit of the revelation of the congruence of his own and von Fluorn's imaginings. Of then the corroboration of his understanding? (That there was one truth about what God had made.) That was absurd. The last drops still fell. It was sufficiently late for the western sky, towards which he walked, to be lit with white and yellow. The sky behind him grew a more vivid and deepening blue. The fruit then of escape from the chapel of Ulpian or from desperate loneliness?

On the bridge he was exposed to the heat of the river air. The showers, even late in the afternoon, provided only a momentary coolness. Quickly they extracted from the earth a greater heat. On the river and its luxuriant banks they raised a wave of humidity. It lay about Dolke's face and head while he paused at the parapet. Today he could not resist the view up the river. In that direction was the site of the illuminations, the memory of skaters and hawkers. Quite unconsciously he had assumed the habit of never stopping to look to the south. He never sought with his eyes that shadow, that indeterminable spot on the bank, from which the desperate concourse from the city had issued over the ice. He could nonetheless face to the north, with sorrow and concern, the damage done by the melting stream. To a height of several feet on both banks the vegetation had been plucked away. There was even a moment's remorse in the recollection of his own inactivity.

But his mind had been infinitely busy. It seemed to him almost as if he had been far away. He could not have isolated himself completely from those events, but he had walked further to avoid the activity on the water meadows beyond the University Gate. He confessed the evasions. Memories of the river during those days remained. The young soldiers and engineers, the townspeople and students – von Fluorn had been there – even the young gentlemen of the Royal Guard, struggling, with ultimate success, to keep the toppled tree-trunks from damming the bridges; all this had struck him even while he remained totally detached, as a commendable and inspiring sight. They retained the vividness of achievement.

Beyond the wreck, in the woods below the palace, the thorn flower was now out. Dolke walked on. From the indeterminate objects at his feet – from the leaves, bark and insects of the forest floor – had been started a musty, almost acrid smell, and over and among them everywhere was light. He had never perhaps enjoyed a wilderness, a chaos, so. He sensed about his feet a sudden scurrying or shifting. A sound in the undergrowth evoked so clear an image of a soft creature that he said aloud:

'That was a vole, I think; and that is all that matters.' Above his head a sharp tapping caught his attention. He paused again and waited, alert in both hearing and sight to the splash of drops of rainwater. Each drop hit and rolled down the extended leaf, bent it down and dripped, and dripped, each drop flat on the lower leaf to the absorbent earth. There was a perverse beauty for him in this undergrowth, one not of familiarity with its secrets, but perhaps of the sense of his own presence there before and of his unawareness then of its life, surrounding him, pervading the ground at his feet, in spite of him. Every surface appeared to him stark and metallic and beautiful – the leaves, the wet, black twigs and the matt pebbles.

At the gate of the garden wall he presented himself at the little wooden box of Gebhard Star, porter there for as long as Dolke could remember, and was admitted through the gate under its arch. Within, all was ordered. Here and there a high pine or a massive oak marked an angle or ended a vista. The other trees were crimped, or stayed with poles to angle their boughs. Some were designed by elegant pleaching of their branches, or transformed by grafting, for a cunning hybridity was contrived of

160

many fruits and flowers. The curious preliminary scents of the lemon and the rich, penetrating odour of orange trees hung in the wide spaces between the lines or filled the arcaded bowers.

Dolke was aware that many of them were dead. The knowledge shocked him and turned his mind momentarily to his walk from the city and to the gradual revelation of the shape and order of what was about him; for that defeat seemed for a moment more incomprehensible than the most tangled confusion of the woods. Scents sprang with the sap, he reminded himself, evidence that much had survived the winter. There was little blossom. Water lapped in fountains and hid the fall of raindrops among the trimmed boughs.

Then the white façade appeared. A single Gothic gable, a slender triangle of white Carrara marble, rose above the wall at the mid-point of the parapet and caught shadow from its own delicately carved moulding; on either side sprang a single firm pinnacle on four shafts. All this surmounted a frame within which the royal arms stood carved in fullest relief. Below, exactly below, where now he could only see the topmost leaves of the trees, was the generous and rounded arch, without moulding or recess and black with shadow, from which ran the way inward.

All was the work of Italian masters: first the white façade, the most ancient structure. Later they had returned to make courts and porticos. Each and every stage, and over so long a period, had been governed, Dolke knew, by an extraordinary consistency of spirit. So pervasive was it that Dolke never distinguished to himself the different parts of the whole. Its beauty seemed to him ancient and venerable, even as it also seemed to him alien and apart.

Behind the marble screen of the façade he came as always on the first of the two courts of the palace with a sense of wonder. He stood, surrounded by three tiers of arcades of an equal order. He gazed at the clustered shafts and rounded arches of the first, of fine-grained stone, the serpentine marble tracery of the second storey and the perpendicular thrust of the topmost, crowned with high pinnacles. Behind them he glimpsed long square-lintelled windows whose tracery hung in their upper corners with the corrupted geometry of torn fishing nets. Within these arcades the perspectives of a Gothic cloister were balanced by a more severe and ancient regularity. He was aware again of the sunlight; the courtyard was a well of light and shade.

In the second court sunlight glared from stone flags and glanced from the water of a swan-necked fountain. He found less pleasure in it. Though he called the third glory of the palace 'imperial', he rarely visited it: secluded galleries clothed the outer walls of the three ranges behind the entrance. Their Corinthian columns were of Parian marble and seemed to him, though he strove to deny it to himself, as exotic as the privy gardens of vines and peaches that spread out below them.

It was in the first court and in particular at one corner, that Dolke stood and stared longest. There, in shadow now, flying arches leaped from shortened galleries, each to a capital on the adjoining range and thereby revealed a glimpse of further bays, windows and pinnacles of that building, the royal library itself. All this was the work, people said, of a local master, having no regard to precept or book of the Italians and seeming to surrender in his design to mystery and to some sense, perhaps derived from the natural world, of how one came, or should come, upon an extraordinary sight. And to reach the library Dolke must enter by a door just beneath these flying arches which outwitted by their individuality the rigorous form of the courtyard.

The claim of art around him, the attempt at something universal and permanently intelligible, was alien. What had power through mutability and irregularity fascinated him, though even now in the library a little frightening in that its power over him lay in something that he clung to, yet could not grasp, even less see into deeply.

He spent little time on his researches. There was already a shifting light on the ceiling of the library. He paused and approved this assertion of the character of the place; and assured himself that this mutability (which was as life in all things) was neither an aspect nor a figment of his loneliness, nor indeed drawn up from within any part of himself.

Von Fluorn! All this somehow reminded him of von Fluorn. That he did not himself so much like the library late and left the place to itself. For a part of his mind this fact was indelibly associated with von Fluorn's power to convince him: with von Fluorn riding and meeting a ghost beneath the city walls, but also somehow with the reassurance he had of von Fluorn. And this reassurance had the force (strangely rational) that is lent to an account of the supernatural whenever it is avowed that two men have each told of some compelling detail of an apparition that neither could have learned from the other. Strangely rational was the operation of corroboration both in heightening the vividness of truth, and in that though his understanding and von Fluorn's *was* strange, yet it was the fruit neither of self-assertion nor fantasy but of perception.

He turned some pages of the manuscript. There was much mystery and some clever phrases. What was this? Architecture become a college tower (Electors' College). Dolke smiled. At first he approached the document dutifully. It seemed decorous enough. There seemed, tactfully, no reference to the Seneschal. What was represented were the places, disciplines, perhaps by reference the persons most worthy of consideration. None on the stage remained too long to the fore. Did they debate for supremacy, or did they dance? Words and movements matched, however, with a strange consonance Dolke's own sense of the hidden movement of his masque. Phrases evoked with a curious familiarity the hidden meaning of his masque, the inspiration of von Fluorn's voice and laughter. As he read closely, he felt it point his masque's details, accuse his masque's caution, mock its contradictions, and, most wonderfully, say what he dared not say.

Dolke paused. Another man's point, he reminded himself, often stands more stark, seems less of a compromise than one's own. It possesses the boldness of an unfamiliar turn of phrase. Was there less, even here, than he dared? There was a minute knowledge of details of his masque. (Had they talked so long together?) But they were telling details. When Vaslav Kutten was young, he suddenly thought: it was almost like that. Both had a way of finding the instance which would unlock the encumbered argument, the compelling phrase.

He was certain. It heightened his own work. It lightened his turgid allegory. It knew more clearly its own feelings. Looking up, Dolke noticed beyond each window the polished but indeterminate outlines of a detached pillar. The pillars ran in a colonnade overlooking, not the courtyard, but a side garden. Each was of a noble dignity, but the gallery they appeared to form was no more than a ledge, an illusion to please the eye. The trick of his masque would be in the light of von Fluorn's little play as transparent as the artifice which arranged those forms so nicely above the garden.

He prepared to go. It was indeed late. He had seen the level sunlight on the profuse capitals of the columns. Something in him, to prove his attention, made him read again and write 'Prolix' against one or two over-exuberant passages. Then he put the manuscript under his arm (it felt warm, he noticed). The last direct rays poured through the windows. The ceiling was spread with gold.

Dolke made his way quickly to the staircase and out into the courtyard. It was deserted. The King and his retinue, their work completed, had a week before left for another city. A guard remained and the Custodian in his lodging. Dolke stood still, very alert. All in him that might have felt the dignity and rationality, the humanity, of the courtyard had left him. He glanced over his shoulder; the flying arches stood out uncertainly against deep shadow. From the distance of the second court came the sounds of muffled waters.

The silence of the great garden beneath the white façade was broken by the evening calls of invisible birds. The scents had died with the day. The sense of his being alone agitated him. That word – 'alone' – had occurred to him as he picked up the manuscript to leave the library chamber. He felt behind him the presence of the white façade lying in its own shadow, but he would not turn to look at it. To either side of him the leaves pattered and rustled softly; he listened to them as if they might at any moment be drawn aside like curtains. Never before had he noticed how different were the evening cries of birds.

Then he remembered that at Gebhard Star's porter's box he would at once be released from this inexplicable anxiety, and he might, he thought, have a companion at least as far as the white bridge. Even when he was still some distance from the gate beyond which the wooden shelter stood, and though something told him that he betrayed himself and his dignity, he stopped and called once, loudly and with authority:

'Star!'

There was no answer. The gate was open. Beneath its arch, surprisingly close beyond it, it seemed to Dolke, was a wild structure of greens and greys, and of different shapes and textures. Dolke waited. The only sound he heard was a sudden evening call of a bird. Two notes followed one another, each like a sliding whistle made with the lips very round but barely apart; almost human sounds then, the first note sliding in a long curve from high to low, the second drawn back through the same range, from low to high, and each in turn swelling and then fading. On a branch above the garden wall was the small, ruffled bird which made the sound, a starling. Star's name.

Dolke summoned himself and called again – 'Star!'

But his voice faded as he missed a breath. Its hoarse whisper seemed incongruous in the wide walks, and seemed to him to echo in the clipped avenues. As he hurried into the wood, he fixed his attention on his anger with the porter. His mind presumed something alien and disturbing. He promised himself bitterly that he would have Star investigated. He stumbled over roots in his path.

When he reached the crown of the white bridge the cool air struck him like water. It was suddenly apparent that it was not even really dark. Below him, the surface of the river, though black, was visible. It ran smoothly but coiled about the piers. Ahead of him he made out the towers of the city and by contrast the light and colour of the sky.

But his own rooms would be too empty. Instead he found himself drawn towards the Close of the Benedictines. The thought of the carvings there, completed and lying there waiting for him, mitigated his isolation. The activity of their manufacture was companionable. Against the silence that had succeeded chaos their calm and delicacy, their humanity and form, their clear function, grew vivid and indisputable. Both of the master carvers lived in the Close. The elder, Pius, would at this hour be talking to the apprentices. Master Pius had drawn him and thus knew him.

Dolke dared not look back. Gardens and palace had led imagination to usurp perception. He could trust only his perception but perhaps his perception was not to be trusted. Standing in the night air Dolke saw this but blamed the place and dared not look back. To his right (he remembered von Fluorn's face with a curious clarity) was another such place: where von Fluorn had wilfully failed, for his emotions' or imagination's sake, to seek the true misery of plain poor men. Dolke remembered this also, but dimly, and dared not look. He arrived at the Close almost tottering. The porter admitted him with no more than a look of mild surprise and reprobation. Dolke managed in gratitude a limp gesture of an old man.

Before him was the cathedral. Its height seemed magnified by the obscurity of its roofs and towers. Below them patches of white stone caught last vestiges of the twilight. Dolke had the strength to pause and wonder whether it was their slight glory that threw the towers into impenetrable darkness. From inside the building the light of candles slightly patterned the windows, marked the red in their glass and broke the regularity of their leads. At the workshop he opened the low door and found Master Michael standing before him.

'Sir! Welcome!' exclaimed the carver, and his pleasure moved Dolke almost to tears.

When Dolke spoke, all he could say was that he apologised but that he had not eaten since the morning. It was now between eight and nine o'clock. Master Michael offered him cheese, bread and beer, and shared some while Dolke ate.

'And Master Pius? I had expected to see him,' Dolke asked, looking up again and calmer now.

'He is dead; in the winter.'

'God have mercy . . . and his drawing of me! I expected to see him.'

The phrases expressed what remained to Dolke of his once curiously intimate bond with the man who had drawn his face in silverpoint; they also expressed the rupture of its meagre mental remnants. There was a pause. He was thinking of the winter, which could not be encompassed by his observation. Its incident and his memory of it had been two quite different things. Sheltered as he was by his imagination, it had passed him by.

Dolke broke the silence:

'The winter was kind to me. Forgive my not knowing, Master Michael.'

'You must see our work. You will remember his drawings? The apprentices will be studying them now. They have been admired, his drawings, by many from the cathedral and from the university, who know your face and look. I have used them constantly these last weeks.'

In his answer there was no strain, from embarrassment or indignation. Doctor Dolke had said all that might be expected; but for a little it was as if he could not keep himself from the subject. Then, in the last words, he felt an uplift in his voice. He stood up.

'Yes, I have three apprentices now. Three young men. You must see them.'

He led Dolke through an inner door. Within, the light of three tallow candles was both dim and glaring. The three young men seated round them could make out little of their visitor as he stood by the door, his own figure extended on a tablet of marble. The candles, raised by the apprentices to illuminate it while they stood behind him, threw their light on to its receptive surfaces of polished stone.

He bent his head to scrutinise its own image. The head of stone was turned slightly outwards, as if in swift observation. With that set to it – also the lips parted to speak and the lower jaw thrust forward with determination – there was suggested all the expressiveness of countenance which it had once possessed in involvement in debate and, moreover, an authority and an urgency of insight. The eyes were wide and distant, but seemed, as did the whole, confident of a clear meaning and an ideal; which, as the statue could only be interpreted, were contained in the book which lay at his side and on which his finger rested.

After a few moments he heard Master Michael's voice saying:

'Here, sir; here was a problem.'

But Dolke scarcely noticed them, nor the sculptor's long fingers before his eyes, pointing vaguely towards the sculptured features.

Every physical detail seemed to be represented. Dolke observed the thin skin, and the forehead deeply lined with concentration – each line in some way inseparable from his whole character. And from those features, this aggressiveness here, this love of controversy for its own sake, and love too of conclusion, there had been created something which was almost beautiful. His traits, neither praised nor condemned, possessed the fascination and virtue of their life, through their synthesis in one ardent, fleeting expression. He appeared an ideal of conviction, perhaps even of achievement: an idealisation then, a figment of flattery? But for the moment Dolke could only delight in it. The characteristics were his; perhaps the inspiration had once been his own.

Perhaps Master Michael, or Master Pius, had glimpsed it in him. If it was not an inspiration that had ever existed in himself, then certainly his features had been lent to the inspiration of the artist.

Dolke turned towards Master Michael, who pointed again:

'These lines – everything – I understood from what Master Pius drew. But what have I taught you, John' (he turned to one of the apprentices with an insistent kindliness), 'how the hand will move when you seek to reduce a stone into a face?'

'That there is a conviction in the hand that those few lines the hand knows how to follow have a peculiar virtue; and that they must be followed.'

'Indeed it is not like reason. And must the carver defeat this?'

'Why, he must not let it defeat him. He must take and use it – being in him – but he must look what more there is to be found and put, and must teach his hand the way to do it.'

'You have it. Yet (as you say) there is a point beyond which it is not in him to get.'

He turned to Doctor Dolke. 'For I saw much more, which I would have put in the carving, but' (and he looked at his hand almost cruelly, Dolke thought) 'my hand is now set in its ways. And cannot be convinced, for my eye is too old to know quite clearly what it has seen.'

'But I have never seen the like,' said Dolke, who had never before seen in a stone portrait the perpetual engraving of an undeniable truth.

Though, while they talked on, he thought again and again of the choices that had been demanded for the realisation in stone of his image, and told himself that it was only a part truth, yet he knew he had learnt the lesson of his limitations. He might have believed more and portrayed more. But it was too late to deny von Fluorn or to seek what was fixed, either at the heart or in the face of the university. He must cling to what he had seen, to his achievement such as it was.

It was painful to leave, but no longer fearful. Two apprentices lit his way to Ulpian.

Chapter 7

In late June there was the sound of occasional music, accompanying a lady across the white bridge. For a month before Saint Libori's Day the music of the city was easy-paced in the heat. However, it remained intricate as always, even when, as was so often the case, it was an improvisation. It seemed always to be heard in snatches and often far away, so much of it being made in courts and gardens, or by a stream, or at a watering place, or in travelling; always apparently spontaneous, but by these characteristics laced with others into a whole. At a lady's carriage there was the sound of piping and of taut, light drums. Between times there was a dry summer wind in the grass and trees.

As Professor Kutten arrived, together with the Visitor, the Very Reverend Sulpizius Heysach himself, at the turning point of their walk – the oak copse which stood on land of the Benedictines about half a mile from the city walls – the professor heard the rattle of a tabor and a murmuring, inconsequential singing.

'Shall we go on, Professor Kutten?' the Visitor requested, with slightly peevish urgency. 'This is not quite so – congenial – a spot, it seems, as I had hoped.'

'Are we late, sir?'

Kutten was glancing up to see if he could catch a sight of what he heard, music, and above him, the slow movement of whole boughs in the breeze. Here he had once come as a young man to consider abandoning the hope of an academic life; he might have married. There was the music again.

Married? There had been an oak tree – taut and splendid – which had seemed to excite a conviction that it would be possible. How absurd mental processes were!

But then it had seemed a beautiful, almost compelling possibility. Unless, surely, the mind was playing a new trick of attribution. There had been at most a reassuring hope. He was not in doubt that he had made the only possible decision in the light of the facts.

The mind cleared of stupidities, what was left here? The place still represented to him a sort of idyll. The oaks gave, as they had given, an extraordinary sense of completeness, an equal impression of the thickness, breadth and height of their stature. They were in their fullest and richest leaf, yet each was distinguished enough from the mass to seem to stand with those nearest in a square or circle about a pale, grass enclosure.

The next moment a young man's singing voice unnerved him. He was at the same time totally possessed by, given to, the sound. Then he shut it out.

'How purposeful – these trees. That is not untheological, is it?'

He was often tempted to add some such irritating afterthought when talking to the Very Reverend Heysach. Now it took his uncertain mind with the compulsion of a habit.

It was a strange affectation, towards an apologetic innocence, the Visitor Heysach was thinking; he gave a silent facial impression of the beginnings of laughter.

'They have, no doubt, a purpose; even if not themselves purposeful,' he added.

Every tree was indeed complete, Kutten thought, and purposeful. For the while his scientific imagination was free of guilt. In both their forms and in this sense of their capacity and will to develop, there was in those trees something scientific. Their variety, which would be as endless as their number and the degrees of their growth, did not detract from his feeling that their forms were equally the correct resolution of a single problem; and that each pursued its way in accordance with a formula, knowledge of which gave them all their present perfection and by means of which they would achieve for each future moment another perfect answer. Something in the house in the Barschgasse, the best of man's efforts, reflected the formula; groped towards it rigidly but stubbornly.

There was no direction in these fitful thoughts. The success of the winter was the meagre success of having fitted a specified problem with a solution. Any glimpse ahead that Kutten had was of a path marred and somehow absorbed by self-accusation and by images of figures startlingly alive.

The Visitor interrupted.

'I have never understood your lawyer's idea of the mental contribution to an offence – how you get to grips with motive and intention.'

'*You* have the benefit of confession.'

'I could not condemn a man who did not confess.'

The Visitor and Kutten soon left the copse to those who sang. They dimly made out their figures, stretched in an indeterminate group under a distant tree.

'Though some men can know guilt. But I would not condemn a man by such means to the rigours of the criminal law.'

Kutten did not respond. He saw in his mind Eberhard Dolke, who was not strictly guilty, but had to be opposed. It was not moreover quite possible to explain why evidence was needed for the first decision which could be dispensed with for the second.

'What would the position be, Professor Kutten – can you tell me – were I to *suspect* that such young men (I suppose they were all young men) might be here to poach?'

'There have been no deer here since the winter.' He almost added: 'Evidence to the contrary would be the absolute minimum.'

He had scarcely invited the Visitor to accompany him. They had met at the gate on to the fields. The Very Reverend Heysach had made conversation until Kutten had felt obliged to state his own goal and to ask the cleric to join him.

'No, my question is purely legal. "Legalistic", if you prefer. I am only too pleased to see young men enjoy themselves.'

He paused, for he had planned to talk to Kutten. To that end he had accosted Kutten when they met, though uncharacteristically 'never at his best' with him. Perhaps it was Kutten's reclusive reputation or the undeniable awe which insinuated itself before Kutten's austerity. ('A born churchman – of a certain type!' He smiled to himself, turning to an ironical whimsy that he shared with many academic colleagues.) Still, his last words might have turned the conversation to his purpose; but he had the common habit of legalistic reflection. To formulate legal propositions was at once to have grasped an abstruse logic and to be close to those situations and that judicial responsibility, the risks of whose outcome were only matched in weight by the temptations of canonical sins (less than crime) and the earthly imposition of the rewards and penalties of the Christian theology.

The Visitor's mind, then, was not sympathetic enough to the aspirations of earthly justice either to understand judicial interpretation or to weigh conflicting rules and principles in a given case; but legal phrases excited him. He could not have abandoned his point, even in what he saw to be his own interest. He continued:

'But suppose there were deer, Professor Kutten, and among the trees at night the loneliness, the opportunity and the – the adventurous, the possibly wilful. I wish to decide like a judge; might I order them off?'

'It is Abbey land. You have the authority, I have no doubt. Suspicion may satisfy you (your conscience, if you prefer).'

'But if I were a judge?'

'If you were deciding their guilt?'

'You have it. Such evidence would not be – "conclusive"? It would not discharge the "burden of proof"?' He was hesitant, deferential before the arcane terms, but there was a note of real pleasure at this summary.

'You might expect something – more to the point; something really bearing on the essential facts. Weapons, for example.'

'But that's my point! Does one have to prove all the elements . . . ?'

They were back on the path; this one crossed the fields and eventually joined the highway near a gate at the north end of the town, convenient for Professor Kutten's lodgings in the Barschgasse. Kutten did not pursue the subject – the Visitor he felt was the sort of man who would not be satisfied by an answer to his first question – and both men fell silent. They moved more or less into step; this and the clean white path soothed Kutten's temper.

But the Very Reverend Heysach had not forgotten his main intention, or that remark of his about the pleasure of young men enjoying themselves. That referred so clearly to the weeks of diversion now enjoyed by those students who remained in the city to await Saint Libori's Day. There was too the flow of people who sought lodgings in the city, at the Court, or with friends at the university, and who also waited. The remark was one which, to the Very Reverend Heysach's ear, might easily be revived and elaborated; it seemed to demand qualification.

'But it seemed to me,' he suddenly began without special

emphasis, as if continuing a sentence, 'that if there has been strict justice, there can have been little pleasure for those who faced a rigorous selection as masquers – even for those who have proved successful. Little point for the selectors if they must find some *absolute* evidence.'

As he spoke he eyed closely the city ahead.

Ahead and to one side, beyond the last harvested fields, he could make out figures scattered over the dry water meadows beneath the walls, moving in company to and fro. To his right, bright, ragged fruit trees pointed the highway. There were carts, leaving the city together. He could scarcely see them above the corn, but he could hear them, and they raised already a layer of powdery whiteness. He thought that their teams must be harnessed for a long, slow journey.

In the opposite direction, a light, quaint carriage hastened towards the city. It slipped in and out of his view, in and out of haze, between the heads of rye. The roof was painted. Outriders in outlandish costume flourished lances as they pursued it or curvetted at its doors.

In the cheerful gardens of Staufen and the severe hall of Electors' the student masquers might be rehearsing. The Seneschal and the committees had balanced the competing choices of colleges; no-one had interfered. The best of the young for grace of gesture, modesty of demeanour, and intelligence and expressiveness of countenance had been gathered at last within a single room. Some of them were to pass through the streets in gilded chariots. With others, they would perform the different stages of the masque.

Kutten only knew God as a judge. He hated Heysach, who mocked his search for some earthly truth.

'All youth seemed to be there,' he said, turning suddenly and kindly towards Heysach.

'Well, indeed, all the university does seem to be involved in one way or another.'

'I was thinking only of the masquers. I felt their selection was praiseworthy.'

It was difficult for him to say this but, once said, it gave him a more profound release from anger, almost pleasure; made his instant forgiveness of Heysach a little deeper.

'I also had in mind the anti-masquers – as I suppose they may be termed.' He glanced sideways at Kutten's expression; it seemed unperturbed. He continued:

'Their rehearsals are conducted with spirit, if not with . . .'

With his left hand he made an elegant passage in the air.

Now was perhaps the first time that Kutten had ever considered the Very Reverend Heysach. He stared at the hand, which remained for a moment poised – and was withdrawn. The fingers were small and strong. They had been held slightly spaced and not quite straight, the position of steady relaxation of someone physically firm. The light turn their movement had described and the slight angle of the wrist had an almost athletic confidence and restraint. Yet there was a consciousness, as in the accompanying motion of the head, of presenting the regularity of the features and of maintaining an appropriate poise. It all reminded Kutten of the Visitor's little rounded habits of formality that were less beautiful and usually accompanied by the sudden affectation of archaic phrases or an inconsistent humour for student idiom.

Today he displayed, perhaps carefully, a certain resilience. When he bent forwards to display his attentiveness, however, a sudden stiffness would sometimes fix his dapper body in a bow. Then he seemed old and paternal in his solicitous courtesy, as if he had been bending to converse with a small child. Kutten, remembering this, felt for a moment a little afraid of him.

'A group of students of the liberal arts were pursuing a – perhaps a rather ambitious scheme. They begged our permission to use the close for their rehearsals. I was obliged to point out that it would only be a "stay of execution". There would still be no place along the route of the masque which could take *their* size of stage! Some are a little inclined to overreach themselves.'

Kutten suddenly felt a nervous alertness like a man about to be stretched.

'It was an inventive piece. Some doctors had a hand in it, I suspect,' the Visitor went on.

He told himself to 'take the bull by the horns'.

'One or two of these – "*jeux d'esprit*" – do perturb me. And all to whom I speak. Comments are certainly made.'

'I can understand, Reverend Heysach, that like the rest of the city you find yourself acquainted with rumours.'

'I hoped to satisfy myself that those in authority are also aware of them. They are not always the first to know – a matter sometimes of misplaced delicacy.'

'You may be sure that I am aware.'

'But you, Professor Kutten, are conscious of your right to be.'

'I am informed by Doctor Dolke. The whole of the Seneschal's household sees his reports.'

That was generous, thought the Visitor, with a start of respect. There was no element in it of irony. The Visitor's own dislike of the anti-masque – and its unlicensed dispersal into vapour of ideas – was not quite confident. It could be overruled by the Seneschal. Nor did he want power, not exactly. He wanted to know whether the Seneschal disliked the anti-masque. He wanted to see into this, and into this man – a new man, he named Kutten to himself; a man only recently emerged from obscurity and made fascinating in the Seneschal's confidence. In his exploration of Kutten now he had no sense of pushing him towards a judgment; but he must know whether Kutten could make a judgment and what that would be.

A wriggling excitement, like that of a romantic but invariably discomfited schoolboy, passed through his body. Knowledge made him intimate with events without the fear and responsibility of decision, of the precipice of ideas. He was aching to know.

'They must all have rehearsals, I suppose? Half the university must be writing. Why, and the other half making suggestions!'

'Indeed. And is the household to be expected to view them all?'

'One, perhaps.' The Visitor wondered why people made it so hard for him to do his duty. 'You may have been considering it. It can be seen this very evening, I gather, in the grounds of the white palace.'

'There?'

The Visitor had been close to irritation with an affectation of delicacy, mounting in their last exchanges, which he had almost pinned down not only in Kutten's words but in his tone. He was startled and almost cowed by the bitterness of Kutten's exclamation.

Until the Visitor's last words, Kutten had preferred evasion, escape in superior dignity. If he dared accuse von Fluorn (though he had known since the meeting in winter near the city wall of an *impurity*), his need to confront, to accuse him (always repulsive, being the preliminaries to destruction), would be transparent – to those, like the Visitor, with eyes that see, though to allow or tacitly connive at that impurity touched him, and prevented that translucency and freedom of thought that could give something lasting.

'The King is away,' he added quietly as if explaining something to himself.

He could no longer keep the Visitor at a distance, keep his eyes above the Visitor's.

He had not intended to press so far, the Visitor reassured himself. The breach between Dolke and Kutten and von Fluorn's well-known influence had interested him no more than to give him a little conversation. His intention was never to arouse. Emotion distressed him almost as much as fanaticism. He spoke apologetically:

'The young man has a cousin in those circles.'

'You are speaking of Friedrich von Fluorn.' In Kutten's mind something was still due to 'the young man', von Fluorn's name among a number of the doctors. He had heard it used (and knew how ancient was the house of Fluorn; Kutten had a sudden picture of a confusing, guilty memory of himself searching through manuscripts). What was due in courtesy should be rendered.

'Yes. Dolke's young pupil,' the Visitor insisted, his patience tired. 'Have you . . . ?'

'I have not seen it yet.'

'You will be present? I dare say it is little more than rumour.' The Visitor had resumed his usual cool affability.

As soon as they passed the city gate Kutten took his leave for the Barschgasse. He did not hurry there. Instead he tried to resume the sense of a solitary expedition, pacing in slow steps and following every curve of the city wall. He loved the warmth of the day. He plunged into the shadow at the foot of the defences.

As the wall followed the rising ground towards the northern apex of the city and the old castle, the way grew narrower. There was less need, he said to himself as if the observation might still strike him, less need for easy passage in what was naturally the most defensible part of the city. And this was its oldest quarter.

All the ways were more confined. Where the sun penetrated,

the air was fetid. Spaces of heat and sunlight gave abruptly into dank shadow. Everywhere there was a rich smell of decay. He had made himself used to it. Now and then as he moved on he stooped to examine the most ancient stonework close to the ground and felt it with his hand.

Gradually evening came. The slow passing of the time compressed and interfered with all the functions of his body. From one end of the Barschgasse he watched in the east the concave yellow, the layered arch of light, of the reflected sunset. It gave a sort of pause, a relief. Then he set out for the white palace.

While he strode and searched ahead in the shadows or slowed, saying that he must let himself breathe, he revived by repetition the pain of the insistently bland words of the Visitor: 'Dolke's young pupil'. 'What a range of voice the Visitor had! How approving, how mellifluous, how possessed of infinite modulation. How excellently tempered by practice in empty aisles and corridors. How complex were the thrusting towers of openwork glimpsed here beyond enfilading alleys . . .' His resentment burst out: for they all knew that Eberhard Dolke waited on a pupil.

Friedrich von Fluorn. A man who was unable, who *failed*, to exert himself towards anything but expression of his self. In an intelligent man this was an unforgivable sin. 'Unforgivable sin!' he heard . . . of this he might justly accuse von Fluorn aloud. A man so intent, and thus so confined, was not capable of judging his own actions, or anything, according to any system of values free of his own desires! Was there more? Kutten hesitated. There *had* to be more to justify this pain. His hesitation passed with a new formula: it was Kutten's own fault but he could not speak of that other.

He decided to cross the river by one of the two bridges at the foot of the castle heights. He would then approach the palace from the north. In the short time it took him to make his way down the steep alleys under the western shoulder of the castle, he had to face one more temptation. There remained the authority of his acceptance, however painful, of Dolke's reading of Marsilius of Padua, to which he had adapted himself: no permanence, no perfection, yet at each glance a workable, a manifest whole; so he could suppress the old resentment. Even at its most intimate – indeed at its most intimate – their friendship had

177

expected the gall of this eventual submission. Yet it had never been quite complete. The greater whole, the greater, more profound submission, had still whispered. He had half blamed the old learning for this new detachment from all sense of what had been well constituted. Moreover he had kept life and theory in isolation, never admitting the evidence of his experience to sustain his accepted intellectual conviction. But the pain and ultimately the penetration of the idea had been profound enough. Surely even Dolke had felt the sting of its confirmation of impurity, or the certainty of the core of decay in everything in the world of men. Was to discover the source, in order to judge and condemn, merely to press one's face in the putrefaction? Or was it to cleanse, to make pure? To make possible perfection, permanence? He would not judge . . . he did not, he told himself, have sufficient evidence.

Kutten's imagination had always been able to leap, or perhaps had remained oblivious to that obstacle, the exoticism of the white palace and the royal gardens. Dense, sprung leaves of the beech trees of the wood, sea green and grey except where the sun shone directly through them down to him, and black, brittle oak saplings against a screen of streaming June light, anticipated the effect of those calculated splendours.

To approach from the north side and glimpse first the nearer corner and then the whole receding length of the great façade; to see ahead of him the varying colonnades of that wing which faced him directly, gave him such joy as when he picked up now a crystal or other intricate geometrical structure and, glancing at a chance angle of it, became aware at once of the regularity, of symmetries and deceptive apparent symmetries to be found through the attentive turning of the object before his eyes, and each of them, being found, confirming the beauty of the whole.

When young, and only recently a doctor, he had observed a fashion among a certain circle at the university, a preoccupation perhaps of a certain type of man, to construct models of perfection – of the motions of the planets or of the constellations of the zodiac. In these gardens an idea had suggested itself, and had even seemed to him about to be made exact and fully realizable, that his surroundings contained, indeed reflected, a formula which would accommodate the force of change within a perfect order. He had but to extract it and build according to it a model.

Its application would be pure and universal. He had considered some relation (for this much seemed clear) of a square or a cube around – or perhaps within – a circle. In the circle would somehow be comprehended the change which the cycle of the seasons brought to the gardens day by day, and thus the inevitable return and revival of each phase and aspect of their perfect forms.

He had deceived himself. When he had laboured to perceive how it was, or seemed, that the square should itself change with the turning of the circle, and in what degree the whole mechanism must depend on the square and in what degree on the phases of the circle – he had laughed and thrown the fashion away.

But here the whole mechanism of the gardens was in shocking disorder. Along the broad alleys the plants of the camellia and the peony of Greece were all dead. Again he anticipated the anguish of the despoliation he would soon witness. As he passed the statues in their recesses of deep green foliage, he fixed his glance on them, one after another. The columns of the library range and the second court appeared, dominant, above the high, clipped hedges of evergreen. Despite the urgency, he walked cautiously, so that when he saw move into the alley a tall female figure he could for a moment only suspect that she was associated in some way with what he had come to see.

She was a lady, or visitor, of the Court and walked without attendants. Nonetheless each and every of her movements and gestures – touching a flower, attracted by another of particular colour – though unconscious, possessed the once-considered self-expression of a person who has lived almost every moment observed; and wishing sometimes to disclose nothing, sometimes to suggest much. She might, Kutten told himself, her robe gathered between her shoulders and from that point spreading long folds to the lawn, have been a figure from a masque.

In the distance from which she had come there sounded music. Wistful and dignified, it was inevitably associated by Kutten with the lady. He determined to reach its source, passed and saluted her, and observed its direction. He turned now here, now there, and came into an enclosure of lawn which spread about the pedestal of a marble basin. Around it were the anti-masquers.

Friedrich von Fluorn was watching from the grass as he lay in the shadow of a hedge. A group of musicians pursued the melody. Kutten stood close behind some casual onlookers and

179

waited. The sun was streaming over the opposite hedge of the enclosure and drove the long shadows of the actors towards him. It dissolved their figures in a radiance; light and outlines seemed elements of a single suspension. They too might have been players in a present masque, with its costumes of gold.

The actors, separating into groups, signalled to one another, to the musicians, to von Fluorn, with bold gestures. They began to move more purposefully to the sound of new improvisations. To Kutten all for a while was meaningless, for, though the figures clearly spoke, he noticed only those superfluous gestures, and could not concentrate on what he saw until he accepted its beauty.

First he heard laughter. The voices of the actors were all at once vibrant, ringing. They fell silent; the figures again moved, but this time ceremonially, ritually. He was beginning to hear, to put in sequence each separate speech and chorus. There was von Fluorn still reclining, nodding the rhythm, and maintaining the emphasis with a tight upwards tension of one hand which he held raised and open. He seemed to Kutten deft yet hesitant, almost vulnerable.

Kutten awoke in horror. He felt only a momentary giddiness. Then the picture was clear and as fixed as any image once the mind has chosen between an ambiguity in it. The only significance of that repeated beat of the hand was its emptiness; and such emptiness – any gabble that was of and for the gabbler alone – once insinuated, was the seed of decay. It was invalid. It was the antithesis of what could last. It was solely of the self, the source of corruption in himself, in his work, in Dolke. It could be defeated.

He watched for some time. He seemed to himself to learn more of the play in those minutes than could have been thought possible. Before he caught again the words of the actors he knew that here was no history, no religion and no permanence; no scholarship, no order and no reverence. Here all the past and all the future were absent, and the tempting faces of each passing moment were presented as the truth and the whole.

From that moment – that vain, appreciative pull of the hand – the speeches, when they came to him, came differently, and he received them with different intent. He sought out phrases and forced them, though they galled his patience, into his memory. Those words, and even tones, which he took to undermine and deride the true nature of the masque, those which denied or contradicted its ideals, he caught vividly. Then the players, at last interrupting their efforts, gathered to talk and sit, and he went away.

It was not too late; there was still time to see Dolke. Kutten returned by the white bridge, drawing over as he went the words he remembered and the heat of his outrage; but he suppressed its energy, forbidding himself to mutter the offending words aloud, suppressing and preserving their power to pain and anger. They appeared, as it were, to his sight, written out on a silent, inward surface.

At Ulpian there was a new gate-keeper. Somehow Kutten was known to him; he made a polite greeting. This perhaps – the disparity in their knowledge – made the courtyard and even the glimpse of the library dome above one of the medieval ranges strangely unfamiliar. He had not spoken to Dolke for half a year or more. Bells chimed, and he hesitated.

He had given way to anger, he told himself. Yet had not his anger and pride always been less alert than Eberhard Dolke's? It was difficult now to bring into focus his picture of Eberhard Dolke. So much time had passed; he must, it seemed, be incredibly old. 'Eberhard . . . Dolke,' he murmured to himself. The words conveyed almost nothing to his atrophied memory. He was shocked that they aroused no warmth (unless perhaps this guilt was evidence of affection). There was detached appreciation and perhaps a certain contempt. No, surely – but a thought followed that he *was* almost sorry for Dolke, the author of a dozen obscure books. Desperately Kutten pressed his finger-tips at his forehead. No! that could not be true. This unreal, unembodied Dolke left him so alone and exposed.

He tried to find a closer view. Had he not intended bursting into Dolke's rooms. By what right . . . ? At once his image of the real Dolke was present; as clear as in past years. He had no right against Dolke. Dolke possessed still a father's rights over him.

Quickly, unsteadily, he made his way to the undercroft of the library. The air was still hot. There it would be cool, as always.

The iron gates on to the garden terrace were a little open. Breathing deliberately, he walked at an even pace out on to the gravelled walk. He had presumed to judge Dolke. How deserved then was his shiver of fear. Yet he *would* see Dolke. A voice told him that to hope to achieve something, even to apologise, ignored Dolke's temperament. His defiance, then, was not quite chastened; it was better to leave.

At the archway to the entrance court he came face to face with Eberhard Dolke. He cried shrilly, 'Eberhard?' before Dolke could pass.

For distinct seconds Dolke remained quite silent. His features squirmed in the shadow and his lips fidgeted. Kutten noticed. He could not even choose a form of address. Eventually:

'Shall we go to my rooms? Or are you busy perhaps?'

There was a moment, Kutten was sure, when they might have spoken. He might have asked Dolke whether he had seen him and come down. Something made him suspect that. And whether Dolke could forgive him. But they remained silent, walking side by side, so that the seal of embarrassment and guilt hardened and could only be ruptured.

In Dolke's sitting-room, sitting opposite him, Kutten tried to describe, dispassionately and without the iciness in his throat which made him breathe in ugly little gasps, what he had seen. But he spoke with an absurd bitterness the silly bantering words that had offended him. He could see that, that his difficult breathing was the symptom of guilt, that he would be discovered, and that he deserved to be punished. His forehead just above the temple on both sides was ice-cold and constricted. Punishment was as inevitable, he told himself, as if for his mother's sake he had stabbed his father. He was prepared for it so long, he prayed, as there was no greater guilt to be confessed than this of loyalty to truth. So long as the insult that had provoked him sat where he had perceived it; and not in himself.

And then, when his description was done, he waited in vain for Dolke's reply and, blaming the inadequacy of his words, believing that Dolke could not ignore him, was suddenly impatient:

'It was a caricature – of itself. Yes. It deserves nothing.'

'The others are better, then?'

'It is true – I have not seen them.'

'And neither have I.'

There was in Dolke a definiteness that Kutten had not seen even when they had first set out together on the masque. The assertiveness, which at Staufen had driven him from the presence of the Seneschal, remained as cruelly mystifying to him as ever. Dolke's expression, though it could not be impassive, was set. He appeared to listen intently, but with the intentness demanded in listening to the obscure argument of a pupil.

'And the problem is that this play is by Friedrich von Fluorn?' Dolke spoke evenly, as if he had just seized the point, an uncontested but still slightly obscured point. But his glance was sudden.

Kutten knew at once that now he too must use his words carefully.

'Perhaps the work *is* typical of him; but that is not the cause of my concern.'

'But you have come to see me about him.'

'You are to some degree responsible for him. You are his tutor.'

'Yes, tutor. And I read his play carefully. Twice indeed. Only once carefully.'

'Yes . . . ?'

'Perhaps his effort is superficial. He presents the university of the passing moment. As a young man, a green young man, may he not be allowed . . . ?'

'His views are – trite. There is no doubt in my mind that von Fluorn has made – and has thought to associate with our celebration – the university's – an unworthy essay.'

'Then you are bound to be disappointed. It will not be bettered by many of the others that will be performed.'

'Does that not raise a question of the advisability of the whole scheme? Of the anti-masque. Leave the masque be. His understanding is unworthy.'

'A moment ago I said it was superficial. I was seeking to do it an injustice. I can not accept that it has no merit.'

'As for its wit, or its metre, I cannot say that I formed an impression. I would leave those to your considered opinion. But surely we attach value to a work – indeed so they tell us – in so far as it suggests more clearly, and brings us to grips with, more than everyday observations.'

'You shall have grandeur enough in the masque. In this instance . . .'

'More than everyday observations,' Kutten interrupted vehemently, 'because more difficult. More abstract, or more complex, and needing therefore to be better seen or understood. The more elusive sense and understanding.'

His voice had given way as he spoke to a bitter and disappointed gravity; and less high-pitched than might have been expected of him, Dolke noticed. As he could not bend a little, he tried to speak lightly.

'It is an intelligent piece for a young man; and avoids vulgarity.'

'Vulgarity! Dare I say that I can show it to be misleading; and that I feel it to be disrespectful and – and above all selfish.'

'It is a joke.'

'Scarcely. Except perhaps . . .' Kutten paused, sensing the first insinuation into himself of a suspicion against Dolke; but his tone remained deeply sorrowful, 'that it makes a fool of *you*. Do you not assume some responsibility for those ideas of his?'

'I recognise that you cannot agree the value he places on certain things, or stand in his point of view.'

'Why do you let him play you?'

There was a curious, distasteful ambivalence in Kutten's words. His whole face and body, Dolke thought, were contracted with a seedy moral strictness; some correction might well be administered. At the same time Dolke was a little afraid and sniffed aloud, wondering whether Kutten was perhaps capable of more active hostility.

To Kutten his own words were again as if he had struck Dolke. He could scarcely understand them, and knew only too well that von Fluorn had not made a fool of Dolke with the play . . . thinking this, something turned in his mind. No fool, whatever parody it was of the masque; in whatever guise it substituted Vice for Virtue; however the ideal of the masque was sullied by piping buffoons. Its offence, which was sinister, was to *reveal* something in the masque – a flaw, a doubt. Suddenly Kutten knew, I suspect *him*, Dolke, as well as von Fluorn.

Dolke was breathing unevenly. His beard was unkempt from his pulling his fingers through it as he listened. He was staring at Kutten, finding it hard to breathe, but seeing that Kutten was at his feet.

'Eberhard, I see only that you accept his play, and without criticism – though you have read it carefully, I accept.'

'And, if I may say so, you seem to have made assumptions – about him – ever since he proposed the idea of the anti-masque.'

There was complete silence. Dolke had scarcely intended to strike Kutten down. The obsequiousness of his last words had made him do it. And indeed only a part of him knew quite what he had said; that he had kept that a secret from Kutten; that it could hurt Kutten so much. He had *never*, he protested to himself, warned von Fluorn to guard his tongue; never sought from him an oath.

In Kutten a fabric of thought was dissolved and seemed to flow out past him in turmoil. He had had his personal explanation of things. It had almost satisfied him: the crisis in Dolke's ideas, even when Dolke had joined with him to work; that only later had their revolution become apparent, and that they could no longer match with his – so that the masque had led to the break, and the anti-masque was the escape of Dolke's imagination from his rigidity. For himself to know – to have believed that it was all von Fluorn . . . that required belief in another choice, in deliberation.

'No need to throw that in my face,' he said like a lamb.

Dolke could see tears in his eyes.

'The whole university knows . . .'

Chapter 8

Nothing more on the subject of von Fluorn's play was heard by Dolke for some time. He was alone one afternoon in his rooms. The announcement which came then was curiously brief.

It verged, he thought, on the discourteous. He gave a snort of laughter, sardonic and disdainful enough to show that something it disguised required fortitude. Then he read the message again. That's all one could expect from them, he seemed to say, throwing up his right arm again and pursing another grim smile.

'They don't even explain what they want,' he said to himself, aloud.

Although Dolke said 'they' and continued to refer inwardly to some individuals, some clique almost, whom *he* at least could identify, the letter was solely in the name of the Seneschal:

'. . . having received numerous inquiries and requests from various eminent members, masters of this university, for reassurances about the nature of these informal diversions, and it seeming a sphere in which you alone are able to give any such answers and reassurances as the facts may require, I see it as my duty to request you to wait on me and on those of my household whom I may select to advise me in any question which seems to me material, on the Monday of next week at ten o'clock before noon in the Library Gallery, so-called, of the old university buildings on the Forum Academicum, and at twenty past ten o'clock in my rooms there.'

Dolke calmed himself with slow breaths, and sought then to extract systematically all he could from the meagre, if prolix, announcement.

If, as a result of these questions, the Seneschal wished to have changes made in the anti-masque or in the student plays, there would be little enough time; ten days after the attendance on him would be Saint Libori's Day. Yet the Seneschal delayed the discussion for three days. This was not for Dolke's benefit. Yet it must be as pressing a matter as any other before the Seneschal at that moment. The delay, he would be wise to assume, was for the Seneschal's benefit. He was preparing his case.

So Dolke argued. But with a revival of his energy after a setback – as perhaps in an argument – he was often possessed by a sudden optimism, whose impulse went beyond reason. It struck him that the Seneschal might be in need of delay. He was uncertain of his opinion; or he wished to accuse but did not have the evidence. He and his household needed above all that their omniscience remain undoubted.

But Kutten knew. Kutten had the evidence, for there was only one thing that interested them, and that Kutten had seen for himself. Fluorn's play. Dolke's arms, defiantly stiffened, slipped to his sides. His steps shortened as he moved about his room and turned in on themselves so that he was driven into circles.

He sat down again. Kutten, the coming man, would decide what the Seneschal should concern himself with. During the next three days they would be preparing a thorough case.

Despite Dolke's disquiet at the prospect of the days he would have to endure before attending the Seneschal and – who knew what others? – the time passed almost pleasantly. There was serenity in the young actors and in the long, surrounding silence of rehearsed, repeated speech; distant glances at a passage of steps, to and fro, or at words spoken in the open air rarely grasp the instant of drama. He watched the rehearsal of von Fluorn's play from the concealment of distance. And as he watched the continuing preparations for the anti-masque, his natural resilience revived. Twice more he saw von Fluorn, once at a rehearsal in the gardens near the river. Fluorn noticed him and waved. Most of all there was the sight of those parts of von Fluorn's play which reflected (Dolke was no longer afraid to use the word to himself) some underlying feeling, some intention, of the masque itself; to see scenes and symbols equivalent to *his* masque's allegory and self-satire; more valuable than its chariots, its costumes, its music. Confident of this, Dolke felt an access of strength. He could face, alone with his ideas, the Seneschal.

On each day in turn Dolke had marked the approach to Saint Libori's Day and the reduction of the time in which the Seneschal

187

might have things changed. These repeated observations could give, however, no honest hope. They were merely the entertainments of anxiety, perhaps the compulsions of an obsessive temperament. His reason told him rather that the crucial day, before which the passage of days was of no significance, was the day on which he would wait on the Seneschal.

The Seneschal had failed to have the courtesy to set out his questions. Dolke's reaction was to dismiss from his mind for most of the time the consideration of his own case. To do otherwise, he would tell himself, must in the circumstances be a waste of time. And during the hot, busy days he felt increasingly that confidence in his new ideas and of the perpetual support and closeness of von Fluorn. At moments he saw himself standing as champion of them both – a champion chosen by chance; von Fluorn would have been just as able to represent them both.

In the daylight there had been, too, a sense of the certainty of the completion at last of the undertaking on which he had persevered so long. His new masque, as if the work of a second cycle of the seasons, would come to fruition.

At other times reason was insistent. Dolke would experience a sensation – the presentation before his inner eye of words demanding whether in truth he had not indulged his fantasy in his ideal masque-world under the pretence of a supposed insight. On what new idea was his masque based? Did the masque care to express it? A sense of von Fluorn's youth? Of his own age? A last onset of assertiveness? A long-frustrated idea, an anciently inhibited legal theory?

To formulate and so buttress his supposed understanding was a task he could not face. Instead the fleeting recognition of a compelling phrase or of some fabric loose from the whole (and made delectable by a vague, geometrical embroidery) provided moments of escape, of delight, of self-awareness, and of justification. Here he was, ready to be champion of a new attitude! That was the word! Not yet a new philosophy, but already a new 'attitude'.

During the final day, the Sunday, Dolke reflected (with little effort of concentration and little sense of crisis) that he were well advised not to take again the line he had taken against Kutten at their last meeting. In this mood he allowed that his position had been untenable. It implied an abdication of responsibility.

And if he were to argue that the masque was a work of the imagination, he would be trapped. For in that case the masque was Dolke's fantasy and did not remotely resemble either the university or the masque of his commission from the Seneschal; or it purported to portray or suggest the true character of the university – and failed. Moreover, if he were to claim that von Fluorn's ideas were not at odds with those in the masque itself, his work would come under closer scrutiny. The day was spent seeking a stance which would acquit his scheme.

Yet, he assured himself during the bright heat of the afternoon, his observations, his new 'attitude', would remain his – and von Fluorn's – secret. That was an aspect of his championship of them. His fight would be defensive. The examples he posed would only be answerable by someone aware of the new principles. He would mitigate. He would evade.

Dolke was too wary and too rational in the calm heat to consider otherwise. The confession of the new ideas at an audience with the Seneschal would immediately be succeeded by his overthrow.

Thereafter, perhaps towards evening, Dolke tried to turn his attention to the points and the aims that might be uppermost in the minds of the Seneschal's counsellors, those at least who were already against him. He knew his opponents! At this he would start or turn quickly as if to catch . . .

He turned from the subject with irritation. Kutten had the whole affair quite out of proportion. It was futile – it was almost ludicrous – to discuss the merits of von Fluorn's play as art, but it would be dangerous to discuss its truth.

Even as he walked into the Forum Academicum on the morning of the Monday – the eleventh of July – he was absorbed by the contradictory whisperings of his personality. He passed under an arch; he glanced up only while its shadow lay on him. But the Forum demanded for a moment his attention. It stood as if it had been decked for his coming. The work was complete. Or the masque might have been over; all on the other hand was so still, even the air. The Seneschal could claim much credit for this early completion.

Three storeys of carved wood touched with gilding – a house

both as full of detail and as insubstantial as a palace which deludes in a dream – obscured the pure proportions of Vitruvius of the Aula Senatus. This stage sprawled and held itself in apparent solidity with a tenacious and theatrical flimsiness. Terms with Emperors' heads, and obelisks, sprang from the ends of each balcony.

Yet it was not entirely illusion. On Dolke's instructions the best craftsmen had designed its details and constructed the whole. It was Dolke himself who had laid down its simple and essential scheme as the stage for his drama: three storeys, each of three lofty and rounded arcades. The topmost parapet supported at each end a statue of a noble female figure. One of these was half turned to face the university church; the other contemplated the Library Gallery.

For Dolke there was in this view a painfulness, a nostalgia. The blue and white of the awning above it, above then the two topmost statues, spread for the length of the Aula Senatus and far out over the square. The colours were repeated above the embankments of seats on every side – along the older buildings of the Forum and at the foot of the university church. Only Tenth Day Street and a way by the north side of the church, each passing under its arch, won the Forum and indicated the separateness of the sections of the whole. All this he had caused to be made. A sense of greeting and of silence from this completeness was all that distracted his train of thought. The solemn fabric, like tapestries heavy on enclosing walls, scarcely trembled.

Although Dolke's movements were constrained by a caution and made close to his body, and although he thought fleetingly of the past, he was not dejected. Saints Ulrich and Afra, the church of the university, sounded a quarter to ten o'clock. Around it other clocks and chapels gave a single concurring stroke. In so far as Dolke was conscious of these sounds they soothed him. Saints Ulrich and Afra had a pleasing double stroke.

It had been a fine day for the walk from Ulpian, though at his favourite view his turn of the head had been the blind glance of habit. In the Forum now he paused again and lightly turned himself on his heels and toes, clockwise through a circle, to survey all his handiwork. There was only a momentary inclination, and no time, to discover the hidden invention of his arrangements – the lighting, behind an embankment of seats, of the

190

arcade under the Library Gallery, and the new galleries for access, of canvas and silk, and of wood cut and carved with Italian pilasters. And so much more!

Dolke again directed himself towards the Great Hall of Convocation. He was admitted and – laughed! Here was Ludwig Aicha! and dressed as a Roman by his sculptor (fifty years after Aicha's death). He had even been placed on a pedestal, the first statue in that Latin fashion. What would he have said, that Gothic man, to this fate? That it was just? He was no philosopher and would not have enjoyed the irony. Dolke threw out his arms, coughed, and stepped to the nearer of those pairs of doors that led into the privy, Gothic world of the old university.

It seemed extraordinary that he had never before found anything incongruous, anything ludicrous, in that statue. Never before, however, had the world and image of Aicha seemed so far away from his new ideas. His own new attitudes, he insisted, were the fruits of reason as well as imagination.

And soon Kutten would try to accuse his old favour for Marsilius; that too would deserve laughter. Almost equal laughter! Had Marsilius ever seen that the inevitability of change made the individual *everything*? The man must die; the institution must change. Life was not to be wasted on the institution! So insistent was this certainty that Dolke could scarcely envisage, without an effort of academic charity, that Aicha too had seen himself as a man seeking through true reason a harmony, but also a lasting perfection in the spirit of the ancient thinkers.

When Dolke reached the Library Gallery, having threaded his way behind an attendant, he was left by himself. Never before, it occurred to him, had he been in the place, that familiar place of resort, alone. It stretched away into a tunnel immersed in shadow. Summer had come, but the Aula Senatus and the Library Gallery would wait empty until Saint Libori's Day. Most of the hangings were drawn and shutters closed against the sun. An Augsburg cabinet of ebony, which on feast days displayed a wealth of ancient cameos, stood shut. Almost every picture reflected a black and silver glow, or grey or brown, through which mirrors only marks of red among the colours beneath sometimes showed. He passed down the line and so made his way the length of the room.

After some hesitation he made out the Adoration of the Virgin.

His eyes were becoming accustomed to the half-light. Though shadow lay directly over the picture, the watery white of the Virgin's shift became visible. He fixed on it with tense eyes his stare until he had distinguished the ideal towers and cities of its vista. Only such an ideal as this, he reminded himself, brought neither regret for the past nor fear for the future. In this room chosen and favoured images of the university revived, images he had never doubted despite the fluctuation, even the dissolution, of his theories.

Two successive sights of such a place (if essentials prove as before and associations are revived) give the sense of a beginning and an end. But like the end of an old romance, Dolke told himself. For a moment a circle, a whole, but then the recognition of at most a phase, artificially distinguished, as could be a different phase, a different interval on another occasion. Repetition threw the latest stance, the latest jink, into relief. Yet it was a persuasive sense. Here he was; he had finished the masque – or he sensed here the completion of his work, as here he had sensed its inception. He had, then, the impression of something complete. That sense, which the mind's straitness granted, was perhaps enough.

Glancing up, he found himself able to distinguish with increasing ease patches of light; they made solid out of the obscurity the firm but subtle camber of the nearest of those beams which spanned the chamber. So vivid was the returning sense of history, of the passage of time in that room and of the proximity of the famous – or once-famous – that the sombreness of the shadow could not dull it. But by now this image of something continuing, the sense of the beginning and life of a *whole*, had come to disturb him. That was inevitable. To command belief, his argument had always been, on any point, to find the compelling phrase. He had since youth seen in the courts how the advocates sought the irresistible way to put their case. A formulation was made, an excision and display of *that detail* which put the facts unanswerably closer to one previous decision rather than another, within this principle instead of that. And his new views seemed incapable of sustaining the return of this invincible image, of the institution and of his part in it.

Ironically, it was to his sympathy with the room and with its associations that he turned to be soothed. For the sympathy was of his – and any like – mind. The awareness, the association, was personal. When he had walked here in a concourse of his fellows, he had often been aware, as if through them, of the room itself. Now as he walked, staring at the shapes of pictures, he glanced sharply, once or twice, the other way, for he felt aware of a shadow in front of him, or of a movement, and half expected a figure to be before him and to pass him by.

From the other end of the Gallery came a distinct sound. Dolke looked up, anxious all at once. Just inside the door through which he had himself entered, stood – he could see against the light – a slim, young man. Behind him was the mannered figure of an attendant. At once both figures withdrew.

Dolke knew it was von Fluorn. By a similar intuition he knew that he must already have seen the Seneschal. The clock bell of Saints Ulrich and Afra struck a double stroke. It was a quarter past ten. The hour must also have struck at ten and the bells of Saints Ulrich and Afra pealed, but he had not noticed them. At that moment he was summoned by name.

He was led, passing through the doors of the gallery by which he had come, and by which von Fluorn, he was sure, had entered and left, first to a staircase, then to a high vestibule on the landing of the upper floor, and so into the rooms of the Seneschal.

The room Dolke was standing in was comfortable and cheerful yet a little formal, very much the type of room the Seneschal must have liked to be seen in. A heavy rectangular table stood in the centre. It seemed slightly out of scale and must, Dolke thought, have been installed for the day's work. A number of people were sitting at it. One was standing. Vaslav Kutten. There was his empty chair.

Another chair stood empty at the head of the table, but fully upholstered in crimson and silver Venice damask with silver fringes.

Kutten, though – he was the instigator. His demeanour, Dolke remarked contemptuously, was designed to suggest that (having set all this in motion) its incident and outcome could mean no more to him than principle required and duty might approve. Did he regret his action, Dolke wondered, and the embarrassment? Embarrassment was the inevitable product, the unforgivable attendant on such behaviour – though himself, Dolke, felt none.

A chair, like that he assumed to be Kutten's, was drawn up for him. It was set facing that upholstered in silver damask. Had he cared to stretch his arms to their fullest extent over the table he might have touched the nearest chairs to left and right. Kutten's and Doctor Feucht's. Dolke scarcely noticed Feucht; he seemed at every moment about to speak to Dolke, but did not. Beyond Feucht, nearer to the damask chair, sat the Regent of Ulpian. As Dolke had sat down, the Regent leaned over towards him to say:

'Oh dear, how these things happen.'

These things, he meant, would have consequences.

Dolke had scarcely heard what he said, but would not have cared to answer. Looking at him, with the advantage at least of not having to turn his head, Dolke felt the stroke of a betrayal. The Regent was not a member of the household and might have explained in advance to Dolke his own position in advising on this matter. Nor was the injury solely one of discourtesy. The Regent was that sort of intelligent man, Dolke knew, who mistakes for impartiality a self-imposed bias against whichever is the side in which he takes himself to have an interest.

Beyond Kutten, on the damask chair's right hand, sat the Visitor, the Very Reverend Sulpizius Heysach. Dolke could bring to mind against him only his rather amusing, erudite and wearisomely repeated anecdotes about the rivalry he had faced in producing his annotation of Saint Polycarp.

Only a slight but irreducible gap between his own and the other chairs denoted that he was the object of an inquisition.

Kutten was thinking of Mrs Wimpfner. When, on the evening he had last seen Dolke, he had reached his home in the Barschgasse, Mrs Wimpfner was standing on the stairs. He had been too tired to do more than avert his eyes. But she had spoken to him. Somehow (he was not sure by what words) she told him that he must go to the Seneschal. At the door of his rooms the smell of cleanness delighted him. He thought of Mrs Wimpfner coming down the stairs and meeting him. He wanted to obey her. The others were the guilty ones. He had decided to go next day to the Seneschal.

But then Dolke noticed someone else. He turned towards a tall figure sitting, rather hunched and uncomfortable, behind a narrow knee-hole table. It was the Advocate to the university, the legatus Andreas Arcute. His table stood at right-angles towards the mid-points of the sides of the big table where the others sat. Perhaps he had been motionless in concentration or had just stepped silently to his place. Certainly Dolke had been unaware of his presence, and felt slightly afraid.

The small table was closely arranged with papers. This tightness of everything on it (slightly disconcerting to Dolke in the exactitude and deliberation of thought and action its management clearly required) seemed to focus Andreas Arcute's concentration and grasp of the present subject. Recovering himself, Dolke took advantage of the silence to attempt to assess him. His previous opinion was informed only by memories of Arcute speaking. Dolke expected him to speak. As the speeches had always been public orations Dolke did not see himself replying. These orations were well known for their confidence, and were delivered with the cadence and accent of the clerical education said to be so marked in many of the sergeants and advocates of the King of England's courts.

Kutten had gone over to his table and they were talking. Arcute's face, so round and boyish from the front, had a strangely intent profile. Its features were young, but the great depth of his head, heavy on his long, crouched body, made this prolonged youthfulness seem almost the child-like and single-minded innocence of old age. This impression was heightened by a tight lawyer's coif of black satin, which fitted over his hair to the nape of his neck. His hair, Dolke remembered, was particularly boyish, short and curled; the close-fitting coif momentarily suggested a freakish baldness. As his head nodded with light beats to express his interest in Kutten's words, he might have been a sage, but his expression even now was not disinterested. If, as was sometimes alleged, the Visitor of the Benedictines was fascinated more by questions and confessions than by the truth, the life of the legatus Arcute revolved round games of the mind and their successful conclusion; and never round the truth.

Doors beyond the damask chair opened. The Seneschal entered, formally. All rose to their feet. He took his place, fluffed out his white summer robe so that it lay boldly over the crimson and silver and, as if some definite stage of the proceedings were thus concluded, relaxed his arms on those of his chair.

'Good morning, Doctor Dolke. I say again "Good morning, sirs," despite our earlier deliberations of today. Doctor Dolke, allow me to explain that I, with the aid of my advisers here, have already considered the content of this unfortunate piece. Moreover, I have been myself discussing this matter during the last hour – quite alone – with Mr von Fluorn, who, as a gentleman, has declared himself unwilling to disoblige me in anything that we may conclude we should desire of him.'

He paused. Dolke said to himself, What then is the problem? They have come to a conclusion about the masque, the anti-masque and the play. He felt himself contract by instinct in the discomfort of anxiety and at the same time in preparation to resist, to spring. What made him anxious, almost afraid, he did not know. It seemed in part related to von Fluorn. He wondered whether his pupil had betrayed him, as if it were his own play that he was intending to defend.

The Seneschal looked as if he had remembered that he was delivering a prepared speech; there was his tongue touching his lips. Dolke fixed his eyes on the slightly flustered figure and told himself with greater assurance that von Fluorn would not have saved the shell of his play by abandoning what was important in it. But he was not totally convinced.

The Seneschal had resumed: '. . . simply to advise me on different aspects of the affair. They are not judges. Nor am I. Nor are we a jury to establish truth by the casting of votes. I, in short, as Seneschal, consider that some reassurances may be needed – the form and the content of the masque, and I include Doctor Dolke's intention of an anti-masque in that reference – and am making inquiry to determine whether this is so.'

It was clear to Dolke that he was expected to make some acknowledgment of this summary. In his turn he stood up.

'Sir, I shall do all I can to assist you. But I remain uncertain about things in general. What is your jurisdiction? – No sir, do not misunderstand me, please; I do not challenge your authority. What I wish to know is your brief to yourself. Then I may help to seek the answers . . .'

Arcute rose, nodding briefly towards the Seneschal, who half turned to hear him.

'Sir,' Arcute began, turning now to Dolke, 'perhaps I may be permitted . . . as we have heard, this is no court. It is not formally constituted. In this university there is no power in the university to try, to punish, to compel. Discipline is for the colleges. There is no question of jurisdiction in the sense of authority.' (No power, no duty, nothing at all! Dolke echoed disdainfully to himself.) 'There is no duty on you, Doctor Dolke, to answer.'

As Arcute spoke, his right hand was held close up to his chin with the finger-tips pursed and pressed outwards as if they would extract the exact and pure words from the air and serve the function of a mouth in both enunciation and emphasis. He turned to whom he spoke, or spoke about – now the Seneschal, now Dolke – and looked them frankly in the face, as if he were granting a point to one, or to the other. The intensity of tone of his pronouncements increased the resemblance to a schoolboy.

'Equally, there can be no limit placed on the scope of your searches, sir,' (he turned back towards the Seneschal) 'you are not bound. And from silence inference is not so strictly precluded.'

'Sir,' Dolke began emphatically, addressing the Seneschal with a directness, as if a moment had come in the proceedings at which forms, barriers, had to be leapt because they were no longer as important as other things, 'if you wish to require anything to be done – by my college perhaps – on the basis of this – this hearing, then authority is a matter for careful consideration.'

'But Doctor Dolke, in the event I act hereafter it will not be on the authority of this hearing, but on my own authority. As I say there can be no judgment here. At most the matter would be one of discussing the state of things with Ulpian, to whom your duty is not only as Doctor and Master. It is also of course owed as tutor.'

There is no space for legal argument here, Dolke told himself. Nonetheless he was frightened of Kutten. He remained silent.

'As we have explained,' the Seneschal continued blandly, 'we have examined copies of von Fluorn's work. As I said, it is – unfortunate. Professor Kutten?' He gave way.

'Sir, may I set out our objections? We have agreed . . .'

'I have accepted your advice,' the Seneschal chided him gently.

'Indeed, sir; and your advice has been unanimous that the masque symbolises your university and its ideals. Your desire for the presentation of a history of the establishment, of its ideals and discipline is well-known.'

'We have much to thank Doctor Dolke for in his achievement of this representation,' said Doctor Feucht, 'and the anti-masque, sir, no doubt provides a foil to the jewel; it is the reminder of the dangers from outside.'

'I would not pretend that all men's hearts here have been immune,' offered the Visitor, with a smile that offended Dolke.

Kutten thanked them both. 'But – the dangers of decay? Or the decay itself?'

'As I said – more a foil . . .'

'More a mockery. Sir . . . ?'

Kutten turned fiercely towards the Seneschal. Almost imperiously, thought the Seneschal.

'Doctor Dolke?'

'In England – I have heard, sir – and in the Court of England, it is said that in such a – picture – a man *must* show structure and history and intangible greatness; but he may also show his sense of change and things passing and passing away, and of the everyday, the merely individual. Even of what is humorous. With respect, that is a more complete image, and the response to it a more complete response. You may consider that man also more complete.'

For if Kutten was a more intelligent man, the Seneschal still had hope that he might become the more complete man. 'Might become', because in him was a degree of genuine humility and honest uncertainty of feeling. The image Dolke presented did not move him, but made him feel that it was something which ought to move him.

'Sirs, in my mind the anti-masque is now one with the masque. In practical terms to abandon one would be to destroy the other.'

And, apart from his secret thoughts and fears, the Seneschal also believed this. When he had finished speaking, he had realized that he had given a judgment on the preliminary question. There would be an anti-masque. He felt a tremor of admiration, even of warmth, for Dolke, as if Dolke had generously shown him something within himself. He felt himself clothed in a strength of office which gave him perception in matters of office. Kutten was passionate and threatened the whole. The Seneschal knew and ensured that there should be a masque of the university, though what that masque should be, what the university was, he had only the vaguest notion.

'And it may serve to entertain a stringent and intelligent mob,' echoed Feucht.

'Whatever is said, sirs,' Kutten suddenly, shrilly, began again, 'we are at least agreed that it is not the part of the anti-masque to contradict the masque. But put aside the anti-masque – put other things aside. Are we not agreed that in its parody, its travesty, of the masque, Mr von Fluorn's essay offends fundamental ideals of the university?'

'We are agreed on its inaccuracies, Doctor Dolke,' the Seneschal confirmed.

'And that it holds up for approbation poor, shoddy diversions?' Kutten insisted.

'Sir, it seemed to me,' said Dolke, feeling a sudden weariness frustrating him, 'that it was a slight piece of fantasy.'

He wanted to exclaim, 'If I had known there would be such bitterness!' but then, he wondered, what would he have done had he known. He might never have produced the masque perhaps; or did he mean that he might never have betrayed Kutten? Instead he continued:

'To him – he has really only a short time here – the sights and personalities of your university pass him like . . .' he paused, 'like a serpentine procession. He hears around him the names of illustrious men and of scandals. It is as difficult to see the importance of one as the other.'

Arcute had stood up again. His hand was poised away from his face, his tone less intense. The cadences of an elegant advocacy were substituted, but also a self-consciousness and an elaborate pleasure:

'Let me disabuse you of what I suspect may be a misapprehension of your own. The nature of this university has been preserved by exact statements. Would it be too much to expect . . . ?'

But Kutten broke in: 'Those of its members worthy of honour – did they ever approve the magnification of the individual or any selfishness of glory? Yes, selfish,' he ended in a murmur.

Arcute could bring himself to continue; the outburst had not after all been addressed to him.

'I am simply an adviser on law, but opinions underlying the

play touch on the very constitution of this foundation.'

'I have observed with some regret,' the Visitor interrupted, 'the absence of any reference in this play to the shaping of this university by Almighty God.'

'It might help the Seneschal,' Arcute continued, 'if you would answer one question, Doctor Dolke. Do you not consider that von Fluorn's play portrays our history as one interminable climbing and self-aggrandisement?'

'And does it not approve it and say that it is witty and inevitable?' It was Kutten, who again interrupted, and his voice was shaking. 'And did it not propose that it is essential for men to climb as part of their greatness. It said that to me.'

'It is difficult to answer all these points, sirs,' said Dolke. 'I do not love change. I know something of our university's history. I am capable of reverence.' He paused, seeing that they had remembered their respect. 'But the progress of its change was not pre-determined, except according to the operation of *all* God's instruments. Many men – many great men – seem to my mind to have contributed to the shape of this foundation. The name of Ludwig Aicha occurs to me.'

'But Doctor Dolke! The office of Seneschal has continued unbroken for three hundred and twenty years,' said the Seneschal with a tone of ingenious pleasure, as if he had put the decisive argument. At the same moment, with a deft hand, he touched the flowing cuff of the Visitor's robe, and somehow forestalled any response.

Kutten waited until everyone was silent.

'Beyond what point, do you consider, Doctor Dolke, does an institution cease to have any identity at all, whether because of constant change or the power of successive individuals?'

'The changing nature of something, if not too rapid, does not prevent our identifying it.'

This was Dolke's prepared answer. He said to himself, I knew he would ask. He went on:

'Something essential remains – so long as that is so. Consider the kingdom, Professor Kutten.'

'Without this essence, what remains? Or is it one of those "essences" which include a little bit of everything?'

'Form perhaps.'

'A serpentine procession?' suggested the Visitor, in a tone

200

which might have been inspired in him by a light but acid wine.

'I spent many hours seeking the image – the compelling image.'

For Dolke his last words possessed the truth of familiarity, and the pleasure of the reassuring, if dangerous, proximity of his secret.

'The model surely,' said Kutten, also with private laughter; and then, 'and in Mr von Fluorn's play?'

'The university remains identifiable.'

This answer, Dolke felt, was weak. He faltered and then added:

'As I said, his view is juvenile; he is a young man of extravagant fancy.'

'He does not even credit the university with form; but merely men with importance.'

'He does not refer to it. It would have been indecorous to mention the offices of the university. I would resent any suggestion that there was anything vulgar in the work, sir,' Dolke went on, turning to the Seneschal. He hoped for the initiative given by the concession of a point, however small. The respite, and the Seneschal's nod, were welcome. More in thanks than in any desire to ingratiate himself, he explained further to the Seneschal.

'There were one or two accidental references to particular colleges. I suggested Fluorn strike them out. He agreed without hesitation.'

'He is a gentleman,' the Visitor explained, with his same ambiguity, as if perhaps passing on some common piece of information while continuing to concentrate on something else.

'For my part,' said Arcute, 'and it may be of service to the others, I saw the piece and thought its form – a dance in effect – must be significant. When you read the work, Doctor Dolke – as von Fluorn's tutor – you may not have been able to envisage it. Or what did you think it signified?'

In this vein Professor Kutten and the legatus Arcute wheedled away at Dolke's stance; at the implications of phrases and whole passages and scenes of von Fluorn's little drama. But by preferring insinuation they were unlikely to lay the principles bare, Dolke noticed. How much he felt, at each quotation, a confirmation of his sympathy for the words! Only the whisper that his whole purpose might be frustrated prevented his confessing – declaring – it.

At last Arcute commented, as if to himself but with a petulance in the movement of his hand:

'It seems to me that these answers are more compatible with von Fluorn's having learnt his ideas from his tutor than with anything else.'

'But would one be right to infer the probability of his having done so?' inquired the Very Reverend Heysach. 'Von Fluorn does not, I am told, enjoy a reputation for the possession of an original mind.'

'Sirs!' The Seneschal's voice remained equable if blandly surprised. 'Our aim is not to judge.'

'Indeed, sir, it is to find a course of action,' said Kutten.

'Which will lead to a satisfactory solution. After our seeing von Fluorn this morning, examination of his work should have been at an end. Doctor Dolke may show us how to effect a satisfactory solution.'

He looked hard at Doctor Dolke, whose face had gone quite white.

'If we have decided what that is.'

Feucht murmured, 'If we keep a sense of proportion.'

The Regent of Ulpian had remained in almost continuous silence. He was without doubt the oldest of those in the room. To him the university meant little beyond Ulpian; little that is but the regal, almost mystical aura which adorned the office of Seneschal. What great names he had known embody it! What autocratic and inspired countenances! His presence at the council of the man who held this office abashed him. He had retained by silence a sense of his own dignity.

Now he chose to speak; and Dolke found himself waiting on his words with a new and sudden urgency. After the almost blinding moment of suspicion – von Fluern – and his suppression of it, everything was clear. The bile and faith of those in front of him had been a painful reminder of the belief that he had once shared – or had told himself that he shared – with them. He was aware too, as he struggled for an advantage of words, that he had scarcely tested his new ideas, that they might be wanting, and – with all his disdain – have been a disguise for some gap, some impediment, in his own mind. But there was something else that frightened him more profoundly, a fear that had in the past accompanied the moments of insight and acceptance of it, and the moments of subsequent examination – that his most extreme convictions might be the whole truth; that the university really was only a form, within which things might be done by individuals, perhaps in its name. And if so, that no thing existed, and its character was but that which individuals saw. That the institution, the idea, was ineed nothing; the object was mere solidity. A common agreement among men as to the character of such things did not make it any more true. As day succeeded day, the time must approach when some individual must give it the lie simply by seeing something different. If so the attribution of character was for each man alone. The meaning of a thing, if any, was for each to choose for himself; what was communicated could not be certain even in the skilful works of men; no certain value, then, could be attached to them. And of what he saw before him, the actions of these men, and even those of the Seneschal, were without authority. It was even agreed that they were without effect – though this did not mean that things would not be done because of them.

If the last step of logic were taken, if the pretence of the institution and the acceptance of its ideals were to evaporate, then the ethics of their decisions would be determined only by reference to the particular case and to their personal taste. The rectitude of their decisions, lacking the sanction of a scheme of law or of long revered and established principle, and without the independent life (or seeming life) of either, must be assessed solely by the count of heads.

And Dolke saw, or thought he saw, that the Seneschal was asking himself whether the foolish play had offended against something of value, something he was bound to defend. How to know? And, if that were the case, what to do?

So Dolke concluded: when the Regent has spoken, the Seneschal will know all their opinions. The Seneschal does not trust his own authority, and will prefer to count heads.

The Regent began, 'As I have always understood it, it is better in matters of good taste (to place no more exact an expression on the difficulties the piece provokes) to err on the side of caution.'

So far he had spoken as if the effort were uncomfortable, glancing meanwhile at Dolke and perhaps at others. His pace, however, now accelerated:

'In maintaining the name of my college – known, I may claim, for the law – I would prefer to err on the side of caution.'

With an invincible finality and soft clarity, more typical of the Very Reverend Heysach, he ended: 'Mr von Fluorn might be informed that the play were better withdrawn.'

The Regent was no longer looking at Dolke. He had fixed his eyes straight ahead, on the ultimate distance. The Visitor, Kutten and Arcute relaxed visibly. The Seneschal turned to Feucht.

'Are you unanimous, Doctor Feucht?'

'Why, sir? We are not a court.'

'We are seeking a course of action.'

'Unanimity, sir, would not give your action greater authority.'

'But it is as well to have agreement among one's advisers before embarking on a course. Remember that I asked for help for the very reason that you – the Very Reverend Visitor, the Regent of Ulpianus, Professor Kutten, yourself – you were all familiar with the events or personages closely concerned in this matter. I do not – I don't want to be left in doubt.'

'If I may ask a question of you, Doctor Feucht,' the Visitor broke in, 'so that we may not stray. Doctor Feucht, do you agree with the attitudes displayed in this play?'

'So far as I have identified them, no.' And Feucht's tone stung Dolke by its usual, almost exasperating humility.

As no-one spoke for a while, Feucht asked the Seneschal whether he was confident that von Fluorn would comply with a request to withdraw the play.

'Having spoken to the young man, as you know, I am fairly – I am confident. These things are best achieved by tact. We would not court embarrassment either for ourselves or for him.'

'But others know all about the play. If it is withdrawn, the whole university will be embarrassed.'

'The play's errors are perhaps esoteric, Doctor Feucht,' Arcute explained. 'There is no scandal. Not that our objections are any the less valid for that! The danger is insidious.' He swept on to his last sentence, allowing no pause in which his insistence on withdrawal might have been compromised: 'Von Fluorn's scheme is incompatible with the masque. He can be brought to see that.'

'Nor, though, is his attitude obscure,' urged Kutten. 'It is vividly suggested. Subtly perhaps. The dance! It is almost fortunate that for its impact it has to have been seen.'

'Until then . . . ?' asked Dolke suddenly.

204

They seemed to have forgotten Dolke's existence.

'If that is explained,' said the Seneschal, 'he will see reason on a tutor's advice. Some arrangement can be made. It could be put to him that the play will receive a performance at a future date?'

'It is its incongruity in the masque which would verge on the scandalous,' added the Visitor, feeling that this formulation would command unanimity.

Dolke was aware that both these remarks had been addressed to him, though not spoken towards him. It was he, then, who was to persuade, or instruct von Fluorn to comply with their 'satisfactory solution'. They had not dared act themselves without knowing his reaction, without crushing him with a unanimous verdict. But how long ago, he wondered, had the Seneschal seen the possibility – the advantage perhaps – of using him, if the need arose. Had the Seneschal had it in mind when he summoned him? Had it only struck the Seneschal, with glancing enlightenment, during this last half-hour – an escape, should no other be up to it. The Visitor seemed to have picked it up with swift hands.

'And I am his tutor,' said Dolke, to round the Visitor's argument for him. Though you know, and I do not, what he has said, Dolke thought more painfully.

'Indeed,' said the Seneschal with a more pleased finality. 'And it is you who know best about the masque; who have in that field a – delegated authority. It would not be remiss of you to reconsider your verdict on the play. After all, you had not been able to see it rehearsed. You have now talked to Professor Kutten – to me.'

'I thought von Fluorn was willing to comply.'

The Seneschal was silent for some moments.

'He is of gentle family. But it is much to ask for – restraint, that is the word – in a young man, when one has required such a, well, a sacrifice, I dare say.'

The Seneschal, then, had to be sure that Dolke did not oppose them and that a small matter would not chance to become a scandal. Dolke was now sure that his own position was as strong as he could bring himself to make it. It was impossible for them to displace him now, despite that lingering over 'delegated'. How could they act against the play without his co-operation, or at least his tacit compliance?

'Sir, I shall talk to von Fluorn,' Dolke ended. His voice was only slightly disfigured by a tremor.

'It is really for you to find a way – a form of words. I did not expect any more exact undertaking from you. Nor peremptory words to von Fluorn; of course. He will have the play performed at some more suitable time.'

Kutten may have wanted revenge, some humiliation of him, Dolke suspected. How little power they had over him! As the Seneschal felt his way forward to his goal (was there not something about him like a cat, after all?), Dolke was almost excited; Kutten's impotence was apparent, and touched Dolke with malicious pleasure. The Seneschal, drying his reticent, sensuous hand on his robe of fur, and sliding it round the gilded protuberances of his chair-arm, had, then, a mind of his own, had seen his course and slipped forward along it. He gave a sort of life to his office.

Or had he indeed tricked out to deceive him, Dolke, with his semi-regal state? Had he counted heads? The expression of the Seneschal's face combined concern with a decent composure. Dolke needed his new ideas, his new individuality, yet he also needed the Seneschal to have decided – in the confidence of his office and on his own determination of what was important to the university.

Dolke's eyes searched the face of the Seneschal for a lapse. He hoped for that half-smile, a parting of the lips showing the mouth, which von Fluorn had noticed as he addressed the Seneschal last Saint Libori's Day and had since mentioned several times – a sudden remembrance, it seemed, of his enveloping robes and thus, perhaps, of the mystery of his office. To Dolke that would now reveal the Seneschal's manipulation of his advisers and of his selection of them, a charade of balance, and the contemptuous certainty of his own policy. Or had he waited, unknowing, for an answer? Waited, praying for unanimity, so that he might not appear to count heads?

Perhaps in a deadlock he might have turned to Arcute.

All of a sudden Feucht was asking:

'Has no-one seen the other plays? How does von Fluorn's compare with them?'

His voice was shrill in his embarrassment and expectation of disdain. Even to Dolke the questions seemed beside the point. With as little delay as was needed to dispose of them, the

Seneschal proceeded to end the meeting. All rose. The bells sounded midday.

When the Seneschal had withdrawn, the others drew Dolke among them, gathering about him as one who was to help them. It would have been too much to have expected conversation with them; by tacit understanding the others found themselves a little ahead of him as they walked towards the door. But the Visitor, Dolke found, was walking with him.

'It would not be just to think the Seneschal an uncompromising man.'

Dolke again slowed his pace; the Visitor slowed down accordingly. He stood still before he spoke again:

'You think he has been persecuted.'

'The attention to him has been exceptional.'

'In his case there might have been scandal.'

The rest of the group were out of sight, descending the stairs. The Visitor began again, more intently, and wisely.

'Yes – Tassillo Aicha came to see me yesterday. He is an intelligent youth; not vicious.'

'He attends my classes.'

'Of course. He came to me for advice on religious matters. I knew his father.' He paused; there was an expression almost of anger on his face: of incomprehension perhaps, and sudden anger against Dolke. 'He is leaving the university.'

Then he added with a really fearful implacability, 'He took himself off to one of the houses near the market – you are aware what I mean – led by our young gentleman.'

'Friedrich von Fluorn.'

'Von Fluorn, I assume, was more fastidious – or more expert – in his selection. I am told the best young gentlemen insist on value for money.'

The Visitor had forced himself to smile; such speech was then possible; to do so he told himself that Dolke had known at once which 'gentleman' he meant, an admission that all along von Fluorn was someone to be suspected. In the space of two sentences his voice had resumed its tone of casual interest, almost of one passing on some possibly diverting academic detail; except the whispered, suppressed 'insist'. He added:

'Poor Aicha has a touch of one of the lesser infections of venery.'

There was nothing to be said. Though Dolke was ingenuous, he did not combine innocence with a capacity to condemn easily. He believed the Visitor; and sought a rational justification for hating him.

'And in my absence as tutor, you felt able . . . ?'

'I have not informed the Seneschal. I felt entitled at that moment to assume that Aicha talked to me as a confessor and not as an officer of the university.'

'The Seneschal would approve your good offices.'

'His reply would probably be that it was entirely a matter for his tutor; and then perhaps of his Head of College.'

Dolke did not at first catch the Visitor's irony, just as he had not seen his new seriousness. Then Dolke smiled, with a grimness made almost sublime by a sense of righteousness. He was sure of his own moral position against – against Heysach at least. And he was confident that he knew von Fluorn. But there was still reason to fear: What had Fluorn said? That was all that mattered.

'And Vaslav Kutten?'

'He doesn't know.'

'Thank God!'

'Why? Had he known he would not have wished me to conceal the strength of his feelings. He will probably know to-morrow.'

'And the play? Its being contrary to fundamental tenets of the university: did you believe that?'

'Doctor Dolke, allow me the justice of your usual understanding. Please do not think that I chose my course maliciously. The Lord forbid it. I believe that the play was incorrect and incongruous. But I refuse to face – do you not see – the greater ill is deep in the mind – I might say "soul" – that the play reflects?'

He looked at Dolke, and began in a muted, cautious voice:

'Doctor Dolke, your ideas and von Fluorn's are not in the least in sympathy. I did not – would not – disseminate this scandal to damage him, but to convince the Seneschal, and to convince you. In his fantasy von Fluorn invents a world, not of achievement, but of licence; an absence, not of empty structures, but of responsibility.'

'Are you intent on trying to prove this – even to me?'

'Are you not appalled then?'

'Yes, I am amazed.'

The Visitor was physically uncomfortable – no more than that. He was convinced of his feelings, but in fact the transgressions of others rarely agitated his deeper indignation. Faced by Dolke's attitude, he had exercised, almost unconsciously, his ability to agitate his feelings in himself.

The two men were at last descending the stairway. Dolke felt curiously sorry for his companion. They entered the Library Gallery and walked its length in silence.

Was there not someone, Dolke asked himself, more truly responsible for the furtive whispers of the Visitor? He could see that the Visitor was not a man of anger. Could he be so implacable? To whisper gave him no, or no further, pleasure. The point scarcely mattered, unless the Seneschal knew. If so, surely the Seneschal had made a decision and all since had been play-acting; all had proceeded according to the particular character of his government.

Yet there was in the Seneschal a worldliness and, it was said, a sensuality which Dolke might have forgiven in others. It was just as likely that, whether he knew or came to know, he would be gradually pushed to act, to leave free those who cared to act. He might do no more than leave a door open to their underhandedness.

While an attendant waited the two men shook hands at the door. Afterwards they parted. The Visitor seemed to identify a change in Dolke. He said:

'I knew I could lift the veil from your eyes.'

Dolke's final words were, 'I shall visit von Fluorn now.'

Dolke's suspicions, about von Fluorn and von Fluorn's accusers, could not be left. He could feel angry with no-one. That must be weakness; or was it perhaps the lack now of any certainties against which he could find them wanting? For, according to the understanding of the nature of things to which he clung, was not the Visitor entitled to determine the ground for deciding, and acting, against von Fluorn, and those principles of moral conduct with which these must comply?

As for Dolke, he scarcely considered the degree of von Fluorn's culpability. Only the first words were obvious: what had he said to the Seneschal? When Dolke reached Ulpian, he remembered that it was almost one o'clock. He was quite hungry. Von Fluorn would not be back in his rooms in Alt-Albertusstrasse after eating at midday. Dolke had something to eat. Then he walked the gardens at Ulpian, but somehow it did not take as long as he would have wished. To go anywhere but Alt-Albertusstrasse was to waste too much time.

The householder's wife at Alt-Albertusstrasse received Dolke with some ceremony. Fortunately von Fluorn often left his keys with her in case friends came while he was out; she was a manifestly respectable and trustworthy person. Dolke was shown upstairs to wait.

'Mr von Fluorn is very careful with his new pictures,' the woman explained. The sitting-room was shuttered. She had a busy manner, but confident in what she did; quite used to rather individual student ways.

'This much will be all right, I'm sure,' she continued, and deftly making her way over to the windows in the gloom, as if she knew the room like the back of her hand, she opened one pair of shutters.

The bright light glanced across the woodwork. The farther wall was illuminated – the rams' heads, garlands. Dolke, hearing the woman thank him as she left, was asking himself the truth about von Fluorn. Aicha's fall perturbed him. But von Fluorn was a young man. Did an indiscretion, even a disaster mean so much? Yet it asked what was at the heart of him: what was in his mind. How dared the others assume they knew?

The beauty of the room, a richness, was astonishing. In the glorious light it struck him far more than on his first visit. The wealth of ebony, and here and there figured reliquaries in coral and amber. No-one could doubt von Fluorn's fastidiousness. If anything here was disturbing, Dolke admitted, it was the degree of refinement and excellence; but then they insisted on value for money, as the Very Reverend Heysach said. He was not himself used to these surroundings; he was reluctant to move about the room, afraid of all that fragile beauty. Eventually he chose the chair where he had sat previously, and stayed there.

Von Fluorn entered. With him was the householder's wife and

210

two of his own friends. By a gesture of respectful excitement, he forestalled Dolke's attempt to rise.

'Sir, one or two friends from . . .' He broke off, and began afresh, 'They have come to see the new painting.'

There was a drawn expression about his mouth, though it scarcely clouded his graciousness. It was a warning of what he knew.

He did not allow his visitors to stay; long enough just to stand in front of the friezes and point out some clever detail here or there. Not once did he mention his own contribution; Dolke clung to the only interpretation he could give to that. For a minute or two they scrutinized and admired a little toy reliquary – a Saint Sebastian martyred, its figure cut in coral – and then, von Fluorn's assured apologies filling their ears, they were ushered away 'until the evening'.

When he turned away, towards Dolke, his expression was set, perhaps slightly aloof with consciousness of self-restraint. His tone remained obliging almost to the point of apology:

'As you may imagine, sir, some new friends from rehearsing.'

Dolke stood up, wondering whether the remark was intended to wound him.

'Von Fluorn, I,' and he emphasised this word rather than those at the heart of the sentence, for it seemed that von Fluorn must expect the rest and he wanted the ludicrousness of the proposal to be apparent in his voice, 'I have been asked to persuade you to withdraw the masque.'

'The masque?'

'The masque – yes, the play, you understand.'

'Then you are persuaded of its faults, sir?' von Fluorn asked, almost as if seeing through Dolke's emphasis. He continued, as if proving his omniscience, 'Perhaps by the news about Tassillo Aicha.'

'The Very Reverend Heysach . . .'

'I dare say all he told you about our little escapade was true.'

'Fluorn, tell me. Did the Seneschal try to persuade you to withdraw the play when he saw you?'

'I think I saw you, sir, waiting in the Old Library.'

'Did he try to force you? What did he say about Aicha?'

'No, no, nothing at all. Tassillo Aicha told me himself.'

'But you were aware . . . ?'

'*Nothing* at all. But Tassillo must have been in a terrible state. I wouldn't have expected it of him – going to the Visitor. I can't imagine how he came to choose him of all men. I suppose the Seneschal did know.'

His voice drifted as if he were totally oblivious of Dolke. Suddenly, however, he turned towards him:

'I can imagine what the Visitor will do. Of course the Seneschal wanted me to withdraw; I suppose that's what he meant. Does the Regent know yet? If that happens he will make sure I go.'

'The Seneschal would not allow it perhaps.'

'The Seneschal was very kind. If I may say so, I think he has a certain fondness for members of the gentry.'

He spoke with his old airiness, but a tension beneath it was easily detected.

Dolke said, 'No, the Seneschal would not allow it. He cannot force you to withdraw the play.'

His mind seemed suddenly as clear as if faced with some purely academic point. It came with certainty that the Seneschal had known nothing about Tassillo Aicha. The correct answer had been given. The conclusion was simple: 'He will not allow them to make you leave; he will not for a number of reasons, not selfish reasons – create a scandal.'

'The risk is a little too great, sir, though I mean no disrespect to the Seneschal.'

'No, I say, Fluorn. They – the Visitor – wanted to prove that they had foreseen – all this. They tried to make me think your work – you! – empty and arid. That was what you thought they had succeeded in doing to me. I understand how you must have felt. You can ignore them. Don't you think it worth it . . . ?'

His voice had risen; von Fluorn was staring at him. The reply came:

'Don't worry about the play, sir. I suppose I can throw that to them.'

'Fluorn, I know that you must feel almost distraught. It would require a quite deliberate bravery.'

In Dolke's imagination, von Fluorn would have been prepared for some sacrifice. There was no danger of scandal, he told himself; the Seneschal's sense of justice could be satisfied by, say, von Fluorn's leaving the university for some months by a tactful gesture.

'I don't want to advise you as your tutor; but if you have ideas you believe in . . .'

'Not if it would sour the mood.'

Despite himself, despite an intense desire to show that he understood, to display the sympathy he believed there to be between them, Dolke found his own voice irresistibly angry with von Fluorn. At this crisis he should declare to von Fluorn the identity of their ideas. He could not. After the meeting the whole of his work might be suspected. The thought almost frightened him; nor was the fear entirely selfish. When he heard von Fluorn – 'not if it would sour the mood' – he must be afraid to deny the forms, the certainties, that he and Kutten had together set out in the masque. There was still much of that, an achievement of a sort, not entirely, he suspected, to be despised. And von Fluorn was looking at him without the slightest intimation of understanding.

'Fluorn, I know that you must feel distraught,' he repeated lamely and without compassion.

Von Fluorn burst out, 'What I could not countenance is any scandal at home! I couldn't.'

His voice, even the words, seemed to Dolke to betray that its unusual passion was partly self-induced.

'And that is your reason?'

It was convenient perhaps, or special self-indulgence?

'Tassillo Aicha told me,' von Fluorn continued distractedly. Then he added in his customary, pleasing voice, 'Aicha – Tassillo – is leaving today.'

Even now it did not occur to Dolke how little he had thought of Aicha since hearing the Visitor's story. The words certainly induced no condemnation of von Fluorn, and no remembrance of Aicha. But for the first time 'von Fluorn' and 'Aicha' were associated, were joined, in his mind. Aicha leaving: a distaste insinuated itself at his memory, as if it had been his fault; von Fluorn was associated with him. A vulgar sexuality joined them. He, Dolke, had been ignorant of it.

He should not condemn von Fluorn for it, and for his own failure; but how could he touch this von Fluorn not of ideas but of the senses. Between himself and von Fluorn, this new man, there seemed a sudden distance. With this he glimpsed them meeting for their expedition – perhaps the very evening of his first visit

213

here. And the richness of these rooms. . . The presence of a female form, even of the housekeeper, gliding in the darkness of the room. . .

'How crass you were, Fluorn! How distasteful!'

How distasteful it was! How remote, how incomprehensible.

'How would you know?'

Von Fluorn said this very slowly, directed by an overpowering need to put distance – to make manifest the distance – between his own mind and Dolke's. Even God made jealous demands of him; was partial. Only women came near Divinity.

Then Dolke's distaste was gone. It was his own ignorance that still offended him. There was a gulf between them.

'I confess I don't want to lose all this now,' Dolke heard von Fluorn saying. Perhaps he had seen Dolke glance round. 'These rooms – Tassillo's work and my own, they are just as important to me as the play. I have another year here. I pity Aicha.'

'But the play. That was also important to you?'

To Dolke it had to be.

'Yes, it was important.'

'Then something shall be done.'

'It's just not important now. I should have liked a part of the masque to be – well – my own. The play had a mood. Perhaps that was rather too much of myself; I hoped someone might say, "I see it as von Fluorn does." Something different might also have been something true.'

'Different from my work? Do you think that?' Dolke tried to give his voice the detachment of mere curiosity.

'I did feel it fitted somehow. I was not quite sure. . .'

'The mood of the masque, do you mean? It had a mood – in tune with yours.' This was the nearest Dolke had yet come to revealing to von Fluorn the extent of his reliance. He went on hurriedly, 'Do you remember your remarks to me? "A serpentine procession". The university might be seen in a new light. But that is not merely a matter of moods, of unrelated images. Our ideas. . .'

His voice was almost triumphant; but he was daring to speak because von Fluorn, he saw, had his glance fixed elsewhere, on a small carving that stood silhouetted on his table by the window.

Von Fluorn had avoided thinking what sacrifice he had tacitly made; he had taken the obsequiousness of the Seneschal in

214

payment. To be aware of sacrifice was to be aware of God's partiality; to be half aware of his fear of fighting against it.

'The play was a slight effort,' he replied, and he turned his eyes back to Dolke.

'The debate was succinct. As I was saying, there are ideas. . .'

'I prefer to see it as a diversion – less even than what the French call *pensées*.' He smiled with something of his old charm of slightly ingratiating innocence, which struck Dolke with an intense pain and loneliness.

'Something at least will be done. After Saint Libori's Day! Minds soon become more equable; and the Seneschal will agree; I shall make sure that a production is arranged.'

'There really is no point. You do not understand, sir.' Von Fluorn's face was red with embarrassment, almost with anger, at Dolke's insistent manner. He stood up. 'I do apologise. The masque will be superbly vivid. It will be like that evening on the ice, sir. The flames, the flames in the distance, and that immense procession. And then suddenly to see their faces!'

Whichever way Dolke looked for some closeness, he was cut across. Von Fluorn would never create, he told himself bitterly, echoing the facility of an opinion he had heard; von Fluorn was not interested in knowing. That was incomprehensible. How had he, Dolke, ever dared to find in him corroboration of the truth of his own fantasy, of the truth of anything? Even the Visitor knew von Fluorn better than he had. Von Fluorn's imagination served to entertain his senses and his moods; perhaps sometimes it diverted his intellect.

They were sitting in silence. Von Fluorn was standing near the Saint Sebastian made in coral, idly fingering its substance and surfaces between the finger-tips. The vast spheres in which their imagination had never coincided seemed to Dolke to encompass each of them, as if he were watching von Fluorn through crystal. There would never have been corroboration there, had he dared to look honestly. On that evening on the ice, when he first questioned the infallibility of his own intuition, he had turned his mind from von Fluorn's distasteful ecstasy at the faces of the poor. Sensuality without sensitivity, without invention, he told himself, giving judgment.

As for the imagery of von Fluorn's sexuality, it remained hidden from Dolke, and so was assumed by him to be furtive. His imagination, Dolke felt – its complete detachment from the search for truth – deserved more condemnation, more derision, than did his own. Dolke had not noticed, or had forgotten, von Fluorn's tone when he had been speaking about Aicha earlier; nor did Dolke understand the curious separation of von Fluorn's sympathy and pleasure.

'What about Aicha?' Dolke suddenly demanded. His own awareness of that person, angry and new, only heightened a false sense that von Fluorn had never mentioned the name during their meeting.

'Tassillo? He would want me to stay in these rooms. You know, I *am* sorry for him.'

It was scarcely important to Dolke – almost unrecognised – that he had lost the will to consider what responsibility lay on von Fluorn and what on Aicha; what discipleship or what casual concealment of necessary prophylaxis; Dolke did not desire to know. Of his disappointments it was hardest for Dolke to recognise his failure to understand von Fluorn. It was not merely that they were so different – in their conduct, their imagination, and their preoccupations; Dolke had certainly learnt this. They had nothing in common. It was harder to accept that he must look to his own intuition, accept the last implication of his own theory, without corroboration; but he would tell himself eventually that he had largely innured his weaker feelings to that glorious loneliness. The worst was – or would have been, had he been able to face it – that his wishful thinking had so lightly usurped the place of insight. In a shifting world he would be a doubtful guide to himself. Even the Visitor had known better von Fluorn's sensuality and the emptiness of his fantasy. Even Kutten had foreseen von Fluorn's inability to escape them.

The truth was that he had never come near to knowing von Fluorn. Dolke was aware of this only as a numbness of his imagination, a profound darkening beneath his more eager and bitter disillusionment.

The two men took leave of each other with repeated formalities.

Even before the light had quite faded the expectation of the crowd on Saint Libori's Day had imbued the mermaids and tritons and

216

varied devices of the chariots with an other-worldliness. The faces of the townspeople, having survived the winter, seemed to say that these sights, but not the death of men or the birth of children they did not know, could stir their emotions to life. The silvered and sculpted machines issued from the Close of the Benedictines into the throng and into the poorest recesses of the city. The muscles of their teams, swathed closely in gold, the sense of almost totally concealed, yet irresistible wheels, the smoothly undulating backs of beasts, mythological beasts and beast-men seemed by turns entirely the work of artifice and then, as the whole strained over an obstacle and the ground gradually inclined, vibrant, flexing, swollen, with uplifted trumpets and conch shells blaring. Each was caparisoned and harnessed in gold and silver – horses, drivers, carriages.

An escort of attendants struck the stones with the slow beat of the butts of their pikes, and so drew to their passage through the press a confidence; the rhythmic fall at each third step filled the silence which each man otherwise maintained. As yet they proceeded without music.

In three of the chariots, however, musicians were seated. But until the train, moving south and east, had passed the market and reached the point at which a first glimpse of the University Gate was possible, their silence persisted. Then, on a flourish of sound, horns, wind and all manner of stringed instruments began a stately music. The strange cries from the crowd (for such had been made, by solitary people) abated, and the melody, filling to the utmost the streets and houses, infused a cohesion and an urgent life, as it were into a new whole.

At the University Gate the nearest masses paused to hear the phrases of clarion and formal welcome and then dissolved, teeming through by every burrow and alley to such places and vantages as remained along the route of Tenth Day Street to the Forum Academicum.

It was still very warm. From Ulpian Dolke watched the legatus Arcute give the thanks of the Seneschal to God, give thanks, indeed, to all, and mention Dolke's name. He also saw the cortège blessed and how the Seneschal with attendants assumed his seat in the midst of the procession.

From the gate-tower of Ulpian emerged the actors and speakers of the drama. They passed below Dolke's window. He reflected that they, and their pages, must pause for a moment out of his sight by a scaffold stage erected against the walls of Ulpian for players of the anti-masque. It faced another, as gaudily festooned, put up against the College of Saint Lorenz on the other side of the open space. None of this had interest for him any longer. Already conscious of each gesture, the masquers allowed themselves to be conducted to their respective chariots. Those who would later dance formed a cavalcade behind them.

Dolke slipped away before they could begin their progress. His attention remained exact but academic. For him there was no exhilaration, either of expectancy, or of any identity between himself and those proceedings which would soon, no doubt, unfold precisely in accordance with his instructions.

Two attendants accompanied him. He was entitled to it, and insisted on this last resort, some slight state which would identify him as having a part; if he felt nothing, still he would not be seen otherwise. He talked to his attendants more than he wished, to excuse to himself his avoidance of the eyes of others.

Before the crowds he felt a rigorous desperation. When he observed the proper figures of the masquers and their excellent bearing, it seemed to him as if they were about to explain some obscurity, but that the meaning must escape him. How then would it not escape these crowds, escape the masquers themselves and the Seneschal, all his work being now so diffuse and contradictory?

Yet, and the two attendants made it certain, he would not deny his part in the masque. Despite the contradictions, the result might somehow justify him; but at the moment he could not say even in what aspects of the work he had any faith left. The part that, as he had liked to think, belonged to von Fluorn? Although he did not hate the Seneschal, the committee, the Visitor, or Vaslav Kutten, he held them (in some vague way quite unrelated to such principles as those on which the law imposed liability) responsible for his broken faith. He could no longer know whether there was any merit in his work to resuscitate him. He looked down, and was repelled by the confirmation of his defeat. Sometimes his hands, usually so robust, shocked him fearfully. They were suddenly white and drained of virtue, almost effete. He clenched them three or four times, spasmodically; the valves of the veins dilated; the colour returned.

'The evening is drawing in,' he explained to his attendants, with a shiver.

No duty required him to see the performance at the Forum, and no fear about the ordering of his arrangements need keep him there. But people gave way before his attendants. Perhaps his face was known, and each of his attendants presented the white staff of an officer of the masque. And when he reached that point at which Tenth Day Street lay before him, empty and fixed clear, like a swathe cut in a cornfield between the foremost ranks of an immense extent of human forms which covered the walks as far as the Forum, and there to his left, between the colleges, was the gap and the wide and varied vista to the white palace, he paused and thought: I cannot hide. I shall watch here.

'I shall watch from here!' he called peremptorily, and his attendants took their places by him.

Although he must turn his back on the view over to the west, he would stay on this side of the street; for he saw how the sun fell from the west and would glance on the chariots and apparel of silk and on the gilded helmets of the actors. At the moment of that view along the whole of Tenth Day Street, before the crowd closed about him, Dolke saw how the crowds on his side of the street seemed motionless in the cool grey shadows of the western façades. On those opposite, however, a glow of gold embellished their faces and figures, and spread a pale and fiery enchantment on their clothes and over their hands. These people, massed and expectant, were also still; except that, in the exaggeration of the deep shadows thrown by every movement in the pervasive light, sudden flurries were apparent, and a constant nodding and shifting along the heads of the front rank.

Behind Dolke were the broken plains and the narrow line, which always, he thought, stood out so boldly, of the path and the white bridge. Of the hill beyond, only a grey-green presence obstructed the streaming evening sunlight. The effect was of something half-formed, waiting to emerge. It seemed to glitter behind the light, and where the rays, clear of the trees, had previously spread a clean, smooth tissue over it, it now pressed into them and split them. In another hour the sun would have set to that point at which this corona was no longer dazzling and at which the form of the palace would abruptly jut into it, black and square.

In ten minutes the pageant would have been marshalled. The hour set for the commencement was nine o'clock. At the insistence of his attendants Dolke allowed himself to take up a slight vantage point. By now he was scarcely aware of the crowd's parting so deferentially for him, a privilege he would have wanted. Again the people pressed together and, though he could now see the route, he was as remote from the masque's unfolding as is a man, lost in the sea, from the ship he watches pursue its course.

Probably it was the cries of those perched on roofs and steeples which made the crowd cluster even more closely, if that were possible, and turn and strain, for the sound of trumpets must almost have been lost in the distance. Dolke could see nothing. But by some chance, perhaps by the penetrating brilliance of the silver clarinos, the people observed the approach of the King.

Perhaps, though, it was by a shifting and stretching of the veil of light over the palace hill. A disturbance, a greater luminosity for more than the height of a man, might just have been made out as it spread along the bank of the river. A figure emerged and seemed, curvetting on his white horse, to release something, to pull aside a curtain. A line of horsemen was standing along the margin of the trees. The crowd heard unmistakably the calls of trumpets and horns.

It was impossible that Dolke should not feel that this scene was indeed a part of his creation. The formalities of the masque at once merged with something wider, of more certain character and purpose. Dolke had even envisaged it, and had allowed for it. Already a messenger would have reached the Seneschal; Dolke had the promise of the Custodian. Just beyond his sight, where a better road ran from Tenth Day Street towards the river bank and the white bridge, the Seneschal would pause to greet the King.

Dolke had often imagined it. The possibility of this conjunction of form with the political heart had always remained in his mind, even when he most strongly felt, and urged most desperately, the isolation of the individual and the insubstantiality of the work. In that office there was a certainty. In the King, or in his attributes, there was an undoubted justification of Dolke's, and Kutten's, masque. The whole – the joint work and Dolke's own – did not contradict that office. The hierarchy, the gorgeousness, the melancholy transience, reverence and insubstantial brilliance, the forms and moods seemed to reflect the emanations, and even the nature of an undeniable authority, and in so doing to receive from that lasting source their own purpose and value. No part of the portrait was, then, empty rhetoric or erudition.

The currents of people pressed and sucked Dolke nearer and further by turns from the meeting place of the King and the university. He broke away, and set his face towards the Forum. People again made way. Dolke lengthened his stride. As he strode, stiff and erect, he dared to hope. He would not risk his confidence by seeing the Seneschal with the King, but he would see the play.

Baboons in white ruffs capered through the twilight, gibbering and mocking to the tune of flutes. At the gates of Ulpian laughing birds seemed to swallow the air with pointed, gaping bills.

Far ahead the Seneschal, as if modest of his entry into the Forum, paused before the Church of Saints Ulrich and Afra, and passed without music under the crosses of the university. They were two of its most revered possessions. The Gothic Cross and the Cross of the Blachernae reached obliquely over the heads of white-surpliced boys and seemed, in sloping up, to extend over the chariots themselves. The first was lowered; it was of parcel gilt set with immense and oily jewels. The Byzantine cross was stretched like the other from a processional staff, embossed with circlets of gold. It waited erect, fell as the other was raised, and was poised above the masquers as they began to pass. Its onyx and amethysts and rare and red enamels were liquid in the faltering light.

At last, before the masters and Regents under their canopies of blue and white, the music played an exultant air. Before tumbling and anarchic rocks the Roman Saint and the Emperor, Liborius and Constantius, famous in the legends of the university, confronted chaos and imposed order. Cliffs were sundered and there were displayed, and dedicated to Religion and Learning, Wisdom and Modesty, the triple tiers of triple arches which were the contrivance of Dolke's dexterity. The helmeted personifications of these virtues contended in arms with intractable Confusion and Pride, and overthrew them. By rhetoric they subdued Ignorance and Doubt.

By now it was dark. The illuminations of the Forum would no longer achieve more than to cast deeper and more deceptive shadows. As the raiment of gold, the swords and crowns flickered black and red, and the actors proclaimed the final and eternal establishment of the university, the windows of the Aula Senatus and the arcades of Dolke's architecture sprang all at once into silhouette as the interior of the hall blazed with illumination.

The music calmed. With confident smoothness and without haste, the central arcade of each of the two lowest storeys of the stage parted at the keystone, and were propelled outwards by some dexterous and unseen mechanism. In this way, from wooden arcades and the windows of the hall, a cloister was created out of a façade; and along its galleries learned figures walked deep in conversation or reflection. Behind them was a throng of figures, less distinct in the immediate brilliance of the hall, and gathered somehow as if their position was in suspense. From among them some approached and showed to the approval of those walking in the arcades objects or writings, and took up new places with them. Of all these men some were sombre, some of them youths gloriously arrayed; many emerged but for a moment, one or two only fixed themselves in pre-eminence. Below still came and went Wisdom and Modesty, Pride and Confusion, the perpetual supporters and assailants. Above this scene Saint and Emperor appeared to take their places, justly enthroned under the topmost arches, until light and music were extinguished.

In the Aula Senatus, later, the most courtly of students, the professors of faculties and the regents of colleges gathered before their seated fellows to dance their solemn revels. In slow and oblique succession they made their paces across the floor. On the first passage the Seneschal led, on the second the Regent of Staufen.

Then they departed, and the return of the masque was as much a celebration as its coming had been a prologue. Every mood seemed heightened and every effect spangled, inverted or made sudden by the light of tapers. Where the masque was gone by, the anti-masquers, dispersed in alleys and in every street, and kindled in the past hour by troupes of satyr-players, mock heroes and rhetoricians, resumed where they could some post in the procession. The time of their own wit and eloquence had come and ended during the drama in the Forum. Their more subtle laughter was exhausted, and it remained for their members to impose themselves on the atmosphere of the night in such ways as they could.

Those who now came in front of Saints Ulrich and Afra, encompassed by the renewal of solemn and ecstatic music, were silent for a moment, and thus passed by. They moved, flanked by student mummers and the amorphous crowd, until all were released between the leaping flambeaux of Tenth Day Street. There some hobbled with awkward wings and wide beaks. Among the herd, Friedrich von Fluorn and some gallant friends – the only company for such a night – loaded an obscene-lipped ape with french cloak, hat and sword. It was von Fluorn's joke, and all laughed, though whether he was also laughing at them, or himself, or both, his companions were not quite certain.

Sometimes the penetrating neighing of the nags on which the generals and tribunes of the anti-masque were mounted subdued the sounds of feet, of hooves and of old leather, the undertones of rattling and scurrying, and even the distant stride of triumphant airs, so that their resurgence seemed, after a pause, a thing to be longed for and, having come, to give reassurance.

Everywhere, and with increasing licence, the anti-masquers decked themselves in the attributes of venerable masters and indulged unrestrained for the shrieking crowd, throughout the night, the imitation of their quirks, their manners and their vices. Only at the University Gate, beyond the pitching fires of tapers and torches, did the crowd hush its cheering, and watched in moonlight and the even brilliance of an enormous circle of flames the homage of the Seneschal in golden robes before his King.

For some time after the departure of the Seneschal, Dolke sat in his privileged place in the Aula Senatus. From there he had watched modesty, grace and youth dance with dignity and eminence the steps laid down by ancient observance. As he sat he recited to himself details that had earlier struck him most – a gesture, an intent expression, the shadows of musicians thrown high on to the parapet of a wall. There had been the half-lit, rapt expressions of his colleagues, first at the play, but most nobly, with most sense of its transience, at the solemn dance. He thanked God he had come. He imagined his chair empty, had he not.

How the crowds and masters had responded he knew; what they had read in what they saw, he could only hope. As for himself, he was possessed, he knew, of a tremendous elation and a fitting melancholy. Already the sounds of triumph were fading into the distance.

'Doctor Dolke! I have been searching for you!'

Dolke turned with a jerk, as if waking from a painful moment of a dream. Who is this officious person? his face seemed to ask.

It was Feucht.

'The dancers here – the students – are to perform our solemn ceremonies for His Majesty. Tonight. His Majesty begged it as a favour. He saw the procession through the river mist. And then from Tenth Day Street. Those were his words. It has been a triumph, my dear Dolke. Tomorrow . . .'

Dolke would have wished to respond to this informality, but at this moment it was impossible.

'You are very kind, Doctor Feucht. Need I come?'

'Tomorrow, if you will.' He paused and repeated, 'If you will. May I congratulate you? Your work is vindicated.'

Neither attempted to pursue the conversation. Should he thank him, Dolke asked himself momentarily, for those few words and for the glances which had expressed conscience, guilt, at their attendance on the Seneschal so few days ago? With a slight bow Doctor Feucht took his leave. 'You are very kind,' Dolke brought himself to say again, and with sufficient feeling that the words were made a sort of general appreciation.

Dolke smiled. For a while he closed his mind to the deeper significance of Feucht's words. It had been a triumph; he felt the elation. And that elation was not only the reward of his art; it was the elation of victory, of vindication.

But tomorrow? To have seen Feucht when he might have expected Kings! For Dolke believed again in magnificence and hierarchy, so long as their object – the pinnacle and the total structure – sustained a worthy purpose. He longed for greatness to persist! He desired that it be perpetual; and unconsciously he hoped that his achievement might be measured in terms of such greatness.

To have heard instead the words of invincibly honest Feucht! Even in his praise, his devotion (Dolke recognised that now, if he scarcely acknowledged it), he was totally honest. He must have chosen his words carefully. So Dolke's forms were vindicated, not his ideas. Feucht's ordinariness, the complete absence in him of anything that to Dolke at least could be remembered, reminded him of his former hope for something, and in particular some achievement of his own, greater, more worthy of sustenance, than himself. Feucht's words told him that his newest ideas were not believed in. They knew he saw nothing. They were not aware of the vibrancy, the demands, of an inner eye.

The new pain insisted on some balm of immediate efficacy. Something more essential to him to his whole life, began to whisper to him that without detachment, without distance, he had no individuality, no power then to achieve. But tomorrow he must face the Seneschal and Vaslav Kutten on the same terms as a day ago. In understanding the human transience of institutions he might have left some lasting work and saved his name from the common fate. His thoughts, like those of Aicha and Marsilius, might have been exceptional. Instead his doubts grew, and would be grown larger by tomorrow. Surely, though, that element of his insight had illuminated the conventional outlines of his masque? Something might be drawn together, a true synthesis made . . . but it was too late. He had not the time, the sense of certainty that the sudden insight gives, the sudden focus to reflection, the impetus to that endlessly repeated process of attempting the marriage of the generalisation to circumstances known and remembered. And he had been *wrong*; tomorrow he must face von Fluorn and know that there had been no communion between them. The Visitor and Professor Kutten had taught him that he could find no corroboration in von Fluorn for his own intuition, itself a comforter, a cornerstone of his new ideas. What he had created was, he hoped, worthy of his own praise; but he might have perpetuated his name. With this idea his elation revived, and died.

Dolke made his way through the crowds of Tenth Day Street. His attendants he left to make their own way. He hurried on, his imagination galling his raw loneliness, and himself bewildered by the questions he found to serve the same purpose. The palace, he saw, flickered with illuminations, as it had on that night when he and von Fluorn had crossed the ice.

To return to Ulpian was difficult, but within his rooms were warm with the memory of solitude which was neither fearful nor imposed. Once there he lit candles and adjusted the reflector on the candlestick he would read by at night. Already his heart seemed to press against his bones, and he drew himself up, to breathe with a curious shudder which he noticed. He was now confident of one event to reward their folly – von Fluorn's, Vaslav Kutten's – and establish in their minds for ever a just regard for his insight; while in his own mind his uncertainty would be ended at a moment when he did not doubt his own achievement.

With a deliberation which served to heighten the pain and expectancy of urgency, he crossed the room and took from his shelves his copy of Marsilius of Padua. The pages were peculiarly white and brittle in the surrounding gloom. When he had found the page, he considered the words once more, that prescription which had once seemed to soothe and satisfy the contradictory demands of his inventive and his critical mind. Now he needed permanence, yet still longed to exercise his mind in endless invention; the compromise of the lesser rôle, of contribution, could not satisfy him as, he must suppose, it had satisfied Marsilius. Having closed the book and placed it far, unmistakably far, out of reach, he lay down on his sofa. With a fleeting smile, grim and tired, he noticed the aptness of his summer robes; they had been rendered so exactly on his effigy. That was how he would appear when they found him. His heart was beating wildly and, though he did not admit anything to himself, he prayed briefly, and waited.

But almost to his chagrin Doctor Dolke did not die. His image of what would be fitting, what just and ironic, and even of what was certain, could still cheat him. In later days he persuaded himself in large part – and for much of the time – that he had not expected death.

The university and his college continued to make demands on his time, perhaps more even than before, but, except at moments when the memory both of the masque and of the laudations and honours of the succeeding days was particularly vivid, he half-suspected that his new commissions were prompted by little more than kindness.

Nonetheless he was not unhappy in his busyness. During the succeeding year he enjoyed something of the amusing and cultivated conversation of Friedrich von Fluorn. Nor later did he neglect the invitations (regular if not frequent) to visit his former pupil. Von Fluorn's periodic air of detachment on those occasions he put down to polite indifference. Once, during an autumn storm, a flash of lightning woke von Fluorn from one of these moods, and he praised, and referred to, the stroke, as if almost he awaited, by just such a means, some affirmation perhaps, or even some object of belief. Dolke affected to observe that he hoped von Fluorn would not find too tedious the inactivity of his well-ordered estates. He spoke without sarcasm and without seeing that consciousness of inadequacy and dread of mediocrity which lay hidden just beneath the appearance of von Fluorn's character. Much of their time together, however, was spent in examination of von Fluorn's collections. He inherited them at his father's death, about two years after he had taken his degree. He never ceased to augment them, in accordance with his own taste, which proved to follow entirely that of his father.

Dolke remained almost totally unaware of the respect in which he was held. He died some ten years after the masque in the last year of the reign as Seneschal of Professor Vaslav Kutten. This Seneschal himself spoke the final apologia. He composed it carefully, without haste and with the glories of the masque of the university again vivid in his mind; and it was by his command cut as an epitaph into the panels of the gilded tomb-table:

'He was a man of great knowledge, which so informed his fantasy as to indicate, to those who watched, new images of the nature of this university. Modest, indeed innocent, of his achievements, he left his work a legacy to others.

In asserting the individual, the apparently transient, view, while seeking to assuage with permanence his insistent creativity, he boldly wrestled with the paradox of the individual mind.

The university receives into itself the name, the works and the memory of Eberhard Dolke.'

So Vaslav Kutten laid him in the tomb at Ulpian with magnificent and devout ceremony, holding this to be his duty.